THE
RAT ISLAND
MURDERS

A gripping crime thriller full of twists

PAULINE ROWSON

The Solent Murder Mysteries Book 14

Originally published as *Dead Passage*

Revised edition 2022
Joffe Books, London
www.joffebooks.com

First published by Fathom in Great Britain
in 2018 as *Dead Passage*

This paperback edition was first published
in Great Britain in 2022

Cover art by Dee Dee Book Covers

ISBN: 978-1-80405-173-3

CHAPTER ONE

Wednesday

The trilling of Horton's desk phone shot a jagged pain through his throbbing head. He reached for it without looking at the display, expecting it to be his boss, DCI Lorraine Bliss, bellyaching about some failure on his part.

'Yes,' he said wearily, his eyes still on his computer screen.

'Is that Inspector Horton?' a woman asked.

It certainly wasn't Bliss. 'It is.' He pulled himself up.

'This is Adele Goldsby.'

'I'm sorry, I don't—'

'Remember me, no, I don't expect you do. I'm Dudley Goldsby's daughter.'

It took Horton a few moments before it clicked. Of course, Dudley Goldsby had been the Member of Parliament for Portsmouth South West. In April 2005, Horton had found the MP's naked body sprawled on a bed in a hotel room on Southsea seafront.

Now fully alert, despite his headache, Horton asked how he could help.

'I can't tell you over the phone. Meet me on the Wightlink car ferry to the Isle of Wight, the St Clare, sailing at eleven this morning.'

'It's rather difficult at the—'

'Please.'

He heard the urgency in her voice. To say he was too busy would be cruel, but also the truth. He was so inundated with work that if he stayed at his desk non-stop for a fortnight, he'd still have a pile of paperwork the size of an Egyptian pyramid. But he didn't like to turn her down or fob her off. 'Couldn't you come to the station?'

'No.' She was adamant. 'There's something I need to show you. Please, just this once. I've never asked you for anything before.'

That was true. He remembered breaking the news to her about her father's death. She had been a plain, chubby young woman in her early twenties, solemn and quiet. After that first time, he'd seen her only once more. That had been at the inquest, because at the time he'd been working on the drug squad and the Goldsby case had been handed over to CID when it became clear the politician's death had no connection with Horton's drug squad investigation.

So why was she turning to him now? He had no idea how she had coped with her father's death or what she had made of her life since.

'Are you sure it's me you need to speak to? If it's about your father, I didn't—'

'It has to be you,' she insisted. There was no sign of hysteria in her voice.

There was nothing for it. With a reluctance that he hid from his voice, he said, 'How will I know you?'

'I'll find you. I've seen your picture in the local newspaper. Meet me on the upper deck by the café.'

The phone went down. He stared at the receiver for a moment, puzzled. When had she seen his picture in the newspaper? He'd made sure to avoid all press photographs since his return to duty eighteen months ago following his suspension over the false allegation of rape when he'd been working undercover for Special Investigations — a memory that still made his stomach tighten. He'd been exonerated, but by then it was too late to save his marriage. Catherine had never really believed that he'd been fitted up. The fact that she could think him capable of such a gross act hurt him deeply.

He rose and called Sergeant Cantelli into his office. 'What do you remember about Dudley Goldsby?' He gestured Cantelli into the seat across his desk. Cantelli had been in CID and on the Goldsby investigation in 2005.

It didn't take the sergeant long. 'Found naked in a hotel bedroom by you and Hans Olewbo of the drug squad. Cocaine overdose. Sad ending for a very good politician. Labour MP for Portsmouth South West. Vocal about housing for the less well off in our fair city, ignored by the powers that be, who saw greater returns on investment by building flats for the better off and for the university students. He was found dead on the Friday thirteen days before the May general election in 2005. He'd have got in with a good majority, too. His replacement didn't fare quite so well but scraped through. Why?'

'I've just had his daughter on the phone. She wants to meet me on the Isle of Wight ferry.'

Cantelli raised his dark eyebrows.

'She didn't say why but she was very insistent.'

'Maybe she needs more information on her father's death.'

'Then she can't get it from me. I found the body, yes, but only because Olewbo got an anonymous tip-off that we'd find Callum Durrant in that bedroom.' Horton let his mind go back to the case. Durrant had been a notorious drug dealer and they'd been trailing him for weeks, wanting to make an arrest. 'When we caught up with Durrant and questioned him, he swore on everything he held sacred, namely his BMW, that he hadn't sold drugs to Goldsby. He claimed never to have heard of him or even to recognize him when we waved a picture under his snotty nose. He was a congenital liar but his alibi held out.'

'I remember. I checked it. He was at a rock concert at the Guildhall and there were witnesses — not all crooks either — to prove that he was there until just before midnight, by which time Goldsby was dead. Before the concert he'd been in the pub, the landlord confirmed it. What happened to Durrant?'

'Died in prison four years into a sentence, natural causes. We finally managed to nail him a year after Goldsby's death. And we never discovered who gave that tip-off.'

'Neither did we. And we didn't find anyone who admitted selling or giving Goldsby that cocaine, which isn't surprising, as they were hardly going to come forward. He probably got it from someone in London or bought it on the internet.'

'Was Goldsby's computer examined?'

'Yes. Both his home PC and the one he used in his constituency office, but there was nothing on either to say he'd bought the drugs online and no dodgy emails, crooked goings-on or looking at porn sites and the like, so I was told. I didn't actually examine them. His phone records didn't reveal anything either. There was no suicide note and the autopsy found no physical evidence around the mouth or jaw to suggest he'd been forced to take the drug, and there was no alcohol in his bloodstream. There was also no evidence that he was a drug user, nor that anyone had assaulted him.' Cantelli tried to stifle a yawn but didn't quite succeed. They'd both spent a very long and unproductive night staked out in a car park on the edge of the marshes bordering Portsmouth to the north of the city, waiting for lorry thieves to show. They hadn't.

'Perhaps his daughter's found a suicide note and wants to give it to you because you were the one to break the tragic news to her,' Cantelli continued. 'She may have information about where her father got the cocaine.'

'If she has then I'd prefer she told me without a ninety-minute round trip to the Isle of Wight.'

'Rather you than me,' Cantelli replied with feeling.

Cantelli got seasick standing on a pontoon. And it would be too cruel of Horton to send the sergeant in his place. It wasn't exactly howling a gale but it was very breezy. Besides, Adele Goldsby had asked for him.

'Did the Isle of Wight or the ferry feature in the investigation?' Horton asked.

'No. And we never found any evidence that Goldsby was depressed, although he had been under considerable strain campaigning for the general election, and the media had been coming down hard on him because of his wife's association with other men. Prudence by name but not by nature. I wonder what happened to her.'

'Probably secretly relieved when she got shot of her husband.'

'Maybe. I didn't interview her. The coroner brought in a verdict of death by misadventure rather than suicide, probably because it sounded better politically.'

'Perhaps that should have been a verdict of undetermined death.'

'We all know he died of a cocaine overdose, either taken deliberately to end his life or, as the coroner said, he could possibly have taken an accidental overdose, not being used to it.'

'But why was he naked?'

Cantelli shrugged. 'Maybe he intended to take a shower.'

'If he was contemplating suicide?' Horton said incredulously.

'Yeah, hardly the most logical thing to do if you were intent on ending it all, but maybe he wanted to go out the way he'd come into the world, naked as nature intended.'

Horton sighed. 'Run Adele through the database, Barney, and check with the Driver and Vehicle Licensing Agency to see if she owns a vehicle.' He wondered if he might catch her in the ferry terminal car park before boarding the St Clare. It would save him time he could ill afford to waste. Bliss would throw a hissy fit if she knew what he was doing, but he saw no need to tell her and he knew Cantelli wouldn't. He felt irritated that he'd been pressurized into accepting such a nebulous invitation, but now he'd said he'd be there, he couldn't see a way out.

He keyed 'Adele Goldsby' into an internet search engine and was surprised to find that the only reference to her was in the newspaper articles written at the time of her father's funeral. She had no social media profile, which he thought unusual these days. But maybe she had married and used her marital name. Or conceivably, like him, she avoided social media like the plague, although it came in useful for tracking criminal activity.

He clicked on a local newspaper article written at the time of Dudley Goldsby's funeral. It had been attended by local dignitaries, including, he noted, the former Chief Constable, Reginald Dyer, who was Detective Superintendent Uckfield's father-in-law. Dyer had retired just over a year ago and Uckfield had been made head of the Major Crime Team shortly before that. But back then Dyer had been a detective chief superintendent and due to leave Hampshire for Avon on promotion to assistant chief constable in May of that year. He had been the senior officer in charge of the Dudley Goldsby investigation. A handful of Labour MPs had also been present at the funeral, as had the deputy prime minister.

Horton's attention shifted to another picture of the mourners outside All Saints Church, close to the city centre and not far from where Goldsby had lived. In front of a group of men were Adele and her mother, Prudence. The latter looked solemn and glamourous in a fashionable, black tailored skirt suit, high heels, black stockings and a wide brimmed black hat. She was an attractive, slender woman, but the pain of bereavement that was missing from her perfectly made-up face was etched on Adele's younger plain one. The article gave Adele's age as twenty-three. She was unfashionably dressed in a black below-the-knee flared skirt, black court shoes with a low heel, and shapeless black jacket. She wore no jewellery or hat. Her mousey-brown, untamed, shoulder-length hair blew around her troubled and serious round face. Her eyes held shock and bewilderment. A deep frown creased her forehead and her lips were drawn in a tight line.

He read a couple more articles and an obituary. They all said the same thing: '*a tragic loss to Goldsby's constituents, to parliament and to the Labour Party,*' and gave a brief summary of his background, his achievements, interests and disappointments. Horton read how Goldsby, a native of Portsmouth born in 1957, had been elected as MP in the April 1986 by-election, prompted by the death of his predecessor in September 1985.

Cantelli entered. 'No vehicle registered in the name of Adele Goldsby and no driver's licence. I can't find a record of her as having married and she's not on the Police National Computer. Do you want me to dig a bit deeper?'

'No. One of us wasting our time is enough.'

Horton glanced at the clock above his door and rose. Grabbing his sailing jacket, he managed to make his escape unmolested by Bliss, whose office door was shut and slatted blinds half closed as he hurried past. Perhaps she was catching up on her sleep from a late-night flight back from her holiday in Tenerife, although she hadn't looked anywhere near as tired as he and Cantelli. In fact, she had breezed into his office looking as crisp as freshly laundered linen, but then she hadn't spent half the night in a freezing cold car waiting for non-existent thieves to show. He'd strangle Billy Jago, his unofficial informant, when he could get his hands on the scrawny little weasel, for giving him duff information.

There hadn't been a glimmer of a suntan on Bliss's fine-boned, sharp-featured face. Maybe the weather had been bad. He'd politely asked if she'd had a nice time and had got the curt reply, 'I'm not here to discuss my holidays, Inspector,' before she'd demanded to know what had occurred in her absence, which didn't please her, but then nothing seemed to. Perhaps her holiday hadn't worked out as well as she'd hoped. He had no idea if she'd gone alone or with a friend, possibly the formidable Eunice Swallows, who ran a private investigation agency in the city. He knew Bliss was friendly with her, but he had no intention of attempting to confirm his suspicion. Polite conversation was an alien concept to Bliss — she considered it to be unnecessary and a waste of valuable time.

He wished her flight could have been delayed for another few days to give them peace from her constant interference in CID. A permanent transfer to the Continent or somewhere as far away from Portsmouth as possible would be ideal, but his wish wasn't going to be granted, certainly not in the short term.

A patrol car dropped him off at the ferry terminal, where he bought a ticket as a foot passenger. After showing his ID he asked the ticket office staff of two if they had sold a ticket to a woman fitting Adele's age, mid-to-late thirties. There was no point in giving a description because she could have changed considerably since 2005. They hadn't had any female foot passengers but had had two men, one in his fifties and the other in his seventies with a bicycle.

Horton stepped outside. Instead of joining the other foot passengers, he walked across the front of the traffic lanes towards the Camber. It was just on high water. The boats were bobbing and swaying in the small marina and the seagulls were swooping and squealing over the fishing boats and around the fish market. He breathed in the salty, chilly March air, hoping it would help to clear his muggy head. It didn't, but then it wasn't only fatigue that was making it throb. It was questions surrounding his private investigations into the disappearance of his mother, Jennifer, over thirty years ago, which were never far from his mind.

He had gleaned some information about her over the last fifteen months since he'd started to question why she had abandoned him as a child, but there were still huge gaps, and he wasn't even certain that much of what he had been told was the truth anyway. Many people had lied to him over the years, right back to when she had failed to return home from the casino where she had worked as a night-time croupier. He'd been told she'd run off with a man because she didn't want a kid in tow. For years he had believed that and had shut out all thoughts and feelings for her until some months ago, when he had discovered that to be a lie. Yes, he believed she had gone to meet a man on that fateful foggy November day in 1978, because according to a neighbour, she had been dressed up and happy. But he no longer believed that she had stayed away voluntarily, leaving her child to the mercy of Social Services. He was certain she had been lured away and killed. But by whom and why? He didn't know the answer to either question, but the answer to the second would give him the answer to the first.

He turned back as he heard the ferry's engines approaching and surveyed the queuing traffic, looking for anyone who resembled Adele Goldsby, or at least matched her age. He couldn't discount the fact that Adele might have a driver's licence under a different name and she could have slimmed down, or got larger, or changed her hair colour. She could also be a passenger rather than a driver, but there wasn't anyone who could even remotely be her.

No one else had joined the foot passengers. Perhaps she worked for the ferry company or for one of the concessions on the ferry, and that was why she had insisted on him joining her on board — she couldn't get away because she was an employee.

With reluctance, he boarded the ferry and took the steps at a run to the upper deck and the coffee shop, which Adele had told him was to be the rendezvous. There was no sign of her and the grille to the café was down. He crossed to the outer deck, where he could view the vehicles loading. Only one more car had joined the queue, and it was with surprise that he recognized the black Range Rover. It belonged to Mike Danby, who had been the detective inspector on the Goldsby investigation and Cantelli's boss at the time.

Was that a coincidence? It must be. Danby had reached the rank of detective chief inspector before leaving the force to start his own private security and close protection company. He'd offered Horton a job on more than one occasion, and Horton had been tempted. Policing had changed in the years since he'd joined. It was now steeped in bureaucracy. Initiative and instinct were increasingly being stifled. The Lorraine Blisses of the police world, a by-the-book copper, seemed to be winning the upper hand. She was clearly destined for dizzy heights and, since her promotion and posting to Portsmouth CID fifteen months ago, she had done her best to oust him. So far, he'd won that battle. He wasn't going to give her the satisfaction of putting in for a transfer, and he knew she'd put the flags out if he handed in his resignation.

He returned to the café and took up a position where he could see those coming up the stairs. No one arrived who resembled Adele Goldsby and no passenger or staff member made a beeline for him. Was Adele deliberately waiting until the ferry set sail before meeting him?

As the engines started up, Horton's gaze swivelled over the boats moored in Oyster Quays marina and alighted on a large luxury motor yacht on the outer pontoon. It wasn't quite in the mega-yacht category, but it was certainly veering towards that. He wondered who owned it — someone extremely wealthy, was obviously the answer. His eyes travelled further up into the harbour to a small clump of trees on a slightly raised knoll. They were situated on a tiny uninhabited island just off the shores of Gosport, opposite the Portsmouth International Port. Burrow Island, or Rat Island as the locals called it, was owned by the Ministry of Defence. Nine days ago, five skeletons had been discovered there. Thankfully, the on-site forensic archaeologist, Dr Lauder, had deemed them all to be from the nineteenth century. Horton hadn't briefed Bliss about it because it wasn't an active investigation.

His phone rang. It was Cantelli.

'I've dug a bit deeper on Adele. It was one of my cases,' Cantelli hastily added in his defence. 'Her last known address is Maidstone in 2006 — after that, there's nothing. Not even with Her Majesty's Revenue and Customs, and she's not registered as deceased or claiming any benefits, which means she either left the country and has just returned, or she's changed her name. She could simply have assumed another name or changed it by deed poll. I'll check if she registered a change of name with the Royal Courts of Justice, but as we both know there is no legal obligation for her to do so. Sounds as though she doesn't want to be found.'

'Until now.' But where was she?

'Any sign of her?' Cantelli asked.

'No. But Danby's on board.' Horton saw the tall, broad-shouldered ex-DCI join the coffee queue.

'Bit of a coincidence that,' Cantelli said surprised, echoing Horton's earlier thoughts.

'He's probably visiting the island on business.'

Danby, spotting Horton, made a gesture offering to buy him a coffee. Horton nodded acceptance. To Cantelli, he said, 'I'll call you if there's anything more to report.'

CHAPTER TWO

'Are you on duty?'

'Sort of.' Horton waved Danby into the seat opposite, noting that he'd put on a bit of weight since he'd seen him in October, and his dark hair had got thinner. He was, as usual, dressed casually and expensively and was sporting a tan that by no stretch of imagination could have come from the Solent in March. Business must be good.

'I was due to meet someone.' Horton took the coffee from Danby.

'Then perhaps I'd better—'

'I don't think she's going to show, unless you've seen her on board and have already spoken to her.'

'Me?'

'Adele Goldsby.'

Danby's eyebrows rose. 'That's a name from the past.'

'You remember the case?'

'Hardly one I'm likely to forget. Labour Member of Parliament and also, as it happened, my constituency's MP.'

But not Horton's. He had been living in Petersfield, eighteen miles to the north of Portsmouth then, and married to Catherine. 'Do you know what happened to Adele after the case?'

'No. Doesn't Cantelli?'

'No. And we can't trace her. She called me and said she had something to show me.'

'Here?' Danby looked around the small lounge area of the ferry, puzzled, as he sipped his coffee. There were only a few people and most of those were engrossed on their phones, with the exception of one, a woman in her mid-sixties, who was reading the *Racing Post*.

'It's where she asked to meet.'

Danby frowned. 'Maybe she saw me and I scared her off.'

'You're not that ugly.'

'Ha, ha.'

'Besides, why should you scare her? I can't imagine you being hard on the girl when her father died, unless there was a reason for you to have been.' Horton recalled how Danby's penetrating green eyes had terrified many a suspect in the interview room. They were still as keen as ever but now were looking perplexed.

'There wasn't. She was never a suspect. No one was. It was a fairly straightforward case. No signs of foul play. There were a few hints that Goldsby took his own life because some kind of scandal was about to break, but our investigation never unearthed anything of that nature.'

'Hints by whom?'

'The press looking to stir things up and smear the election campaign. But they soon moved on to the next big story of the day, whatever that was. Why has she contacted you? You weren't on the case. If she'd found something belonging to her father that throws light on why he died, I'd have thought she would have got in touch with . . .'

'Yes, who? You're no longer in the job and Dyer's retired.'

'There's Cantelli.'

'But he was very much in the background on the investigation.'

'DCI Ingham then. He was in charge of the case.'

'Ingham died six months ago. Heart attack.'

'I didn't know! Poor sod. She must have contacted you because you found her father's body and broke the news to her. Your name stuck in her mind.'

Horton's thoughts exactly. 'What do you remember of her?'

Danby thought for a moment. 'Quiet, solemn, mousey.'

'And her mother?'

Danby grinned. 'The opposite. Voluble and lively. I haven't seen anyone resembling Adele Goldsby on board, but then it was years ago and she's probably changed a lot since then.' His phone rang. He glanced at it. 'I've got to take this.' He rose and hurried towards the outer deck with his phone pressed to his ear.

Horton drank his coffee and stared out at the grey, increasingly choppy sea. There were only a couple of hardy sailors braving it. A launch was making its way towards the solid circular granite structure of one of the four Solent forts built to protect Portsmouth from the marauding French in 1867. The French had never made it to Portsmouth in the 1800s, but they did now on the ferries that sailed into the international port. In the Second World War, the forts had played their part in helping to defend the dockyard. After that, they had lain derelict for years until Spitbank Fort, where the launch was heading, had been converted into a luxury hotel like its larger sister, No Man's Fort, further east and closer to the Isle of Wight. Horton had never been on them.

Danby was still pacing the deck with his phone pressed to his ear and a scowl on his rugged face. Horton turned his thoughts to Adele Goldsby. Why had she called him, if indeed it had been her? But why would anyone wish to impersonate her? Why hadn't she shown? He had no answers, nor was he likely to get them by staring out to sea.

Danby returned looking troubled.

'Business problems?' Horton asked.

'Nothing I can't handle. I'm just a bit pushed for time. I could have done without this last-minute appointment, but you can't turn down an opportunity for business. I'm meeting a prospective client at Totland.'

That was on the opposite side of the island to one of Danby's many prestigious clients, Lord Richard Ames, who owned a property on the northern shore between Fishbourne and East Cowes and who Horton believed was connected with the disappearance of Jennifer, his mother. He had no proof of it, only a photograph taken in 1967 of six men at the London School of Economics, where she had been working as a typist. The picture had been left on his boat by Andrew Ducale, his foster mother's twin, without any explanation and shortly before Ducale had vanished. The photograph had kicked off Horton's tortuous journey trying to unearth the truth behind Jennifer's disappearance.

He'd discovered that all the men in the picture, with the exception of one — Lord Ames — were dead. But after his visit to Guernsey in January to Andrew Ducale's aunt, he now questioned whether the sixth man in the picture really was Richard Ames. From what Violet Ducale had intimated in Guernsey, Horton wondered if it was Richard's wayward brother, Gordon, who had died of a drug overdose in Australia in 1973. Horton hadn't yet had the chance to challenge Ames about it and he wouldn't — not until he had more evidence to back up that idea, and he wasn't certain when or if he would get it.

He brought his mind back to the purpose of his trip. 'What do you remember about the Goldsby case?'

'It was opened and closed very quickly.'

'Because of the general election?'

'Because there was nothing to find.' Danby took a sip of his coffee. 'The election in Goldsby's constituency was postponed — you can't catapult a replacement candidate in that quickly. Apparently there are rules about these things. We had to show proof of death to the returning officer, and no, I don't mean dragging him off to the mortuary. There was the autopsy, the death certificate and the coroner's decision at the inquest. If I remember correctly, the Portsmouth

South West election was held a month or thereabouts after the inquest. There was no evidence to show that Goldsby had been murdered and the coroner seemed satisfied he hadn't been. We didn't cut corners, Andy, because there weren't any to cut. The autopsy showed that he'd taken cocaine and hadn't been forcibly fed or injected with it. There were no fingerprints in the room save Goldsby's. Nothing was missing from his briefcase. No shady deals, no affairs. All his personal papers and the data on his computers and mobile phone were squeaky clean.'

'Perhaps that was what you were meant to find.'

'Trust you to be suspicious.'

'I am a copper.'

Danby smiled. 'I know what you're implying. You mean Special Branch were nosing around and cleaning up and removing anything controversial.'

'It's been known to happen. Did Goldsby have a government laptop issued to him?'

'If he did, we didn't get to see it.' Danby frowned. 'I don't know why you're bothering, Andy.'

'I wouldn't be except for the phone call.'

'And it looks as though she's stood you up, unless she's boarding at Fishbourne.'

Horton hadn't considered that she could be getting on at the Isle of Wight terminal.

Danby continued, 'Goldsby wasn't very high up in the parliamentary pecking order. He was only a backbench MP, and I don't think he was silenced or taken out because of some misdemeanour or past association. I suppose his phone could have been tapped, and maybe he had been under surveillance, but I can't think why.'

'Did he have any enemies? Was he lobbying against anything significant that would have put someone's nose out of joint?'

'Not according to his agent, Harry Belling, and his personal secretary, Frieda Chillerton. They both thought the sun shone out of his backside. I can't think what Adele could have that she'd want to show you which would suggest her father's death was suspicious. Maybe the call to you is a hoax from someone else.'

'Designed for what?'

'No idea. You're the detective.'

They fell to talking about other matters — the job, Danby's business, which was thriving, and how Danby thought Horton a fool not to go and work for him. Horton would have liked to have asked Danby if Richard Ames ever talked about his brother, but by doing so, he'd have to explain why he was interested and he couldn't do that.

The announcement came for passengers to return to their cars and foot passengers to make their way to the front of the ferry, where they would disembark first. 'Which is everyone bar you, Andy. Hope you solve the Adele Goldsby riddle.'

Horton stepped outside and rang Cantelli. He told him about the no-show and asked Cantelli to trace the call. 'Is Walters back?'

'Just arrived.'

'Put him on.'

When Walters grunted, 'Guv', Horton asked him what he'd picked up on the latest Somerstown robbery. There had been five in the area, all on business premises, which was five too many.

'It's got the same MO as the others. The lock on the door wasn't forced, not that it would have needed much strength — Sergeant Cantelli's little boy could have smashed it with his toy hammer — and there was no alarm system. They should have hung up a sign saying, "Help yourself".'

'I hope you didn't tell the proprietor that.' DC Walters was not renowned for his tact.

'Not in so many words.'

Horton winced, thinking that a complaint might land on his desk.

'It looks to have been a quick in-and-out job. Yeah, like my sex life,' Walters added, pre-empting Horton's remark, which he hadn't been about to make.

Instead, he said, 'I didn't know you had one.'

'Not with the time this job takes up,' Walters grumbled. 'The thieves took the usual — computers, printers, phones, some tools, anything they could carry and throw in the back of a small van or car. No one claims to have seen a vehicle in the area, but then you are dealing with the three monkey syndrome in that part of town.'

Horton knew the area well. It was where he had lived with his mother in a council tower block and where he had gone to school before she had vanished. After that, he'd been taken into care and uprooted to another part of the city, an area where the three monkey syndrome equally applied as far as dealing with the police was concerned: nobody ever saw anything, nobody ever heard anything, and they certainly weren't going to talk to the police even if they had.

That brought him back to thoughts of his unofficial informant Billy Jago. He might have heard something on the street about the Somerstown robberies. Horton also needed to find him to ask why last night's tip-off about the lorry thefts had gone tits up.

Walters said, 'I'll check the internet to see if the villains are idiot enough to try and offload the stuff there.' He sounded as though he was eating, but then when wasn't Walters filling his face with food?

Horton rang off. The ferry eased its way into its narrow berth close to the Royal Victoria Yacht Club pontoons on its right and the shores of the small hamlet of Fishbourne to the left. The wind was strengthening and the clouds rolling up from the west were dark and bulbous, full of rain or sleet even. Horton was certain it had grown colder since that morning.

He watched Danby's large black Range Rover drive away. The foot passengers boarded. There were four, and none of them were Adele. If she was an employee on the ferry, she would have made contact by now. Unless she had seen him with Danby and that had frightened her off, as Danby had suggested. If that was the case, she'd have ample time to make contact on the return trip.

She didn't, though. The ferry seemed to take an age to reach Portsmouth, and his irritation grew with each minute. He didn't like to be made a fool of. This had to be some kind of practical joke, but he failed to see the humour in it or the reason behind it. Dudley Goldsby's death was, as both Cantelli and Danby had said, a tragic accidental overdose or possible suicide.

His phone rang. He expected it to be Cantelli with the news that he had traced Adele's call, but he was surprised to see it was Dr Lauder, the forensic archaeologist.

'Those skeletons that were found on Burrow Island,' Lauder abruptly announced.

Horton rapidly brought his mind back to the unusual discovery nine days ago that had excited the media, historians and archaeologists. He rose and crossed to the front of the ferry where, further up Portsmouth Harbour, he could see the tiny uninhabited island. 'What about them?'

'Four do indeed date from the nineteenth century, as I initially conjectured at the scene, Inspector. However, the fifth is far more recent.'

'How recent?' Horton asked, not sure that he liked the sound of this.

'Certainly within the last fifty years,' Lauder replied. 'What's more, there is clear evidence that it is homicide.'

And that meant it would be a current investigation.

'I thought it politic to inform you, as you are named as the officer in charge. But as this will quite clearly come under the remit of the Major Crime Team and therefore Detective Superintendent Uckfield, and as I am not in the habit of repeating myself, I will meet with him, and whoever he deems fit to be on his team, in an hour, by which time no doubt you will have informed him.' Lauder rang off.

Horton stared at the small clump of bare-branched trees and shrubs on the small island just off the shores of Gosport, the town he believed Jennifer had been making for the day she had disappeared. His belief was based on a set of numbers on the back of a manila envelope bequeathed to him by Professor Quentin Amos, a lecturer at the London School of Economics in 1967, who had known Jennifer. The numbers could, with some manipulation, correspond with the grid location of one of the marinas on Gosport, which he could see on his left. But the marinas hadn't been there in 1978. Rat Island had, though.

His brow furrowed as the ferry swung into its berth. Was it possible? He didn't yet know how long the skeleton had been on that island. He didn't know if it was male or female. He had no idea of its age, but as he punched in Uckfield's number, he felt a cold sinking sensation in the pit of his stomach. Was he about to learn that the fifth skeleton on Rat Island, murdered within the last fifty years, was in fact the remains of his mother?

CHAPTER THREE

'What do you mean you couldn't tell how old those bones were when you were at the site?' Uckfield demanded, his stern gaze boring into Lauder's haughty one.

'It was hardly wearing a tag declaring when it died, Superintendent,' came Lauder's smart reply. 'And strangely enough, there's not a great deal of evolutionary difference between someone born in the nineteenth and twentieth century. Of course, if it had been clutching a mobile phone in its skeletal hand, we'd have known it straight away,' he added with heavy sarcasm.

Horton smiled despite his anxiety that the remains could be those of his mother. Uckfield sniffed loudly and shifted his large arse while Bliss frowned and pursed her lips. Across the conference table, Cantelli continued chewing his gum. Sergeant Trueman's expression remained inscrutable and DC Marsden's eager.

Lauder eyed Uckfield over the steel rim of his spectacles. 'And it's not as simple a process as the layman believes it to be to identify human remains, never mind to date them and certainly not in situ. Which is *why* the Ministry of Defence forensic experts needed to remove the bones and *why* I and my team needed to examine them thoroughly before tying up a lot of valuable police time unnecessarily.'

Uckfield grunted. 'You've had nine days to discover this.'

'And *five* skeletons to examine,' came the brisk retort. 'All of the bones had to be labelled and removed from the earth then carefully reassembled and tested.'

Horton could see they were in for a lecture. Why didn't Uckfield just let it go instead of baiting Lauder? But then Uckfield was never one for tact. And when he was in a bad mood, which he obviously was, he was even worse.

'First it has to be determined that we are looking at human remains. It may appear evident, but animal remains, including skulls,' Lauder stressed, as Uckfield's eyes flicked down to the photographs spread out before them and his finger came out to stab at one, 'can be mistaken for human ones, even to the trained eye. And although these skeletons *looked* to be human, tests needed to be conducted to confirm that they were. We wouldn't want you going on a wild boar chase now, would we?' He smiled silkily.

Uckfield glowered.

'I won't bore you with relaying the details of all the tests that were conducted — you can have the pleasure of reading that in my report,' Lauder said. 'I'll just give you the highlights. From these pictures, which were taken where the skeletons were found, you can see that four of them were lying fairly close together. The fifth was a short distance away and, when laid out on the slab, it transpired that it wasn't as complete as the others.'

Horton could see that from the photographs spread out before him. He took a silent breath while telling himself there was no reason that these were Jennifer's remains. But it was someone who had once been as alive as Jennifer, as alive as them all around this table.

'As I have already said, the four more complete skeletal remains date from the nineteenth century. I hesitate to label them convicts because I don't have any records to say they were guilty of any crime or even convicted of one.'

'Then what were they doing there?' exploded Uckfield. Horton could see the Super was getting more exasperated with Lauder and his pedantic manner by the minute. Lauder remained unperturbed. Horton got the impression he was enjoying himself.

'The harbour contained a prison hulk, HMS *York*, between 1819 and 1854 after she had returned from serving time in the West Indies and the Mediterranean, so it is possible they were either convicts or French prisoners captured during the Napoleonic War. The *York* would have had about 500 men on board — many were transported to Australia. Some would have died of typhoid and cholera before they could be transported. Others served their time out on the *York*. During the day they were put to hard labour working on the fortifications around Gosport, on Burrow Island and in Portsmouth. At night they would have been chained to their bunks to prevent them escaping ashore.'

'If I'd wanted a history lesson, I'd have gone to the museum,' Uckfield growled. 'This recent corpse, how—'

'Burrow Island or Rat Island, as it is more commonly known, was used as a burial ground for these convicts, guilty or not, and for French prisoners. Further tests will be conducted on the remains to ascertain from where they originated, which might give us more information. Working with historians, we can try to piece together their lives, but it's not their history as you so rightly and eloquently pointed out that concerns you, Detective Superintendent.'

Uckfield's scowl deepened and his mouth opened to protest, but Lauder continued. 'It's our fifth skeleton. This one.'

Horton stared down at the picture Lauder was indicating with a long, slim index finger. His heart raced with the fear that he was staring at the remains of his mother. If he was, it meant others would know about her past and his, and he abhorred anything connected with his private life being made public. Only Uckfield and Cantelli knew how he'd been abandoned and taken into care. Uckfield had dismissed it as being of no consequence years ago and had probably forgotten it because only what was important to Uckfield concerned him. Cantelli, though, knew what it meant to Horton and how it hurt. But as yet, Cantelli hadn't made any connection, and why should he have? He didn't know the half of it. His dark eyes were staring at the pictures, his brow creased in thought.

Horton steeled himself for more. Maybe Lauder would reveal the remains were those of a man.

'As I have just mentioned, this skeleton is not as complete as the others and neither had it been buried as deeply, which made it easier for some of its bones to be dispersed by animals. Those bones then have possibly been swept out to sea. But the island is uninhabited and, as you know, the property of the Ministry of Defence, so there has been very little disturbance on it over the years. You might find more remains from a further search of the island.'

'I can just see the Assistant Chief Constable authorizing that,' Uckfield replied caustically.

But he would have to, thought Horton. A search of the island, although small, would nevertheless be costly and tie up resources but it *was* the scene of a crime.

It was Uckfield who voiced Horton's unspoken question. 'OK, is it male or female? And when did it die?'

Judging by Lauder's set and superior expression, he was not going to deliver the answers until he was good and ready. For once, Horton just wished he'd get on with it.

'Having ascertained the remains were human and that one of them was more recent than the nineteenth century, the next question we needed to ask was are the remains contemporary and did this person die within the last fifty years? If not, then they are of no interest to you, but if recent, then they will indeed be the focus of a criminal investigation.'

'And you wouldn't be here if the answer was no,' retorted Uckfield.

'A more recent death can show up in the colour of the bones, and this is the case with skeleton number five. It is of a lighter colour, which means it hasn't absorbed as much of the surrounding soil as the other bones. So immediately it looked to be more recent.'

'Pity you didn't spot that before they dug it up,' Uckfield declared.

No one else commented. Horton dashed a glance at Cantelli, whose dark-featured, tired face was still studying the photographs intently.

'The bones were dirty and earth-covered at that stage. In addition, bone quality is far more superior in our fifth skeleton. There were no personal items found with any of the skeletons, including number five, but further exploration might reveal jewellery, buttons or zip fasteners, hence the need to excavate that area.

'Next, I considered the biocultural aspects of the remains — the teeth, for example — and here we were fortunate to have the skull. High levels of carbon-14 in the tissue can indicate that the remains date within the last sixty years. This is due to the fact that the United States and several other countries tested nuclear weapons above ground during the fifties and sixties, but the Nuclear Test Ban Treaty of 1963 effectively ended this. Since then, atmospheric carbon-14 levels have been declining as the radio carbon is soaked up by the oceans and the biosphere. So the longer someone was born after 1963, the less artificially high levels of carbon-14 there would be. However, in this case, testing for levels of carbon-14 was exacerbated by the fact there was no soft tissue present. But as I said, we do have the teeth, and we focused on tooth enamel, tooth collagen and bone collagen to help determine year of birth.'

Uckfield huffed loudly. Horton fought hard not to show his own rising impatience and tension. He wanted to scream his questions at Lauder.

'Adult teeth are formed at known intervals during childhood, and if we assume tooth enamel radio carbon content to be determined by the atmospheric level at the time the tooth was formed, then we can deduce the year of birth. The radio carbon level in skeleton number five was particularly low and, judging by the level found, we estimate that number five was *born* sometime between 1950 and 1956.'

Horton's heart leaped into his throat. Jennifer had been born in 1950.

'Next we come to gender,' Lauder continued.

Horton took a silent breath and tried to appear relaxed, but he was as tense as a steel rod. His eyes flicked around the table but no one was looking at him. All eyes were focused on Lauder.

'Here we are fortunate to have the pelvis.' Lauder stabbed the relevant photograph. 'The female pelvis is smoother, lighter and more spacious than the male pelvis, and the body of the pubis is quadrangular rather than triangular. The sacroiliac joint is small, all of which indicate skeleton number five is female.'

It could be Jennifer.

'OK, so when did she *die*?' demanded Uckfield, voicing the question that was hammering through Horton's head.

'On the basis of our analysis of cortical and trabecular bone, we estimate the year of death to be between 1980 and 1985.'

It was very close to when Jennifer had gone missing. And just because she went missing in 1978, didn't mean she had actually died then. He told himself there was no reason why this should be her but the small voice inside him kept saying it could be.

'The skull is the only reliable bone in determining race,' Lauder continued, 'and again, we are fortunate to have that. But that doesn't tell us where female number five originated, just that she was Caucasian. She could be British, but equally she could be German, Swedish or French.'

'Great, that narrows it down,' muttered Uckfield.

'We can determine her stature from the femur, tibia and humerus. She was approximately five feet five inches.'

Jennifer's height.

'And examining the fusion of bone ends to bone shaft, I would say her age is more likely to be thirty, possibly a little younger.'

Jennifer was twenty-eight when she vanished. Lauder's description was getting closer. Did Horton want it to be her? If he could keep the investigation from focusing on his tormented childhood, then maybe.

Lauder said, 'We'll scan the skull into the computer and flesh out her face, which will give you an idea of her appearance, but we can't determine the colour of her eyes, hair, or the shape of her lips, although we'll give you several variations, which might help to identify her. It's clear she wasn't washed up where she was found but buried, as were her neighbours. But whoever buried her probably didn't know how close he was to the other four skeletons. The fact that she was buried indicates foul play, and from my examination, I can confirm that. From the pattern of markings on the bones, the probable cause of death was sharp force trauma to the thorax.'

'She was stabbed?' asked Cantelli, concerned.

'With a sharp-edged knife, Sergeant. There are several more tests we need to do. I might in due course be able to tell you a little more about where she came from. Different geographical locations are known to have different, often distinct isotope ratios. I won't bore you with the details,' he added as Uckfield sighed heavily, 'but there are four stable isotopes, and because their ratios vary between different geographical locations, people and animals will ingest food and water from those locations. Therefore, the analysis of the ratio of isotopes found in the bones could indicate where she lived.'

'A DNA profile would be helpful,' said Uckfield.

'Bone contains little nuclear DNA. However, all is not completely lost because bone does contain mitochondrial DNA inherited from the maternal bloodline, which lasts longer than nuclear DNA. We might be able to give you something to compare with living maternal relatives but not the paternal bloodline, that is, if it can be successfully extracted and analysed and if you can find someone to match it against.' Lauder rose. 'Keep me informed of anything you discover during your investigation, Detective Superintendent, which might assist me in determining more about the weapon used, the manner and the circumstances of her death.'

Lauder made no effort to extend his hand, nor Uckfield to proffer his or rise from his seat. Horton thanked Dr Lauder and got the twitch of a smile in return.

CHAPTER FOUR

'OK, so we need to know who female number five is,' Uckfield declared as soon as the door was shut. He stretched his hands behind his head and spread his legs.

'Can't we give her a name?' Cantelli said.

'What do you suggest? Bones?'

No one laughed, although Marsden looked as though he might. A glance from Trueman silenced him. Horton prayed, *Not Jennifer*. Cantelli, in a serious tone, replied, 'A girl's name that means five.'

'Know any?'

'Plenty. Before the twins were born, Charlotte and I researched names for them, one of the twins being our fifth child, but we chose Molly instead of May, as in the month. Don't ask me why, but one of my favourites was Quintessa. Sounded grand to me.'

'Bit of a mouthful. But if you say so. Trueman, pull off all the women aged between twenty-eight and thirty reported missing between 1980 and 1985. See if any of them fit the profile Lauder's given us. Get Marsden to help you.'

Horton breathed a sigh of relief that the search excluded Jennifer. But he'd still keep hold of the possibility that Quintessa could be her. Yes, he believed Jennifer had been heading for Gosport on the day she disappeared, but that didn't mean to say she had ended up there or on Rat Island. She might have boarded a boat and been taken out to sea. She could have met someone in a car and been driven away. She could in fact be anywhere, or rather, her remains could be because Horton was convinced that she was dead.

Trueman said, 'How did the killer get the body there?'

'By boat, obviously,' Bliss answered.

But Horton corrected her. 'You can walk onto Rat Island at low tide from Gosport at Priddy's Hard, although it is only a soft shingle spit and not that easy to do. And in the dark it would have been particularly difficult, especially if pulling or pushing something with a body in it. The killer might have had an accomplice, though.'

'By boat then is the most likely method.' Bliss fixed her stern gaze on Horton as though daring him to contradict her.

'But why go to the trouble of burying her? Why not simply dump her body at sea?' he said. 'That way, she might never have shown up, or parts of her might have washed up miles away with little left to say who she was or how she died. Rat Island isn't exactly isolated. It's right in Portsmouth Harbour — there would have been vessel movements in and around it. The killer would have taken a chance that he wouldn't be seen heading there or landing there.'

'It was dark,' Bliss said.

'Boat movements don't stop just because of that, although there wouldn't have been as much activity at night as during the day.'

'And this was in the mid-eighties,' Uckfield added. 'The harbour wasn't as busy then as it is now.'

That was true. The international port had expanded greatly since then, with cross-channel ferries and small cruise ships and a thriving trade in shipping fruit and other cargo — as he knew all too well from his and Cantelli's abortive stake-out last night waiting for would-be lorry thieves, who were making a nasty habit of stealing valuable goods destined for the port. And further up into the harbour, what had once been marsh land had been reclaimed and turned into a housing estate with shops, a cinema and a substantial marina, where Uckfield kept his motor cruiser.

'She could have gone there willingly with her killer unsuspecting she was going to be killed,' Horton said. 'If she did, I think it more likely she'd have gone by boat rather than walking across the spit in the dark. It's not exactly the place for a romantic moonlight stroll.'

Bliss frowned. 'Wouldn't she have thought it strange to be going out at night with a man in a small boat to a deserted island?'

'Probably,' Horton agreed. 'Unless they went regularly or she trusted him implicitly. If our killer is local then he could be following the news of the discovery, worried in case we discover his crime. He could make contact with us on some pretext in order to find out how we're progressing with the investigation.'

'Then we keep this from the media for the time being,' Uckfield said. 'And that means we can't go back there digging up the island with flapping blue crime-scene tape, white-suited SOCOs and uniformed police all over the place.'

'But we can return under the guise of further archaeological exploration, based on the fact the skeletons are of historical interest,' Horton said. 'We'll need the Ministry of Defence's cooperation not only to access and seal off the island but also to keep quiet about Quintessa.'

'I'll talk to whoever's in charge. We'll contain this for as long as possible, but you know what it's like — some bright spark will a smell a rat.' Uckfield grinned at his pun.

Marsden smiled politely, but he was young and keen on promotion.

'They might very well find some,' Horton said.

'As long as they don't dig up any more recent corpses. Who found the skeletons?'

Horton answered, 'A Neil Brandon.'

'What's he like?'

'I don't know. I didn't interview him.'

'Why not?' Bliss asked, surprised and clearly with disapproval, judging by her sour expression.

'Because it was Ministry of Defence land and therefore, strictly speaking, not our jurisdiction. Sergeant Dai Elkins and PC Phil Ripley attended because Brandon called Elkins direct. Brandon keeps a boat on the Cruising Association's pontoons nearby and has the marine unit's number. Elkins informed the Ministry of Defence marine unit, but because they were busy escorting an aircraft carrier into the harbour, a bunch of ancient skeletons was not high on their list of priorities. Elkins rang it through to me and I told him to take Brandon's contact details and get shot of him quickly. It wasn't in our best interest to have him on the island when the experts arrived.'

Horton didn't add that Elkins had told him Brandon was a bit of a pain in the arse, the type of man who was an expert on everything, or thought he was. 'I notified Inspector Jenkins of the Ministry of Defence CID, who said he'd call in their team of army forensic experts.' But Horton knew as well as Uckfield that the Ministry of Defence CID's main area of investigation was in developing intelligence on suspected terrorists and saboteurs, not homicide, and particularly not ancient ones. This would be their baby. Uckfield would still need to notify them and clear it with them, though. 'Sergeant Elkins met with Brandon later and obtained a statement from him.'

'He *was* trespassing on government property,' Bliss stressed. 'Aren't the Ministry of Defence going to prosecute him?'

'That's down to them but I doubt it.'

'So he gets away with breaking the law?'

Horton raised his eyebrows. 'You want us to charge him?' he said, managing to inflect incredulity in his voice, which made her eyes narrow even further.

'He could be the killer revisiting the scene, claiming he'd found the skeletons as a way of forcing us to help him confess. What was he doing on the island in the first place?'

'Looking for artefacts, according to Sergeant Elkins.'

'Huh!' she scoffed. 'I suppose he informed the press of his find.'

'No law against that,' Horton replied, but if there had been, Bliss would have said Brandon should have been charged. 'If we interview him now, he'll know there's something not right about one or more of those skeletons. Yes, I know we could say it's routine,' he hastily added when she opened her mouth to reply, 'but he could go running to the media, thinking he's got a juicy story.' Horton looked pointedly at Uckfield, who had just ordered them to keep the news contained.

Uckfield hauled himself up. 'We'll speak to Brandon later. I'll break the bad news to ACC Dean.'

But Bliss wasn't going to give up yet. Rising, she addressed Uckfield. 'We should run a check on him. Sergeant Cantelli can do that.'

Uckfield agreed. Dismissed, they returned to CID, leaving Bliss with her small victory.

'Did you speak to Danby about Goldsby?' Cantelli asked.

Horton hadn't had the chance to relay that conversation to the sergeant yet. 'I did. He had nothing to add to what you had already told me.'

'Adele's call came from the public payphone at Portsmouth Harbour railway station,' Cantelli said.

Which wasn't far from the Wightlink car ferry terminal. The call had been made ninety-four minutes before the sailing. Perhaps after making it she had changed her mind. She'd got on a train and disappeared back to where she had come from. He said as much as they stopped at the drinks machine outside the CID office.

Cantelli pressed the button for tea. 'The call didn't come through the general switchboard. She rang your direct line. The only way she would have known that number is if someone gave it to her or she has one of your business cards with it on.'

Horton gave them out to many people, including those in the community and those connected with the investigations he was involved in. For all he knew, he could have given it to Adele Goldsby himself without recognizing who she was.

'Well, if she's still burning with a desire to tell me something, she'll call again.' He selected coffee, black, no sugar.

'What do you make of Quintessa?' Cantelli asked.

Walters looked up briefly from his computer then fixed his eyes back on it. Horton hesitated, wondering whether or not to confide in Cantelli, but he had nothing to go on that could confirm the basis of his suspicions that it might be Jennifer. It was too nebulous. He was probably being a bit paranoid.

'I'm not sure, but I'd like to see where she was found. I'll get Elkins to take me over to the island on the RIB. It's OK, Barney, you're not coming,' Horton added. 'Bliss has ordered you to do a check on Brandon and far be it for me to go against her commands.'

Cantelli smiled. 'That'll make a change.'

'Brief Walters. I can see how keen he is to know what's going on.'

'Huh?' Walters didn't even glance at them.

In his office, Horton rang Elkins, who said they were on the launch at Hamble but that they'd transfer to the RIB. They'd be at the secure berth at the port within half an hour. That gave Horton time to finish his coffee and check his messages. There was nothing from Adele Goldsby.

He stopped off at the canteen to buy some sandwiches. He didn't for one moment believe he would uncover anything from seeing the burial place of Quintessa that could help them progress the investigation, but as he walked under the motorway subway towards the port, he knew it wasn't inspiration on Quintessa's untimely death that he hoped to stimulate, but Jennifer's. And the two could very well be the same.

CHAPTER FIVE

'Lucky for her Neil Brandon got nosy, otherwise she might have lain there for many more decades,' Elkins said as PC Ripley swung the craft out into the harbour. Horton had updated him.

'Unlucky for whoever killed and buried her.' Horton unwrapped his sandwiches.

'Think he might still be around?'

'The 1980s aren't that long ago.'

'Depends who you're talking to. To Ripley, they're as ancient as the Second World War.'

Ripley tossed them a smile.

Elkins continued, 'The killer could have been in his late fifties or even older when he killed her, which would make him in his nineties, *if* he's still alive.'

None of them had mentioned that at the briefing. Horton didn't think Uckfield really believed they'd catch Quintessa's killer, or that they'd discover who she was or why she'd been killed. But he had to make sure it wasn't Jennifer who had lain in that grave for over thirty years.

He bit into his sandwich and gazed around the harbour as Ripley manoeuvred the RIB across it. The sky was heavy with clouds. The air felt damp. It wasn't the kind of weather for sailors — save the exceptionally hardy or mad ones, or those from the sailing schools, and there weren't many of them about. He thought back to how the harbour had looked in the eighties. None of the marinas he could see now lining the shores of Gosport and to the north-east of the harbour had existed then. Instead, there had been shipbuilding, a greater presence of both the navy and the army, marshland, fishing boats, the commercial quay and, of course, a much bigger dockyard.

As Rat Island drew closer, Horton addressed Elkins. 'You said Brandon claimed to have come here looking for artefacts. Is it a regular hobby of his?'

'So he says. He said he knows he was trespassing but no one takes any notice of that, not where Rat Island is concerned. He said the MOD have long lost interest in the place and are not bothered about anyone landing on it.'

'So he comes armed with a metal detector?'

'No. He just mooches around to see what he can find. Even Ripley's found a clay pipe. Not sure he's handed it in, though — probably smokes it in private.'

Horton doubted it. Ripley was a fit, healthy and active officer.

'Brandon saw what he thought might be a bone. He cleared away some earth and realized he was looking at a humerus.'

'He has knowledge of skeletons.'

'And more,' Elkins said pointedly. 'He says he called me immediately and didn't touch anything, which, when we arrived, we saw to be true. It didn't look as though he'd poked around and covered it up. I saw the bone he was referring to and carefully cleared above it and found the skull. That's where the remains were found.' Elkins pointed to the clump of trees and bushes to the south of the small island on a slight knoll as Ripley brought the RIB up onto the shingle.

Alighting with Elkins, leaving Ripley on the RIB, Horton made towards it. The place of burial was at the furthest end from where the island joined the mainland by the spit at low tide. In the dark it would have been difficult to transport a body from there. But how did they know it had been dark? She could have come here with her killer in daylight, just as Brandon had done. Perhaps she and her killer had come in search of artefacts, although in the early eighties that would have been more difficult because of the large military presence in the area. The island would have been better protected and anyone landing in daylight could have been spotted and intercepted. No, it was much more likely to have been dark or dusk with perhaps poor visibility such as fog or driving rain. But if the latter then Quintessa must have already been dead, because she'd hardly have agreed to set off for an archaeological exploration or clandestine meeting with a lover in such inclement weather.

'If the killer brought her here by boat, already dead, why bury her? Why not dump her at sea?'

'Maybe his boat was too small to take out into the Solent. It might have been a dinghy or a rowboat.'

There was that. 'I suppose the weather could have been bad. But that could have made ideal conditions for ditching a corpse unseen and undetected.'

'They didn't have sophisticated navigation systems then and perhaps chummy wasn't a sailor and couldn't risk taking her out any further.'

If so, then he could have kept his boat in this area on a mooring or on the shore somewhere. But tracing that boat and its owner from way back in the eighties was impossible.

They drew up in front of the red-and-white tape flapping in the wind and strung out on thin poles, marking the area where the skeletons had been found. The earth where they had been excavated was exposed. The fifth grave was set a little apart from the others, as Lauder had said, and as Horton had seen from the photographs on Uckfield's desk. He gazed down at the wet earth, wondering if he was looking at Jennifer's final resting place, but he got no kind of sensation, premonition or gut feeling.

'Do you think Brandon could have killed her and buried her here?' he asked. If so, then Quintessa certainly wasn't

Jennifer because Horton couldn't see how Brandon could have known her. But he rapidly revised that opinion. He had no information on Brandon's background. It was wrong to make assumptions.

'I guess it's possible,' Elkins answered. 'But if pushed, I'd say he wouldn't have the guts, the passion or the drive to kill, but he does have an ego and that in itself can be enough. He thinks he's a cut above the average but he isn't. He didn't look uneasy or anxious, more triumphant, I'd say. But that's because this is probably the biggest thing that's ever happened to him. He'll be able to bore everyone rigid about it for months — years, even — and he's got his face and name in the local newspaper. Probably miffed he didn't make the nationals.'

Horton recalled the pictures he'd seen of the skeletons. 'They were all buried in the same direction, head to the west and feet to the east. Why not positioned north to south?'

'Maybe there's a certain way people are meant to be buried.'

'I'll ask Cantelli. He knows about that sort of thing.'

Horton wondered if the killer had known that the other skeletons were here and how they'd been buried, and whether he had laid out Quintessa in the same manner because of it. If so, was he some kind of historian or archaeologist? Had Quintessa been a fellow archaeologist and therefore eager and willing to come with a colleague to the island at an unsocial hour? Had there been previous excavations on the island and skeletons unearthed? Horton made a mental note to ask Trueman. 'Let's take a stroll round the island.'

'Won't take long.'

They walked further down to the shore. The wind had risen dramatically in the last twenty minutes and was now gusting up the harbour, bringing with it a fine, icy drizzle, the kind that seemed to seep right through to your bones. Ahead, to Horton's right, were the masts of the boats in Gosport Marina, which had been the Camper & Nicholsons shipyard in the eighties. It had closed down some years ago but the company still existed and was thriving worldwide, particularly in the manufacture of luxury yachts like the one he'd seen earlier at Oyster Quays. Beyond that were more masts, this time of the boats in Haslar Marina. A tugboat was ploughing through the restless waves, making for the quayside to Horton's left, towards a grey naval ship. Cranes dominated the dockside of Portsmouth and beyond them, he could see the tall buildings of Oyster Quays and the dome of Portsmouth Cathedral, both of which were rapidly becoming obscured by the fine, salt-laden, freezing rain.

They rounded the southern tip of the island and Horton was glad to be out of the full force of the wind and rain. Boats were moored on the pontoons of the marina across the narrow stretch of water that separated Rat Island from the mainland, and several were on buoys in the channel.

Elkins said, 'This would have looked a bit different in 1980. No mooring buoys back then, no pontoons and no marina.'

Horton knew that, and the brick building he was now gazing at across the water had been the Royal Navy Victualling Yard. He nodded towards it. 'Do you know when that closed?'

'About 1990 or 1991, I think. This was all owned by the armed forces then. That low brick building over there—' Elkins pointed further north where the spit joined the mainland of Gosport at Priddy's Hard — 'was an armaments depot for both the Royal Navy and the army in the eighties. It's now a naval warfare museum where Brandon works as a volunteer. He lives close by, is retired and keeps a boat on the pontoons at the Cruising Association just over there.'

Horton looked to where Elkins was indicating. There were several craft berthed and many others moored up on buoys. They walked on and were soon back on the RIB. Viewing the scene hadn't sparked any new ideas or given Horton any confirmation that this was where Jennifer had ended up. He hadn't really expected it to. He asked Elkins to keep him posted if he or the Ministry of Defence marine unit found anyone attempting to land on the island, especially Brandon. 'Now he's found five skeletons he might be tempted to return to see if he can locate any others.'

'And if he did bury Quintessa then he might return to the scene of the crime,' Elkins replied. 'Or try and pump us for more information.'

* * *

Back at the station, Walters was still engrossed in his search for stolen goods on the internet. Horton thought he was spinning it out and said as much.

'The phones have been busy,' Walters offered up as his excuse.

Horton updated Cantelli about his trip to Rat Island, which didn't take long because there was nothing to tell him. He asked him about burial rituals. 'Is there a special way that bodies should be buried?'

'Graves in Christian churchyards are usually arranged so that bodies can lie with their heads to the west and their feet to the east.'

'As in the case of our five skeletons.'

'Yes, but burying convicts in consecrated ground would have been out of the question.'

'Hence, they were dumped on Rat Island. I'd have thought there would be more there.'

'There probably are.'

'Did the killer choose to bury Quintessa facing that way because he knew that was the way Christians are usually buried, or was it just a fluke?' Horton mused.

'Maybe he found the other skeletons and just repeated the pattern, thinking that if she was ever found her remains would be construed as being just those of another convict.'

Which was what had originally been thought but closer examination would always have decried they weren't. And Quintessa could have been discovered years earlier with the flesh still on her bones, making her identification easier.

'What have you got on Neil Brandon?'

'Very little. No criminal record. No driver's licence, retired, aged sixty-six, living on the state pension, owns his house in Gosport.'

'And has a boat, according to Elkins.' Horton wondered if Brandon had owned a boat in the eighties. 'Have you told Bliss?'

'Sent her an email. She's in a meeting.'

'When isn't she?'

Horton rose. In his office, he quickly checked through his messages, wondering if Adele Goldsby might have phoned to explain why she hadn't made the rendezvous. She hadn't. Neither was there any message on his mobile phone from Billy Jago asking for a meeting to explain why his tip-off about the lorry thieves hadn't materialized into action. Horton rang Trueman and asked if there had been any excavations on Rat Island before 1980 up until the estimated time of Quintessa's death.

'Probably not, it being Ministry of Defence land, but I'll check with them to make sure. Their team is going in tomorrow to carry out a wider search for us. And we've come up with three missing women who fit Lauder's profile — Margaret Telham, aged thirty-four, from Reading; Kathryn Cutler, aged thirty from Luton, and Karen Klixby, aged twenty-eight, from Basingstoke. We're getting more on them tomorrow.'

Will one of them turn out to be Quintessa? wondered Horton, turning his attention to his paperwork.

It was just before seven when Walters waddled into his office to say he was off home. He couldn't find any of the stolen goods from the Somerstown robberies for sale on the internet; Uniform were out and about on the estate making enquiries and listening out for any gossip; and the fingerprint bureau hadn't come up with a match. Horton thought they might still strike lucky on that score because the thieves could get careless on their next job.

Cantelli popped his head around the door to say he was leaving unless there was anything else that needed to be done.

If there was, Horton didn't think Cantelli would stay awake long enough to do it. He might not either. His head was throbbing again and his eyes were itching with fatigue. He postponed his idea of going in search of Billy Jago in the pubs and amusement arcades and shut down his computer.

Grabbing his leather jacket and helmet, he made for the rear exit and had just reached his Harley Davidson when his phone rang. He was tempted to ignore it but it could be Jago.

It wasn't. It was Mike Danby. 'That potential client I was going to see — there wasn't one,' he curtly announced. 'The call was a hoax.'

Horton was suddenly wide awake. 'What happened?'

'I'll tell you over a pie and a pint. The Still and West, Old Portsmouth.'

'Be there in ten minutes.'

CHAPTER SIX

Danby was at the bar drinking a non-alcoholic lager. The pub was fairly quiet, it still being early evening, and the bitterly cold weather and icy rain were keeping many indoors. They ordered some food then, taking their drinks, retired to a table overlooking the narrow harbour entrance.

Without preamble, Danby began. 'A woman rang me this morning just after eight. She apologized for the early call and asked if I could meet her boss on the Isle of Wight at his house in Totland Bay on the south-west of the island. He had an urgent security requirement that he wanted to discuss with me. She knew it was short notice but it was extremely important, and my company had excellent testimonials. She sounded genuine. She gave her name as Sophie Kranton.'

'And you've checked her out and she doesn't exist.'

'She does, but I don't think a ten-year-old from Market Harborough could fabricate such a story.' Danby took a pull at his drink.

'You think it was Adele Goldsby?'

'I think it damn queer that you and I end up on the same ferry at the same time and we're both there on a wild goose chase. Once I realized the property was empty, on the market, and had never belonged to Peter Jarvis, I—'

'Jarvis?' Horton sharply interjected.

'Yes. The alleged client. Why? You know him?' It was Danby's turn to look surprised.

'If it's the same man, he's the owner of an international packaging and food processing company in Gosport.'

'*Was* the owner. He recently sold it for a fortune. How do you know him?'

'He's my ex-wife's boyfriend.'

Danby's expression turned to one of puzzlement. 'That makes this even more intriguing. You seem to be the connection.'

'For what, though, and why?'

Danby shrugged.

'Tell me more about Jarvis,' Horton said eagerly, trying to make some sense of this.

'He now runs a fund specializing in start-up companies and has a major share in a bioplastics company, based here in Portsmouth, which he founded and which is attached to the university, pulling together some of the best brains in the industry.'

'And what's bioplastics when it's at home?'

'I asked him that,' Danby said with a grin.

'You've spoken to him?' Horton asked, surprised.

'Of course. I called Jarvis's company and got his PA, his real one, who said she had never heard of Sophie Kranton, but she would pass on my message. Jarvis called me back within twenty minutes, confirmed what his PA had said and asked if I would meet him on his boat at Oyster Quays.'

Into Horton's head flashed the picture of that large luxury motorboat he'd seen from the ferry that morning and his heart sank. 'Don't tell me, he owns that superyacht moored up there on the outer pontoon.'

'He does.'

Horton felt a wave of bitterness mingled with despair, not because he was jealous of Jarvis's wealth or the fact that Catherine had bagged herself a rich boyfriend, but with thoughts of his daughter, Emma, on board that giant luxury yacht. She'd spent last Christmas with her mother and Jarvis on a boat on the Côte d'Azur but he'd had no idea it had been so luxurious when she'd chatted on innocently on the phone to him about the big boats all around them, not realizing how dismal and inadequate it had made him feel. Now he felt even more dejected. How could the small sailing yacht he lived on compete with Jarvis's palatial one? It couldn't.

'Why does he want to see you?' he asked, trying not to show his feelings.

'Why do you think?'

'For security purposes?' Horton thought anxiously of Emma. 'Why should he need protection?'

'I'll know that after I've seen him. My appointment is at ten tomorrow morning. Perhaps the alleged Sophie Kranton has done me some good.'

'Or rather Adele Goldsby.'

Before Danby could answer, the waitress arrived with their meals. After she had checked they had all they needed and left, Danby continued, 'Why would Adele use a phoney name *if* she set this up?'

'Because she knew you wouldn't agree to spend an hour and a half on a round trip to the Isle of Wight without something at the end of it.'

'You make me sound mercenary.'

'Aren't you?'

'No, just realistic and businesslike. I have to be, Andy. I no longer draw a salary, like you. If I don't get clients, I don't get paid and neither do my staff.'

Horton shrugged and sprinkled his chips with salt and pepper.

'OK then, why the hoax phone call in the first place?'

'Because we are both connected with her father's death,' Horton said. 'I found the body and you were one of the investigating officers.' But that didn't answer why she had used Jarvis's name to draw Danby to the ferry. 'Did the ferry feature in the investigation?' Horton repeated the question he'd put to Cantelli earlier, expecting the same reply.

'It never came up at all. Neither did anything connected with the Solent. And although Adele Goldsby managed to get us on the same ferry, how could she know we'd meet up? I could have stayed on the lower deck and you on the upper.'

'But she knew I'd be looking out for her and that I'd see you. Even if you hadn't come onto the upper deck, I would have found you before you disembarked.' Horton took a swig of his Coke and continued eating, trying to puzzle out this new development as he watched the Brittany ferry edge its way into the harbour, lights blazing. It seemed so close he felt he could almost touch it. To add to his concerns over Quintessa possibly being Jennifer, he was now worried about Emma's contact with Jarvis. He had nothing to indicate that Jarvis was involved in anything criminal, and perhaps a rich man like Jarvis did need additional security. Perhaps bioplastics was a dangerous field to be involved in — he didn't know — but why would Adele have used Jarvis as the phoney client to lure Danby to the ferry? Had Adele been in a relationship with Jarvis and this was her way of getting back at him for ditching her in favour of Catherine? Was she eaten up with jealousy and stirring trouble for him? *It has to be you.* Why? Because of Catherine and Jarvis?

Thoughtfully, he continued, 'You could have been anywhere in the UK, abroad even, working with a client. I could have been on holiday or on a course, or working elsewhere in Hampshire, so she must have checked us out before ringing us. She called you first at eight o'clock and me an hour and a half afterwards. Did you trace the call?'

'Yes. It was made from the harbour railway station.'

'Same here and probably from the same payphone. But not immediately afterwards — why not?'

'Maybe she thought you wouldn't be at your desk until after nine o'clock.'

'Did she call you on your mobile?'

'Yes, but my number's no secret. I give my business card out to clients, prospective clients and to those I meet at conferences, exhibitions and seminars. I gave you a card a few months ago.'

'And I've still got it in my wallet. I certainly haven't given it to anyone, and neither have I lost or misplaced my wallet at any time. Ask Jarvis tomorrow if he knew Adele or her father.'

'Are you kidding? He's got nothing to do with this.'

'Then why did she use his name?'

Danby didn't answer.

Horton asked a question that had occurred to him earlier and which he'd postponed. 'What made you think the Peter Jarvis you were supposed to meet on the island was the same as the one currently on his boat in Portsmouth?'

'Because this Sophie Kranton said that her boss was the former owner of a food processing and packaging company based in Gosport and was now involved in a new business venture which needed certain security checks to be carried out, hence the contact with me. It wasn't difficult to put two and two together and come up with this Jarvis at Oyster Quays, especially as he was featured in all the business media and it *is* my job to know about the rich and influential. My company has access to certain databases. It was easy getting Jarvis's telephone number. I was once a detective, you know,' he added caustically but with a smile.

Horton continued eating in silence. He saw what Adele must have been getting at when she'd said, *There's something I need to show you*. Yes, an expensive superyacht in Oyster Quays, and she'd used Danby to deliver that message. But why play such an elaborate game? Was it to make him more inquisitive about Jarvis? If so, she had succeeded.

'Did Jarvis's name come up during the Dudley Goldsby investigation?'

'Of course not. Look, Andy, she could be a nutcase, hell-bent on stirring up trouble for Jarvis. Maybe she worked for him and got sacked, or had an affair with him and he ditched her. Perhaps that's why Jarvis is looking for more security — she could be sending him abusive emails or letters or pestering him with phone calls.'

'In which case, her name will come up during your meeting, unless you've already mentioned it to him.'

'I haven't. I didn't know then that Jarvis was connected with you, or, to be more accurate, with Catherine. I asked him on the phone if he'd ever heard of Sophie Kranton. He said he hadn't, and neither had he owned a property on the Isle of Wight or even thought of buying one there. He said he couldn't think why someone would have used his name but suggested that she had probably plucked it out of a newspaper article and that the hoax must have been destined for me for some purpose. That obviously made me wonder about our allegedly coincidental meeting on the ferry. I apologized for troubling him and said I'd look into it. He said that as I had made contact, and as my company had an excellent record and glowing testimonials from some people he knew—'

'How did he know that?'

'He obviously looked me up after his PA told him I'd called. He asked for a meeting while he was in Portsmouth.'

'It all sounds a bit tenuous to me.'

'It would. It's what you're paid to think.'

'But you must admit there has to be something behind this.'

Danby shrugged. 'It's a strange coincidence.'

'It could be more than that.'

'Look, if it transpires that Jarvis is receiving threats or being stalked by some mad female called Adele Goldsby then I'll get what I can from him, but if he needs my services for some other reason then I'm not mentioning her.' He pushed away his empty plate and consulted his expensive watch.

Horton took the hint. He hadn't finished his meal, but he'd lost his appetite. They headed out into the blustery, cold night. The rain had thankfully stopped for a moment. Turning towards the High Street, where he had parked his Harley alongside Danby's Range Rover, he said, 'Was there anyone she was close to when she lived here in Portsmouth?'

'Not her mother. They hated the sight of each other. She worked with her father, though.'

'His agent or secretary might know what happened to her after her father's death, then.'

'You'll need a clairvoyant to speak to Harry Belling, his agent. He died nine months after Goldsby. I'm not sure where Frieda Chillerton is or what she's doing now.'

Horton would be able to trace her. 'You'll call me tomorrow and let me know how the meeting goes?'

Danby said he would.

Horton watched him drive away before climbing onto his Harley. He hesitated, wondering whether to make for Oyster Quays to take a fresh look at Jarvis's superyacht. But where would that get him? Nowhere, was the answer, save that he might discover if Catherine was on board. How would he know that though unless he boarded the yacht? He didn't think he'd be very welcome. He doubted he'd be able to see who was on board from the quayside or the pontoon. He might find her car in the car park, but what did it matter if she was there or not? Emma was at her boarding school. He had been against her going away to school originally but now he was thankful.

He swung east and made his way slowly along the deserted seafront towards the marina where he lived. He thought of Jarvis's yacht at Oyster Quays, large, comfortable and opulent while his was cold, small and basic. Emma had never even slept on board. He had no overnight access to his daughter, while a man who had no blood ties with her had the right to whisk her away to expensive locations, share Christmas with her and spend as much time with her as he wished.

His stomach knotted in anger and anguish. It wasn't right and fair, but then when had life been fair? He had to do something about it. A good lawyer might get the family court to give him more access to Emma, but so far, he had avoided that, not wanting his personal life to be aired in public. He'd have to steel himself for that, though. Emma meant more to him than his personal feelings and the shame that he felt at being abandoned by his mother.

He pulled over at the pier and stared across the road — this time not to where Jennifer had worked at the casino, which had long gone along with the nightclubs and bars that had once surrounded it, now replaced by flats, but at the elegant and large hotel where Dudley Goldsby had ended his life. There had to be some reason for Adele's antics this morning and there had to be some connection between Peter Jarvis and her father, otherwise why mention the man? He needed to know more about the Goldsbys.

He reached for his phone and called the station. When Sergeant Warren came on the line, he asked him to get an address for Mrs Frieda Chillerton. Tomorrow, if she was still living locally, he'd pay her a call.

CHAPTER SEVEN

Thursday

It was just after eight when Horton knocked on the door of Frieda Chillerton's house on the outskirts of Portsmouth. The smartly dressed, slender woman in her late fifties wearing black trousers and a short red jacket looked momentarily stunned at finding a leather-clad man on her doorstep and a Harley Davidson parked in the road by her driveway, but as Horton quickly introduced himself and showed his warrant card, her expression relaxed.

'I'd like to talk to you about your former employer, Dudley Goldsby, if you could spare me a few minutes,' he said. He had considered overnight how to approach her and thought she might be more forthcoming if he began the interview discussing her late boss. Then he could steer it towards asking about Adele and Peter Jarvis.

'I can spare you a great deal more than that, Inspector, as it's about Dudley.' She stepped back and Horton entered a wide hall with two doors off either side and a door ahead that led into a bright, modern kitchen. He apologized for disturbing her so early.

She dismissed that with a smile. 'It's lucky you caught me. I was just leaving for work.'

'Do you need to phone to let them know you might be late?'

'No. It's my own business and the staff can manage very well without me for a while. I run a recruitment agency in the town. Come through to the lounge.'

She showed him into the room on the left and invited him to take one of the sumptuous armchairs. Her taste was contemporary. The room was immaculate.

'Are you reinvestigating Dudley's death?' she asked eagerly, sitting opposite him and folding her well-manicured hands in her lap. Her hair was short, straight, grey-steaked and flicked out level with her chin. Her eyes a pale blue. They were keen, intelligent and friendly, but there were heavy bags under them — although they didn't look tired — and lines in the corners and around the mouth. Her skin had lost the lustre of youth but was carefully made-up. He thought she might once have smoked quite heavily.

He was surprised by her natural assumption and his curiosity surrounding the former MP's death increased. 'No, but something has come up that I'm puzzled over.'

'Such as why a man with no signs of depression or any reason whatsoever to kill himself would take an overdose of illegal drugs, or any drugs, which he abhorred.' Her crisp tone had a hard edge to it.

'You don't believe he took his own life?'

'I do not,' she declared. 'I didn't then, and I don't now.'

'But the alternative is—'

'Someone killed him, yes.'

Her conviction was persuasive. He stilled his racing thoughts and watched her carefully. 'Any idea who?'

She held his gaze steadily, almost defiantly, then sighed and relaxed. 'None. That's the bewildering and frustrating thing about Dudley's death. There was no one I could even remotely suspect of committing such a terrible act. I know what you'll say, and I agree — even the most mild-mannered person can be driven to extremes. But I've gone over it so many times, both when it occurred and over the years, and I still can't think who could have been so desperate as to do that. And neither can I come up with anyone who Dudley could have hurt or angered enough to provoke such retribution. Oh, there were those who didn't agree with his views, or his politics, but that wasn't a reason to kill him. I'll admit, Inspector, that it is sufficient reason for some extremists and terrorists, but Dudley wasn't killed in any kind of display of outrage or terror. He was a diligent, thoughtful and intelligent backbencher and a highly respected and extremely good constituency MP.'

It sounded like hero worship, but Horton knew it wasn't from what he'd read and heard about the politician from Cantelli and Danby.

'There were those both on the extreme right and left who didn't agree with Dudley, but no one I could even begin to suspect of wanting to kill him. Nor can I see how anyone could have made him take those drugs unless he believed they were something else.'

'Any ideas of why he went to that hotel room or why he was naked?'

'He wasn't there to meet a woman,' she answered crisply.

'How can you be so sure?'

'Because I knew him. He wasn't having an affair and neither was he the sort of man to pick up a prostitute.'

But did she *really* know that? Maybe Goldsby was good at hiding that kind of thing. 'Did anyone threaten him, either verbally or via the post or email?'

'Not that I'm aware of. I opened all the post — there was nothing, not even crank letters. But he would have received emails direct. He never said that anyone had threatened him, and the police went through his computer and his hard drive and never found anything, or if they did, they certainly didn't tell me or make it known at the inquest.'

'Did he have a government-issue computer?'

'No, only the one in his office and one at home.'

'What was he like as a person?'

She answered without any hesitation. 'Quiet, thorough, kind, intelligent.'

'And on the debit side?'

She smiled. 'There weren't any, not unless you count being too kind and too trusting as debits, and they certainly were when it came to Prudence.'

'His wife.'

'In name only. Dudley couldn't believe she was being unfaithful to him, although it was blatantly obvious to me and to Harry Belling, his agent, but then Prudence thought Dudley was having an affair with me. He wasn't. I was and still am happily married. My husband is a sales director for a technology company and has never had the slightest interest in politics.'

Horton wasn't sure he believed the bit about her and Dudley not having an affair. But he let it go. 'Tell me about Dudley's background.'

'You must know it already.'

'Only from what I've read. I'd like to hear it from you.'

Horton watched as she composed her thoughts. After a moment, she began, 'Dudley had a Christian upbringing and remained a devout Christian, like his parents and grand-parents, all through his life. His mother was an intelligent woman who taught at adult education colleges and was very keen on women's education. She stood for parliament in 1950 in Surrey but wasn't elected. She remained a lifelong Labour activist and did a great deal of support work in Portsmouth with prostitutes, working primarily in Portsea and out of St Agnes's Church in the city centre.'

Horton knew it well, and the Portsea area. He'd spent some months there in a shithole of a children's home, con-fused, bewildered and hurting. In fact, it had been from that children's home that Eileen and Bernard, his foster parents, had rescued him. Or rather, Andrew Ducale had — the man who had left the photograph from 1967 on his boat — and had placed him with his twin sister, Eileen, for her to look after him. There was no official record of it, though, because the file on him being in care had been destroyed long ago.

'Dudley's father was a strong socialist and an active trade unionist,' Frieda Chillerton said. 'Dudley was their only child. He was never spoiled, though. His parents didn't believe in private education and neither did Dudley. He sent his daughter to the state schools in Portsmouth. Dudley passed the eleven plus and went to grammar school, another thing he despised — the very idea of labelling children as failures at the age of eleven was abhorrent to him. He went on to become a naval architect at Camper and Nicholsons shipyard at Gosport before leaving to stand for parliament. Stop me if this is irrelevant.'

'It's not.' But the mention of the shipyard brought back thoughts of his visit to Rat Island yesterday. He wondered if anything further had come in on Quintessa's murder, although he suspected it was too early unless Trueman and Marsden had got something more on the missing women fitting the age of the remains. He'd spent a restless night trying to shut out the images of those bones being Jennifer's, and Emma being with Peter Jarvis on that damn great yacht. He hadn't succeeded. Even when he'd drifted into sleep, his dreams had been confused and haunting.

'Dudley was selected as the Labour candidate for the Portsmouth South West constituency for the by-election in 1986 following the previous MP's death in 1985 and was elected,' Frieda went on. 'He held the seat until his death and would have secured it again in the 2005 election had he lived.'

'When did you start working for him?'

'Just after the 1987 general election. I'd met him at a business function in Portsmouth at the Guildhall earlier that year. I was responsible for organizing the event on behalf of my then boss, a company director involved with the Chamber of Commerce and the Institute of Directors. Dudley was the keynote speaker. He was a powerful orator, not blustery and bullish but quietly convincing, earnest and genuine, and it was that sincerity that won people over.'

'Including you.' Horton smiled.

She returned it. 'Yes, I was also struck by his total commitment. I told him that if he was looking for a secretary, I would be very interested. He offered me the job there and then.' A shadow crossed her face. She paused before continuing, 'He was a good constituency MP, Inspector, but he always said he never felt part of the Westminster club. He said that politicians were ambitious and careerist, and he was right, but he was neither. He genuinely wanted to make a difference to people's lives and change things for the better.'

'An idealist.'

'There's nothing wrong with that,' she retorted, although he didn't think he had uttered it scathingly. Less harshly, she added, 'But he was also realistic and he had a genuine vision. When Labour were in government he became spokesperson for the Department for Environment, Food and Rural Affairs, something he took very seriously. He was particularly keen on environmental matters, especially those connected with marine life, and he took a special interest in the fishing industry, not just UK-wide but our own fishing fleet here in Portsmouth, which he felt was as much part of the city's heritage as HMS *Victory* and the *Mary Rose*. He was also a member of the Defence Committee, which was equally important to him, Portsmouth being a naval city.'

'How did he get on with his agent, Harry Belling?'

'Fine, although Harry always tried to push him harder, urging him to be more ambitious. Dudley had a brain but he just didn't have the thrust and that ruthless edge to climb the political greasy pole.'

'And his relations with his family?'

She shook her head sadly. 'Do you know Prudence?'

'No.'

'Then you're lucky. She was then and probably still is a selfish, self-centred, heartless and feckless woman. In 1983 she thought she'd married a rising star in the political arena. Although she was never political herself, she envisaged Dudley being the next prime minister or chancellor of the exchequer. Instead, she ended up with a backbench MP, a spokesperson and a man devoted to his constituents, many of whom she considered were common and a waste of his time and talents. Dudley gave a lot of his time to Portsmouth — too much for Prudence's liking, and probably too much for Adele, his daughter. I felt sorry for her, having a mother who was more intent on having fun and a father who spent more time with his constituents than with his daughter.'

She had brought the conversation around to Adele. Good. 'Tell me about her,' he said.

'Dudley didn't mean to be a remote parent but that was the way it worked out. She came in for a lot of bullying at school because her father was the local MP. She was a shy, plain little creature, and although she never openly complained, I could see that it hurt her. She went to the local college to study for her A levels, but her heart wasn't in it. She did well despite that because she was always studious. Dudley wanted her to go to university but she refused. She said she didn't know what to study. She ended up working for me in the office. She was efficient, quiet and thorough. She helped her father in the general election campaign of 2001, the backroom stuff, and again in the run-up to the 2005 election. She was a bit of a lost soul, really.'

'Boyfriends?'

'None that I know of. I thought she'd be devastated over her father's death and she probably was, but I never saw her cry once.'

Horton recalled that Adele hadn't cried when he'd broken the news to her. Her face had turned ashen and he had seen the shock and horror in her eyes. He'd asked her if there was anyone she'd like him to call, but she'd said no, she'd be all right on her own. Prudence Goldsby hadn't been at home.

'In fact, Adele never showed any emotion at any time following her father's death or at the funeral, but I guess it went inside. Some people are like that. I tried to help her, to get closer to her, get her to confide in me, but she wasn't the confiding type. She didn't get on with her mother and there were no other close family members. I don't think she had any friends either. After Dudley's funeral I never saw or heard from her again. Do you know where she is now?'

'I was going to ask you that.' So, dead end there. 'Have you any idea as to why Mr Goldsby was in that particular hotel on the seafront?'

'None. As you probably know from your files, he'd held a public meeting that night in St Paul's Church hall at Somerstown. It was a good turnout for the area, just over fifty people.'

'Did he look or sound different that night? Did he seem worried or upset?'

She brushed back a strand of hair that to Horton hadn't looked misplaced. 'I've thought back to that night many times trying to see if I missed something. He was tired, yes, and he looked it, but there didn't seem to be anything worrying him and neither did he seem particularly elated or excited.'

'Perhaps he was just an expert at hiding his feelings.' *He was a politician*, Horton added silently.

'It's possible,' she acquiesced. 'He confided in me occasionally but never to the extent that he was despairing or depressed. He was essentially a very private person.'

Like him. But then he'd learned how to be private — it stopped you from getting hurt and exploited. Or did it?

'After the meeting ended, I collected my notes, put them in my briefcase and turned to talk to Adele who was sitting beside me. We were in the front row on the far left of the hall, facing the door that led up some steps on to the stage where Dudley was with Harry. After his talk, Dudley came down into the hall. I said a few words to Reverend Pilbeam about the meeting. It had gone well, there hadn't been any hecklers. Then I went into the lobby and to the ladies' toilets, after which I chatted to a few people and waited for Dudley and Harry to come out of the hall. Adele was with them.' She frowned as she recalled the night. 'Dudley looked drained. I told him to go home and relax. I gave Adele a lift home but Dudley declined. I assumed Harry would take him home. I didn't know that Dudley was going to that hotel and neither did Harry. Dudley told him he wanted to walk and get a bit of air.' Her mobile phone rang. She glanced at it. 'Do you mind if I take this? It's a client.'

'Of course.'

She left the room and Horton could hear her talking in the kitchen but not what she was saying. He glanced around the perfectly arranged and spotlessly clean lounge with its modern furniture and comfortable soft furnishings. Frieda Chillerton was obviously a lady who liked order and was organized and efficient. Had she always been like that, he wondered, or had there once been a rebellious streak in her? There was no evidence there had been, except that the lines on her face told him there might have been, not just because he thought she had been a smoker — that meant nothing — but he just had that feeling about her. There was a determination about her, that once she had made her mind up to have something, she got it, like securing the job with Goldsby. Despite her reassurance that there had never been anything sexual between her and Goldsby, he thought there might have been.

He rose and crossed to a silver-framed photograph on the oak unit. He assumed the square-set, affluent-looking man in a well-cut, light grey suit and standing next to Frieda was her husband. The picture had been taken recently. She was wearing a lilac dress and matching bolero jacket. They were standing in front of a vibrant display of rhododendrons. Neither was sporting a buttonhole, but the picture had all the hallmarks of a wedding photograph or perhaps an anniversary celebration. He noted there were no pictures of children or pets.

'Sorry about that,' she said, returning. 'I'll have to leave, but you're welcome to come back any time.'

She showed him to the door but there Horton paused. 'Would there have been anyone Mr Goldsby would have confided in aside from you and Mr Belling?'

'The only person I can think of would be the Reverend Simon Pilbeam. He was vicar of St Paul's Church,

Somerstown — probably still is. Dudley and he were good friends. I expect the police spoke to him at the time.'

Maybe they had. Neither Cantelli nor Danby had mentioned him but then there was no reason why they should have done. Horton had two more questions to ask. The first was where Dudley Goldsby had been buried, if he had, and not cremated.

'Kingston Cemetery, next to his parents and his grandparents' graves. It's on the far eastern side close to the railway line about halfway down.'

And his final question. 'Do you remember Mr Goldsby ever mentioning or talking about a man called Peter Jarvis?'

'Yes.'

Then it *was* Jarvis whom Adele had wanted to show him. With barely disguised interest, he said, 'How did they know each other?'

'They were at school together. Peter Jarvis went on to study science at Bristol University and Dudley naval architecture at Camper and Nicholsons, as I said, but they kept in touch over the years. Peter worked for the government as a research scientist before starting his business. His company was very active in the community in Portsmouth and Gosport, and he used to live in Portsmouth. He came to Dudley's funeral, which I helped Prudence to arrange. When I say "helped", she did practically nothing, but then I didn't expect her to — not out of grief, may I hasten to add, but idleness and disinterest. Let me know if I can be of further help, and if you're reopening the investigation.'

Horton said he would, but asked for her discretion in saying nothing about his enquiries for the time being. He gave her his business card with a request that she contact him if she thought of anything more that might be of interest. He rode further up the road and turned onto the hill that bordered Portsmouth to the north. There he pulled into a lay-by overlooking the flat urban sprawl of the city, the grey of the Solent and the hills of the Isle of Wight beyond it. The March wind was still bitingly cold and held the hint of snow. Officially it might be spring, but no one had told the weather that. He didn't envy the team excavating on Rat Island today. He called Cantelli.

'Has Bliss asked for me?' he said when Cantelli came on the line.

'Not yet, but she's bound to at any moment.'

'Tell her you don't know where I am.'

'I don't. Where are you?'

Horton told him. He relayed the news about the hoax call to Danby and that Frieda Chillerton had confirmed that Goldsby and Jarvis had known each other rather well.

'I don't remember the name Peter Jarvis coming up in the investigation,' Cantelli said, concerned. He knew that Jarvis was Catherine's new boyfriend. 'Or Reverend Pilbeam, but then none of Goldsby's friends or acquaintances were interviewed. I'm not sure we even had a list of them.'

Horton would have dearly loved to get his hands on the case file, but to request it would probably sound alarm bells in the hierarchy.

Cantelli said, 'We asked for last sightings of Goldsby, aside from those at that public meeting, but no one came forward to say they had seen him walking to the hotel or being driven there and he didn't take a taxi.'

'Has Adele left a message on my voicemail?'

'I'll check.'

Within a couple of minutes Cantelli came back on the line. 'No.'

'Contact the Transport Police, ask them to send over any CCTV footage from Portsmouth Harbour railway station for yesterday between 7 a.m. and 11 a.m. We'll see if we can spot Adele Goldsby, or anyone in the vicinity of the payphone at that time.'

'I take it we keep this from Bliss.'

'For now. Anything new come in on Quintessa?'

'Not that I'm aware of, but I'll check with Trueman. No new lorry-jacks last night.'

That was something at least. And Billy Jago hadn't been in touch, maybe because he was keeping a low profile after the false tip-off.

'And no further robberies in Somerstown reported,' Cantelli added.

That was where Horton was heading. Not to the small business estate where the robberies had occurred, but to the church of St Paul.

CHAPTER EIGHT

Horton thought he'd entered hell as the screams and squeals of what sounded like 200 children assaulted his eardrums. He'd been told by a woman cleaning the church that he'd find the Reverend Simon Pilbeam in the adjoining hall. He wondered if talking to the vicar now was such a good idea, but when he stepped into the main hall from the lobby, he saw the source of the clamour was in fact only several children, along with some mothers and the occasional father. Ahead, in front of the stage, a scrawny, silver-haired man wearing clerical dress and a concerned expression was talking to a stooping, thin man in his early sixties whom Horton instantly recognized — Keith Harnley. Horton had had the pleasure of nicking him several times for housebreaking.

The adults' conversations stopped as Horton crossed the hall and a man in his mid-twenties sneaked out, hiding his face. Horton didn't think he looked like a copper in his leather jacket and trousers, carrying a motorcycle helmet, but he obviously did. He noted the door to the stage that Frieda Chillerton had recently described to him.

Spotting him, Harnley stiffened and his small grey eyes narrowed with hatred and suspicion. 'What the f—?' But he quickly staunched the abusive language as he cast a sideways glance at the vicar, who was looking a little bewildered. 'What are you doing here?' Harnley amended with a snarl.

'I could ask the same of you, Keith. But you'd probably demand a lawyer.'

'Ha bloody ha. But if it's any of your business, copper, which it isn't, I bring my grandson here on Tuesdays and Thursdays and I help the vicar.'

'Quite the family man.' Horton raised his eyebrows and swivelled his incredulous glance from Harnley to the Reverend Pilbeam, who was now looking a little annoyed. 'And a reformed character, which I find very hard to believe. Are you sure you're not after the lead on the church roof — oh, but that's already been stolen, sold and replaced with tiles.'

'We're not all cynical sods like you,' Harnley hissed.

Pilbeam quickly interjected. 'I take it you're a police officer,' he said somewhat stiffly. His eyes darted nervously at Harnley and then around the room.

Probably wondering which of his flock I'm after, thought Horton. He reached for his warrant card. 'I'd like a word, vicar, if you can spare me a moment.'

'Me?' Pilbeam said, alarmed.

Harnley quickly jumped in. 'You're scraping the barrel, copper, if you think you've got something on the vicar.'

Pilbeam hastily addressed Harnley. 'Keith, I think it best if you see to your grandson. He looks as if he's about to hit that other little boy over the head with a plastic sword. I'll see what Inspector Horton wants.'

'Well, don't let him fit you up, he's good at that,' was Harnley's very loud parting shot.

Horton had never fitted Harnley up, just caught him in the act, and with stolen goods in his flat. He'd had a search warrant.

Pilbeam said, 'Shall we step into the church?'

'With pleasure,' Horton replied with feeling, eager to get away from the noise of the children, despite the fact that empty churches always depressed him. They made him feel claustrophobic, and the memory of almost being fried alive in the vestry of one fifteen months ago during a murder investigation didn't help.

They entered the gloomy interior, where an icy wind seemed intent on penetrating every nook and cranny in the echoing Victorian edifice. Pilbeam, looking worried, gestured Horton into one of the wooden chairs at the back of the church, to the right of the font. Horton felt cold even through his leather jacket — Pilbeam must have been freezing in his threadbare corduroy jacket over his cassock. Maybe he was wearing a woollen jumper under it and thermal underwear. His face was thin and drawn, his eyes ringed with fatigue and fraught with anxiety. Perhaps that was his natural manner. Perhaps the police made him nervous. Or perhaps he was worried about the havoc being caused by his young flock in the adjacent hall with no one in authority to oversee them. The woman who had been cleaning the church had disappeared. They had the place to themselves.

Pilbeam began, 'Keith Harnley has been out of trouble for five years, Inspector.'

Maybe, thought Horton, *or perhaps he just hasn't been caught.* He wondered about the most recent spate of robberies on business units in this area. Harnley usually went in for domestic properties but perhaps he'd branched out.

Pilbeam continued a little stiffly, 'I can see that you don't believe me, but I can assure you that he has reformed. Being diagnosed with bowel cancer and having a grandson on whom he dotes has helped him to stay out of trouble. His daughter, Bethany, works on Tuesdays and Thursdays and Keith looks after her child.'

'It's not him I've come to talk to you about, vicar. Or any of your parishioners. It's Dudley Goldsby.'

'Dudley?' Pilbeam's tired eyes widened, then narrowed with bewilderment. 'Are you reinvestigating his death?'

It was what Frieda Chillerton had asked, and it wasn't surprising that Pilbeam should have jumped to the same conclusion. Horton avoided answering the question. 'What was Mr Goldsby like?'

'Kind, genuine, dedicated to his work and the community,' came the instant reply.

More or less what Frieda Chillerton had said. Could someone be that perfect?

'The city lost a dedicated and caring politician when he died, and I lost a very good friend.' Pilbeam paused and eyed Horton keenly. 'The manner of his death was totally out of character. He would never have taken drugs and he would never have committed suicide. It would have been totally against his faith.'

'You think it was an accident?'

'I can't see what else it could have been. He must have picked up a bottle to drink from, which contained the cocaine.'

'No bottle was found with his body.'

'He must have thrown it away or it was picked up by someone else, the owner of it perhaps, who was unaware of what had happened or was too frightened to come forward.'

'You know who that is?' Horton asked eagerly, watching him, but Pilbeam shook his head with a small smile.

'No, Inspector. And no one has confessed to me.'

Pity. 'Did you see Mr Goldsby pick up a bottle and drink from it during or after the public meeting?'

'No. There was a jug of water on the stage. I put it there myself and both Harry Belling and Dudley drank from it. There were questions following Dudley's talk, then Harry brought the meeting to a close. I exchanged a few words with Mrs Chillerton, who was sitting at the front of the hall with Adele, and then I got called away by a parishioner, but I saw there were a few people around Dudley as he came down from the stage — the journalist from the local newspaper, Sam Kidlington, was one, and a couple of parishioners, Vera Rackton and Nigel Steller. And Vic Fisher was making a beeline for Dudley. Sadly, those parishioners are not with us any longer.' And neither was Kidlington, who had died a few years ago of a massive stroke.

'As I left, I remember thinking that Dudley looked drawn,' Pilbeam said. 'He'd been campaigning hard. I should have stayed and spoken to him. But I didn't. A regret I have to this day.'

'Did he speak to you about his concerns?'

'Only general ones to do with the city, sometimes political ones.'

'Any personal ones? His marriage, for example.'

A shadow crossed Pilbeam's long, gaunt face. 'He never openly spoke about it but it was a difficult and unhappy marriage. It troubled and upset him. He did his best but Prudence wasn't an easy woman to live with. She was restless and ambitious for her husband. She became increasingly frustrated and embittered by his lack of ambition. But Dudley was besotted with her. He knew of her affairs — not that he ever confided that to me,' he hastily added, 'but I could see the pain and hurt etched on his face.'

Pilbeam studied Horton in a way that made him feel slightly uncomfortable, but before he could speak, the reverend continued, 'Dudley always hoped they could be reconciled, but sadly that was never going to happen, even if he had lived. It upset him greatly that he'd failed in his marriage. He took his vows seriously but that's not much good when the other spouse doesn't do the same.'

Horton thought of his own marriage. He'd taken his vows very seriously. He'd been overjoyed that at last he'd found the love and stability he craved, and when Emma had been born, his joy had been complete. How wrong could he have been? At the first sign of trouble, Catherine had chosen to believe the worst in him. But now, as he looked back, he knew that things had started to go wrong between them long before that false allegation of rape.

Pilbeam said, 'And before you ask, Inspector, there was no one else in Dudley's life, man or woman. Dudley would never have been unfaithful.'

Horton nodded contemplatively. Never was a big word. Everyone was still singing from the same hymn sheet. 'And his daughter, Adele?' He was curious to know if Pilbeam's description of her would match that of Frieda Chillerton.

Pilbeam shook his head sorrowfully. 'Dudley loved his daughter, although I'm not sure that Adele fully realized that. He spent so much time with his constituents and on parliamentary business that he didn't have a great deal left over for Adele, and what he did have he gave to Prudence in the hope of trying to keep her. I think Prudence knew that and used to play on it and take pleasure in squeezing Adele out even further. It was as though she was jealous and resentful of her. Although she didn't want Dudley for herself, she didn't want him to love anyone else.'

Pilbeam's words struck a chord. It was what Cantelli had said about Catherine being jealous of his love for Emma as one of the reasons why she was being so obstructive.

'I've often wondered what Prudence would have done if Dudley had fallen in love with someone and had an affair. Dudley showed Adele love in the best way he could, but it wasn't a demonstrative love. Adele never complained, but I always got the impression that she was looking for and hoping for that one gesture that would show her how much her father loved her, and sadly she never got it, not to my knowledge anyway. At the funeral there was a hardness about her. She didn't show any sorrow and she wouldn't accept any comfort from me. She was polite, told me she was all right and not to bother with her. It was as though she'd erected a barrier around herself. You couldn't penetrate it. It happens sometimes. She left immediately after the wake. I don't know if it was that very night or the next day, but Mrs Chillerton told me that she'd gone.'

'Do you know where she went?'

'No. I haven't seen or heard from her since the funeral. I asked Prudence shortly after it but she said she didn't know where her daughter was or what her plans were, and I'm sad to say she didn't seem to care much either. She sold the house as soon as she could, and that was the last I saw of Prudence. Have you spoken to her?'

'No.'

'Will you?'

Horton wasn't sure. He'd like to, but interviewing her could lead her to inquire at a high level why he was asking questions about her daughter and nosing around her former husband's death. 'I don't think there will be any need,' he said, making to rise, but Pilbeam stalled him.

'There must be a reason why you're asking these questions now.' He ran a bony hand through his fine silver hair. His tired eyes looked deeply troubled.

Horton hesitated. Should he tell Pilbeam that Adele had been in touch and that he was concerned about her whereabouts? He decided not to for the moment. There was still a chance she might call him today. He took out his card. 'Will you let me know if you hear from Adele?'

'Is she in trouble?' Pilbeam asked, concerned.

'Why should she be?'

'When a police officer asks, it's rather a natural assumption, sadly.' He rose stiffly.

As they walked to the door, Horton elaborated. He thought he owed the vicar some kind of explanation and he didn't think Pilbeam was going to go around blabbing about it or stirring up trouble for him. 'I'm here unofficially because something was said to me recently about Mr Goldsby's death. I can't say more than that, vicar. If I get further information then maybe we can reopen the case, but at the moment there is nothing new to indicate that he didn't take the cocaine himself with the purpose of ending his life.' He paused and studied Pilbeam. 'Perhaps it was a cry for help and Mr Goldsby thought he'd be reached in time to be saved. Could he have left a message for his wife, only she didn't act on it?'

Pilbeam considered this with a forlorn expression. 'I don't think Prudence would deliberately have let him die. I suppose it's possible he could have said something to her about being depressed but I still don't believe he would have taken his own life. She never mentioned anything to me about it and nothing was raised at the inquest.'

'Would she have done so if it put her in bad light?'

'No, you're right, and perhaps Adele knew it. It could explain why she appeared so hard and why she left so quickly.'

And was that the reason for Adele's phone call to him? Horton wondered as he returned to the Harley. Was she pointing him towards a connection between Prudence Goldsby and Peter Jarvis? Did Adele have something in her possession that showed Prudence Goldsby had known that her husband was going to kill himself? And could Jarvis have been involved in Goldsby's death? According to Frieda Chillerton, Jarvis had studied science. Had Jarvis, through his contacts, been able to get hold of cocaine? But why would he want to kill his old school friend or aid and abet Prudence in doing so? Had they been having an affair?

Horton thought it was time he talked to Jarvis, but first, he had a graveyard to visit.

CHAPTER NINE

It took him longer to locate the final resting place of Dudley Goldsby MP than he'd anticipated. It was a plain affair, over-grown with grass and weeds. In front of the headstone was a small fresh bunch of daffodils, and despite there being no card attached to the elastic band holding the flowers together, he knew that Adele must have placed them there.

He made his way to Oyster Quays, hoping that he'd be in time to catch Danby leaving his meeting with Jarvis. It all depended on how long they had discussed security matters. He was very eager to learn from Danby why Jarvis felt the need for protection.

Parking the Harley in the underground car park, Horton made his way up the escalator and through the shopping mall to the waterfront. The biting wind had taken the edge off al fresco coffee. There were only a few people about on the boardwalk. The grey cloud was building to the west, the sky darkening, and along with it the sea outside the harbour was very rough. It wasn't that calm inside it, he thought, trying to study the sleek white motor cruiser dispassionately. But he couldn't. In his mind's eye he saw Emma on board, sleeping in one of the many cabins, playing on the deck or in the salon. He envisaged her on the rear diving platform or the flybridge beside Jarvis at the helm, Jarvis laughing and talking to her, with his arm around her.

God, why was he torturing himself like this? He felt sick with bitterness and brushed a hand across his face as though trying to erase the painful images.

Two men stepped out from the main cabin. One was Mike Danby and the other had to be Jarvis. He was stouter than Horton had imagined, with a paunch. His hair was cropped short, almost balding, and what remained was grey. He was tanned and dressed casually, and although Horton had guessed Jarvis's age from Frieda Chillerton's remark about him being at school with Dudley Goldsby, he was still surprised to find himself looking at a man in his late fifties. Or rather, the surprise came from the fact that Catherine was attracted to Jarvis, who was at least twenty years older than her. Horton also wouldn't say that by any stretch of imagination Jarvis was good-looking. But then wealth was an attraction and an aphrodisiac.

He watched the two men shake hands, all smiles. Danby alighted and Jarvis returned to the cabin. Horton made his way to the entrance of the marina and waited for Danby to emerge.

Danby looked momentarily surprised, then irritated when he saw him. 'Jarvis has got nothing to do with Adele Goldsby,' Danby said, striding towards the shopping mall.

'You asked him?'

'No, because he's not being stalked by anyone. That wasn't why he wanted to consult me. It must have been just coincidence, you and I being on the same ferry and getting mysterious phone calls.'

'Coppers don't believe in coincidence.'

'Like I said, Andy, I'm not a copper.'

'But you were at the time of Goldsby's death and Goldsby was best buddies with Jarvis.'

'How do you know that?' Danby's head whipped round.

'Frieda Chillerton told me.'

'Well, she never said anything about that at the time of the investigation. Still, there was no need for her to do so.

Goldsby must have had lots of friends, and none of them were questioned because—'

'Yes, I know, it became clear he killed himself,' Horton replied somewhat wearily. 'Frieda Chillerton doesn't believe he committed suicide. Did she express that view at the time?'

'She might have done. It's a natural reaction. There's nothing here for you, Andy. Jarvis is a decent sort.'

'Just because he's given you a contract,' Horton sneered.

Danby flashed him a hostile glance, then exhaled and slowed his pace. 'I've got the chance to pitch for a security and surveillance system for his possible purchase of an apartment in a new luxury marina complex in Port Ferdinand, Barbados. Jarvis is sailing there at Easter.'

'With Catherine?' Horton asked tersely. He didn't give a damn where Catherine went or with whom, but he did care if his daughter was going with her.

'I didn't ask.'

No, but Horton could see that Jarvis had volunteered that information because Danby avoided his eye contact.

'And my daughter?'

'You'll have to ask Catherine that. I'm travelling on board. I'm to do the survey and then fly back.'

'Nice work,' Horton said, tight-lipped.

'Better than dealing with the low-life scum you have to associate with, Andy. I've told you countless times you should work for me.'

'But not on Jarvis's yacht.'

'No. A bit too close for comfort, don't you think?' Danby smiled. They dodged a man on a mobility scooter who seemed to have a desire to run down as many pedestrians as possible.

'How long is Jarvis staying here?' Horton asked.

'Until tomorrow afternoon. Then he's leaving for No Man's Fort. He's hired it exclusively for the weekend.'

The larger of the two forts in the Solent that were now luxury hotels. 'Why?'

'Business and pleasure. He's invited investors for his new business venture that I mentioned to you.'

'Bioplastics. Did you find out what it meant?'

'Yes. It's about developing plastics from renewable sources, such as vegetable fats and oils, and agricultural by-products. Most of what he said on that score went over my head, but it's a growth area and environmentally friendly.'

'So it ticks all the boxes.'

'Probably.'

They'd reached the top of the escalator leading to the underground car park. Danby halted.

Horton said, 'Do you remember a Reverend Simon Pilbeam coming up in the Dudley Goldsby investigation?'

'No.' Danby glanced at his watch.

Horton ignored the gesture. 'He was another of Goldsby's closest friends and he doesn't think the politician killed himself.'

'Then why didn't he come forward at the time and say so?'

'It was at his church hall that Goldsby gave his last talk, after which he left for the hotel where he was found dead. Why didn't anyone interview him?'

'As I said last night, Andy, there is no disputing Goldsby took that cocaine and there was nothing to indicate his death was suspicious. Don't go looking for trouble when it isn't there and don't let—'

'My personal feelings get in the way.'

'That's up to you, but if you do need to speak to Jarvis, which I can see you are determined to, then I'd appreciate it if you didn't mention me.'

'But he would know that you were on the original investigation.'

'Why should he? Like I said, he was never interviewed because he had nothing to do with what happened. Must go.'

Horton watched him descend before turning back to the waterfront. He punched in the code to the marina, showed his warrant card to the security guard at the entrance and made briskly for Jarvis's boat. Climbing on board, he was about to call out when a man in his mid-thirties descended from the flybridge, fit, tanned and affable. Horton introduced himself without stating he was a police officer — he was certain that Jarvis would know exactly who he was. He asked to speak to Mr Jarvis.

'I'll see if he's available, sir,' came the polite reply before the man pushed open the glass doors and disappeared inside an immaculate grey-and-white salon.

Horton was certain Jarvis would see him, if only out of curiosity. He wondered what Catherine had told her boyfriend about him and their relationship and what Emma had said about him. He took a breath as his eyes travelled to the salon. There was a lean, bespectacled man in his late fifties sitting on one of the sumptuous leather sofas reading a newspaper. Beyond the living space was a dining area and a bar. The galley must be behind that and the cabins below.

His entire yacht would fit in the space of the salon. His gut churned. How could he ever compete with this where Emma was concerned? The answer was he couldn't. Did he need to, though? Emma was his daughter — surely she would love him no matter what. But the silent tormented voices of his boyhood taunted him. *You thought your mother loved you but she left you.*

She hadn't left him, though. Someone had taken her from him, and he was going to make damn sure that someone was going to pay for it. He wanted revenge.

Jarvis was heading towards him through the salon. He stopped to address the other man, who looked up from his newspaper and threw a glance at Horton. His expression showed no curiosity and he returned to his newspaper. A skinny blonde woman in her mid-thirties approached them. The lean man put down his newspaper to talk to her while her eyes flicked to the deck and focused on Horton before she quickly looked away.

Horton drew himself up. Roughly he pushed aside the mix of angry and despairing silent voices running through his troubled mind as Jarvis stepped outside and slid the door shut behind him. Jarvis had no intention of inviting him in.

Maybe he's scared that I'll make a scene in front of his guests, thought Horton.

The wind was hurtling around them, changing direction every few seconds. Now that he was close, Horton could see an air of puzzlement and wariness in the light blue eyes in Jarvis's round and lined face. Horton called on all his police training, making sure his expression betrayed none of his swirling emotions.

'How can I help you, Inspector?' Jarvis's crisp tone and the use of Horton's police rank made it clear that he couldn't see any need for this visit to be anything other than official.

Horton couldn't quite keep the sharpness from his voice. 'Adele Goldsby.' He watched Jarvis's reaction closely. His surprise seemed genuine, but then it would. He wouldn't have expected anyone, especially a police officer, to come asking about his late friend's daughter. 'When was the last time you saw her?'

Jarvis's expression turned to one of bewilderment. 'I don't understand why you're asking.'

'Just routine.' Horton gave the stock answer and saw, with pleasure, as a flicker of annoyance crossed the man's face. But Jarvis swiftly controlled himself, although Horton could see it cost him effort not to snap back.

'If you must know, Inspector, it was at her father's funeral.'

'Has she been in contact with you since then?'

'No. There's no reason why she should have been.'

Was that the truth? Was Jarvis involved in the death of Dudley Goldsby and the disappearance of Adele? Or was it as Horton had considered last night that Adele was stirring up trouble for Jarvis out of some kind of quest for revenge that had nothing to do with her father's death?

'But you were a friend of her late father.'

'Yes, of Dudley Goldsby, not his daughter,' Jarvis stressed.

'Would you have said he was the type of man to kill himself by taking an overdose of cocaine?'

Jarvis's eyes narrowed. 'Why the interest in Dudley after all this time? And don't tell me again that it's just routine — I think you can credit me with more intelligence than that.'

Horton answered the question with one of his own. 'Have you heard of a woman called Sophie Kranton?'

He noted Jarvis's annoyance. *Good.* He wanted to provoke some kind of emotion in this overconfident man. Jarvis evidently didn't like the fact that Danby had told him about Sophie Kranton. Maybe Horton had queered Danby's pitch. Well, tough. Danby was old and ugly enough to look out for himself.

'Not until yesterday, and before you ask, I don't know who she is or why she should have used my name to deceive Mike Danby.'

'There's the possibility her real name is Adele Goldsby.' Horton let that sink in before adding, 'Mr Danby was one of the investigating officers on the Dudley Goldsby case.'

Jarvis's mouth tightened. 'I can't help you, Inspector. I have no idea where Adele is and I have nothing to say about Dudley Goldsby's tragic death. Now, I have guests arriving.' His eyes swept beyond Horton to the pontoons.

Horton followed his gaze. Heading towards them were two men. One he recognized as Dominic Keats, the owner of the Superyacht Training and Recruitment Academy. Keats was in his early fifties, an impatient, ambitious man who measured people's worth in terms of their wealth. The other was a short, broad man in his mid to late fifties, expensively dressed with short, greying cropped hair and a round, lined, suntanned face. He walked with a slight rolling gait as though he'd spent his entire life on board a ship.

'When was the last time you saw Mr Goldsby?' Horton said.

'I really don't see—'

'Did he confide in you that he was depressed or concerned about anything?'

Jarvis's irritation deepened. His eyes flashed fury and his jaw clenched. 'No, he didn't. Now I must ask you to leave.'

Horton held his gaze. 'Of course,' he replied, with a tone that intimated that he'd be back if he needed to. He alighted as the men drew level with the boat. Keats looked surprised and then worried to see him, while the other man studied him with a frown as though trying to place him. He heard Jarvis address the short, broad man as Alex.

A few flakes of snow started to fall as Horton made his way along the pontoon. They dissolved the moment they hit the wood. By the time he reached the boardwalk, Jarvis and his guests had disappeared. Horton stared at the super-slick motor yacht. Would Catherine marry Jarvis or was this just a passing affair? If she did marry him, what would that mean for Emma? The answer was clearly a life where she would have everything she asked for, where she would mix with wealthy people and the children of affluent individuals. She'd have a privileged upbringing that would make his background, that of a poor child from inner-city Portsmouth, so alien to her, and his job and his way of life seem so inadequate and meagre that perhaps she'd have less to do with him as the years passed.

A cold dread that Jarvis would steal Emma from him filled him with despair of the kind he'd experienced when Catherine had thrown him out. In those dark days of his suspension, he'd taken his small yacht out to sea in a storm without caring if he ever came back, but his instinct for survival had proved to be stronger than his desire to enter oblivion. What if he never got to see Emma, though? What would he do?

His phone rang and he snatched at it eagerly, glad to stop the terrible black thoughts from crowding his mind. He was even pleased to see it was Bliss.

'Where are you?' she demanded.

'St Paul's Church, Somerstown,' he lied — well, he could still have been there. 'The spate of robberies in the area,' he explained.

'I know what the crimes are,' she snapped. 'I thought Walters was handling that?'

'He is, but I thought it important for a senior officer to show his or her face in the targeted community.' She was always banging on about being seen and getting involved at ground level without actually doing much herself, unless it involved meetings with the higher-ups.

'That's as maybe, but—'

'I have contacts here and a long memory for faces of those involved in this kind of criminal activity. I wanted to ask around, see if there was any intelligence on the streets.'

'And is there?'

He thought of Keith Harnley and the vicar's assertion that Harnley was going straight. Maybe he wasn't. 'Possibly.'

She sniffed as though she didn't believe him.

'I'm just heading back.' He rang off, annoyed that she obviously thought he needed his hand holding. If he had wanted confirmation of his earlier thoughts that the job had changed, here it was. Even someone of the rank of inspector wasn't to be trusted and let out alone. But then perhaps that was just Bliss's way where he was concerned. He'd given her no reason to be distrustful and suspicious of him except for the fact that she despised his methods and was afraid they would reflect badly on her as a manager and therefore hinder her chances of promotion. She also resented his friendship with Uckfield, which went back to their days at police college. Horton knew she was very keen to wrangle her way on to the Major Crime Team and she was wary that he might queer her pitch. He wouldn't. And besides, even if he tried, Uckfield wouldn't take a blind bit of notice of what he said. Uckfield was equally as ambitious as Bliss.

His phone rang again just as he was about to start the Harley. This time it was Elkins.

'Neil Brandon's boat has been broken into along with three others on the pontoons of the cruising club. Various items have been stolen. Ripley and I are dealing with that, but the reason for my call, Andy, is that Brandon was very nosy about why the forensic archaeological team were back on Rat Island. He tried to pump me for what they'd found, and for more information on the skeleton he'd unearthed. It might be natural curiosity, or he might want to go running to the press again, but he asked if we had discovered anything "funny" about the remains. When I pushed him a little harder on what he meant by that, he quickly dismissed it and brought the subject back to the vandals. There's definitely something not right about him, Andy. My copper's nose is twitching and I haven't got a cold.'

'Thanks, Dai.' Horton called Uckfield and relayed what Elkins had said. 'I think we should interview him. If he's got nothing to hide then at the least I can warn him off speculating to the press.'

Uckfield agreed. Horton then called Cantelli, asked him to run off a copy of Brandon's statement and to meet him in the station car park. As he headed back there, he was glad to have something to distract his mind from thoughts of Peter Jarvis.

CHAPTER TEN

'There's a light on,' Cantelli said, peering through the grimy glass panel of the front door of Neil Brandon's small terraced house. He'd parked in a nearby side street because Brandon's property fronted directly onto the busy main road. The traffic thundered past, almost drowning out Cantelli's voice.

It had taken them over an hour to travel the twelve miles to the Gosport peninsula. The traffic had been backed up on the motorway because of an earlier accident. Horton thought they could have walked it quicker. Going by the police launch would certainly have been faster, but he wouldn't have inflicted that on Cantelli.

The inclement weather was making it darker than usual for the time of day. It felt more like four o'clock than two. The few flurries of snow earlier had come to nothing, but the sky remained oppressive and the shadow of Peter Jarvis hung over Horton. He'd said nothing of his interview with Jarvis to Cantelli. He didn't want to go over it again and he wasn't comfortable with confiding his fears and emotions even to Cantelli, who was the only person he was likely to do so with. Life in the children's homes had trained him well.

He peered through the filthy front-room window but could see nothing but grit and gloom. He straightened up. 'Try again.'

Cantelli did, this time ignoring the bell, which obviously didn't work. He lifted a crusty pitted knocker and hammered it persistently. Horton was surprised the door didn't cave in. He would have surmised that Brandon was out and had left the light on to deter would-be burglars if it hadn't been for the blare of a television. A shadow hove into view through the glass.

'About time,' Horton muttered. The door opened to reveal a squat, heavily overweight man with collar-length straggly greying hair, a bushy and none-too-clean grey beard, and jowly features. His navy-blue jumper was stained with beer and food and his breath smelled of nicotine and something else that Horton wasn't going to get close enough to analyse. Elkins hadn't warned him that the man was so unkempt. Maybe a large sailing jacket had disguised his appearance when Elkins had talked to him.

Brandon studied them guardedly.

'Mr Neil Brandon?' Cantelli said, showing his warrant card.

'Yes.'

'We'd like a word.' Horton stepped forward, forcing Brandon to spring back. Horton had read Brandon's statement and there were a few things that didn't quite add up. That, along with Elkin's copper's nose and his own instinct on seeing the man told him that Brandon wasn't 'right'. He couldn't say why yet — it just happened that way sometimes. But was he right about Jarvis being mixed up with Dudley Goldsby's death and Lord Richard Ames being involved with Jennifer's? Or was that just prejudice talking because he disliked and mistrusted both Jarvis and Ames?

The scruffy, malodorous man in front of him was as grubby as the narrow hallway with its peeling faded wallpaper, filthy paintwork and dust. If Brandon was involved with Quintessa's death, then Horton couldn't see how she could possibly be Jennifer.

'If it's about my boat—'

'It's not.'

'Then what—'

'Shall we go through.' It wasn't a question. Horton stretched out an arm in the direction of the lounge, leaving Brandon little alternative but to turn and plod, slightly splay-footed, down the short passageway.

They followed him into a small sitting room that was so crammed with shabby dark furniture that there was little space to move. The room reeked of cigarettes, stale food and sweat. An open door led into the kitchen beyond, which looked to be just as dirty. There was a large television on a chipped cheap wooden cabinet, and dust on every surface that wasn't covered with newspapers or books. Cobwebs hung in the corner of the almost brown ceiling.

Horton picked up the television remote control and switched it to standby.

'Here, what do you think—'

'Rat Island.'

'So that's it. You're persecuting me because of a small matter of trespassing when hooligans go scot-free after breaking into my boat and thieving from it.'

'Who said anything about trespassing?' Horton said.

'Eh?' Brandon looked confused and shifted uncomfortably as Horton held his gaze.

'Tell us how you found that skeleton.'

'I've already told Sergeant Elkins and I've made my statement.'

But through his bullishness, Horton could see apprehension in Brandon's small brown eyes before he averted them and retrieved a packet of cigarettes from the small table. The sound of the traffic thundered on the main road and reverberated around the small house.

'Tell *me*,' Horton insisted.

Brandon looked about to retort then sighed. 'I put the boat up on the shore and walked around the island—'

'For how long?'

'Don't know. Not long.' He removed a cigarette from the packet and flicked his plastic lighter at it. After inhaling, he continued, 'I walked up to the trees and then just wandered along the edge of them, looking on the ground. I stepped inside the copse for a . . . well, a pee if you must know.'

'Your boat doesn't have a sea toilet then?'

'No.'

'And you have a weak bladder, a prostate problem maybe?'

'No.'

'Ah, I see, you forgot to go to the toilet before leaving home and before taking out your boat.'

'I didn't want to go then. Look, why are you so fascinated by my toilet habits?' he declared belligerently. I just happened to need a pee while I was looking around for—'

'Yes, I know, artefacts,' Horton finished for him sceptically.

'I saw something that I thought looked odd.' He glanced away and picked some tobacco from his uneven yellow teeth.

Horton studied him unfailingly.

'I bent down, began to uncover it and found a humerus. I was gobsmacked.' His short legs shuffled. 'I called Sergeant Elkins on the marine unit mobile number, then waited for him to arrive.'

'And you found just the one skeleton?'

'That was enough.' He exhaled and made to sit down, but as neither Horton nor Cantelli made any attempt to take a seat, Brandon hesitated, probably knowing he'd be at a disadvantage if he sat. 'The reporter who interviewed me told me they'd found five.'

'Did that shock you?'

'Of course it did.'

'Why?'

'What do you mean, why?'

'I thought you were interested in local history. Didn't you expect more convicts to be found?'

'Yes. No. I guess it was possible.' He shrugged. 'I didn't stop to look for more.' Ash dropped from his cigarette onto the stained carpet.

Brandon was looking decidedly uneasy by the barrage of questions. Horton knew there was something wrong with the man — he could smell it above the stench of grime and nicotine. He considered what Bliss had said about Brandon deliberately finding the skeleton.

Evenly, and in a matter-of-fact tone, he said, 'Did you go to Rat Island because you had a prick of conscience?'

'Eh?' Brandon tried to look puzzled but his furtive body language and darting eyes said something else. 'I don't know what you're talking about.'

'Did you think she'd lain there long enough?'

Cantelli flashed Horton a look.

He knew why. He'd just defied Uckfield's orders by alerting Brandon to the fact they were interested in one particular skeleton. Well, tough. There was something wrong about Brandon and tiptoeing around him wasn't going to get whatever it was out of him. Horton was rewarded by the pallor of Brandon's skin — it paled visibly. The smoke dribbled from his hairy nostrils and he licked his lips. But he still wasn't ready to cough.

'What are you talking about?' he asked airily, but he was a very poor actor. Horton could see the perspiration beginning to prick on his furrowed brow.

He'd let him sweat a little longer. 'Where did you work between 1980 and 1985?'

'Eh?'

Horton said nothing. Under his steely glare, Brandon twitched before answering. 'The Royal Clarence Victualling Yard, if you must know, but what has that—'

'Did you own a boat between 1980 and 1985?'

Brandon looked at them, confused. Cantelli remained silent with his pencil poised over his notebook.

'Yes,' Brandon answered reluctantly. 'A small motorboat for day fishing. I kept it on a mooring in the harbour.'

'Easy enough then for you to motor to Rat Island.'

'Well, yes, but you didn't do it in those days because the navy were all over the place.'

'Not in the dark they weren't.'

Brandon's hand came up as though to mop his brow but froze under Horton's unrelenting scrutiny. 'I didn't have any need to go to Rat Island then.'

'But you did ten days ago, because you needed to check that what you put there in the dark in the eighties was still there? And when you saw that it was, your conscience finally got the better of you, which is why you led us to the remains.' Horton said, his pulse quickening. He sensed Cantelli's excitement beside him, though he showed no visible sign of it.

Brandon's nicotine-stained fingers plucked at his beard. The sweat was pouring off his face now and his body emitting a sickly smell. His eyes darted between them and a small pink tongue snaked out of his fleshy, hairy lips. With an attempt at defiance, which came out as a plaintive bleat, he said, 'You can't arrest me for lying about how I found that skeleton.'

Horton was puzzled but Brandon quickly continued. 'Look, I'll tell you the truth. I didn't stumble across it. I was told where it was. I got this phone call.'

'When?' Horton barked. He didn't think Brandon was making this up.

He drew heavily on his cigarette and his anxious eyes flicked between them. 'It was late on the Sunday night, the day before I found the skeleton. She said she knew how keen I was on local history—'

'*She?*' Horton's thoughts leaped to another female caller who seemed intent on mystery. But why should Adele Goldsby be interested in a woman who had been murdered in the early 1980s?

'Yeah. She said she knew I was something of an expert on local history, which was why she wanted to tell me about the skeleton.'

'*The* skeleton, single not plural?'

'Yeah.'

'How did this caller know you?'

'No idea.'

'You didn't ask her?'

'No.'

Horton found that hard to believe. And again, Brandon's body language betrayed the lie.

'Before I could say anything, she rang off.' Brandon leaned down and stubbed out his cigarette in a silver foil cake wrapper before shaking another from the packet, but he didn't light it. His fingers twiddled at his beard. 'I haven't heard from her since.'

'What exactly did she say?'

'I can't remember her precise words, but it was something like, "I've found some human remains on Rat Island. You might find them interesting."'

Cantelli chipped in. 'Why didn't she report it herself?'

'Don't know.'

'Oh, come on, you must have asked her,' Horton said derisively.

'She muttered something about not having the time and didn't want to get involved with the police and the media.'

'How did she know the remains were there?'

'Dunno.'

'So you just went out with your shovel and dug around?' Horton sneered.

Brandon shifted his weight on his stout legs. He lit his cigarette. 'Just a small trowel,' he muttered, inhaling.

As if that makes a difference, thought Horton. 'So you dug with your small trowel all over the island until you found it?' he scoffed.

'She said it would be somewhere on the western edge of the copse.'

Cantelli said, 'Did she ring your landline or your mobile?'

'Mobile.'

'How did she get that number?'

'She might have got it from the Explosion Museum, where I work as a volunteer.'

'She gave you her name?'

'No.'

It was a lie and Cantelli could see that too. It sounded like a cock and bull story and Horton would have thought it was if it hadn't been for what had happened to him and Mike Danby — a mysterious phone call from a woman.

'I'm telling you what happened, all right?' Brandon wheedled.

Horton stepped forward. Coldly, he said, 'No, Mr Brandon it is not all right. In fact, it is far from all right. Your story stinks, and shall I tell you why? Because that skeleton you found is not that of a nineteenth-century convict but a twentieth-century woman, and one who was killed in the eighties. Now I suggest you think very hard about the fairy tale you've just spun us and start telling the truth.'

Brandon's face turned ashen. The smouldering cigarette drooped in his hair-lined lips. He just managed to save it from falling on the carpet. 'That's not possible. It can't be. I'm telling you, I had this phone call from a woman. She told me where to look. I know nothing about any woman being killed in the eighties.'

Horton wrenched the cigarette from Brandon's fingers. Stabbing it out on the silver cake foil curtly, he said, 'Get your coat.'

'You can't arrest me. I haven't done anything!'

'Your coat, Mr Brandon.'

'OK, so she did give me her name,' he gabbled.

'How do we know you're not making this up? Why did you lie and say she didn't tell you who she was?'

'I don't know. I panicked.' He ran a hand through his straggly hair.

'Your coat.' Horton turned away.

'Adele, that's who she said she was. Adele Goldsby.'

CHAPTER ELEVEN

Brandon's announcement was surprising and yet, as the interview had progressed, Horton had been half expecting it. As they took him to the police station in Portsmouth, Horton wondered if the 'thing' that Adele had wanted to show him on the ferry wasn't Peter Jarvis's boat but Rat Island. But why not report the skeleton to him? Why use Neil Brandon to deliver the message? There could only be one reason: somehow Brandon was involved in the death of Adele's father, and the skeleton must also have some connection with the late politician. Where did Mike Danby, the mysterious Sophie Kranton and Peter Jarvis fit into this? Horton didn't know, but he'd find out. Now how to explain all this to Uckfield and Bliss without being shunted off the case because of his personal connection with Jarvis?

He thought it best to keep quiet about Danby's call and his interview with Jarvis earlier. He'd have to reveal the call he'd received from Adele, and his interviews with Frieda Chillerton and the Reverend Pilbeam. First, though, he and Cantelli would interview Brandon in the formal setting of the station under caution, on the grounds that he had lied about the discovery of the remains, and on suspicion of being involved with Quintessa's death. Four hours later,

Horton was reporting back to Uckfield. Bliss was present. Cantelli was drafting Brandon's statement.

Uckfield looked blankly at him when he mentioned Brandon's call had come from Adele Goldsby, Bliss even more mystified. Neither had been working in Portsmouth at the time and Horton quickly brought them up to speed with the late politician's death and how he had found the body. When he also mentioned that Uckfield's father-in-law, Dyer, had been the senior officer in charge of the very quick and seemingly cursory investigation, Uckfield's scowl deepened.

Horton said, 'Brandon denies killing Quintessa, or having anything to do with her murder, and claims he'd never heard of Adele Goldsby before that phone call, nor her father. Dudley Goldsby wouldn't have been his MP. But the fact that Adele told Brandon where to find those remains must mean Quintessa's death is connected in some way with her father.' Horton could see that didn't please Uckfield very much. It meant that Dyer had possibly overlooked some vital evidence.

'But Quintessa's death was twenty years before Dudley Goldsby's.' Bliss said. 'I can't see how it can be connected.'

'And as Goldsby's dead we can't interview him unless we hold a séance and his spirit returns to tell us who killed her, so we're stuck with a skeleton and a woman who likes to play games,' Uckfield chipped in. 'Brandon could have made up the name.'

'I can't see why he'd have chosen that particular name, plus the timing of Adele Goldsby's call to me makes that even more unlikely.'

'What call?' Bliss fired at him.

Horton explained, which drew a look of incredulity from her, while Uckfield frowned. Horton said nothing about Danby having been on the same ferry.

'We need to find out how Adele got hold of Brandon's mobile number.' Horton continued. 'He says few people have it. He claims he hasn't got any friends, which isn't so surprising after meeting him — the smell is enough to put most off.' As it was, Horton thought they might need to buy another can of air freshener for the interview room and one for Cantelli's car, unless he decided to wash it out with disinfectant when he got home. 'The Cruising Association secretary has Brandon's number and so does the curator of the Explosion Museum, where Brandon's a volunteer. They come under the auspices of the National Museum of the Royal Navy in the dockyard. Someone might remember a woman in her mid-thirties asking for the number. Elkins and Ripley can check out the Cruising Association. Cantelli can interview the museum staff tomorrow. I've also requested CCTV footage from the Transport Police and Walters will look through that to see if we can spot a woman who could be Adele making that call.'

'But why all the song and dance about it?' Bliss asked. 'Why didn't Adele come forward and tell us what she knows, or what she thinks she knows?'

'Maybe she's too scared. She knows who the killer is but can't say outright.' Horton thought of the bunch of daffodils lying on Goldsby's grave, which meant that Adele was in Portsmouth, or had been. There was no point mentioning the flowers, though — Uckfield would only say they could easily have been left by someone else. 'Perhaps Adele had intended to keep her rendezvous with me on the ferry and explain everything, but she got frightened or was prevented from meeting me.' And that worried him. Was Adele safe?

He then revealed that he'd spoken to Frieda Chillerton, Goldsby's former secretary, and the Reverend Pilbeam, the late politician's friend, both of whom had claimed not to have seen or heard from Adele since the day of the funeral.

Bliss opened her mouth to speak but Horton swiftly continued, 'Frieda Chillerton believes that Dudley Goldsby was killed but doesn't know why or by whom, and Pilbeam says Goldsby must have taken the cocaine accidentally. In the light of this latest development, we should re-examine the Goldsby case.' He studied Uckfield carefully, knowing he'd be reluctant to do so because it might cast aspersions on his father-in-law's competence. 'And we should ask Adele's mother, Prudence, if her daughter's been in touch. She lives in Old Portsmouth.' Horton had asked Walters to get the address.

'No,' Uckfield stoutly replied, dashing an impatient glance at his watch. 'No one is to mention any connection with Dudley Goldsby or go near Prudence Goldsby until I get authority to do so. Will this Chillerton woman and the vicar blab that you've been poking your nose in?'

'No, but Brandon might when we release him, and we'll have to because we've got no evidence to charge him.'

'Then tell him if he so much as breathes a word to anyone, including the media, he'll be booked for trespassing, spying on the navy and anything else you can think of.'

'Have the forensic team at Rat Island discovered anything new?'

'Not yet. They're going back tomorrow. Rather them than me freezing their bollocks off in the harbour.' Uckfield's mobile phone rang. 'That's it for now,' he quickly dismissed them, glancing at his phone and not answering the call until they were outside. Horton wondered if it was the latest in the seemingly endless line of Uckfield's lovers. He seemed to change them almost as often as he changed his socks. To date, Uckfield had been lucky not to have been caught. Horton thought him a fool to risk his marriage and his career, but Uckfield wouldn't thank him for saying so and would have ignored the advice anyway. Horton pitied Alison Uckfield, who, as far as he knew, was totally unaware of her husband's serial infidelity.

As soon as the door was shut, Bliss rounded on him as he had anticipated. 'Next time I ask you where you are and what you are doing, Inspector, I expect to be told the truth, not a pack of lies.'

'I *was* at Somerstown and I *was* following up the robberies.'

'Yes, and interviewing a man who is *not* involved in a crime that we are *not* actively investigating. Stick to your duties, Inspector, or you might find yourself relieved of them.'

He held her hot, angry gaze evenly but didn't bother to reply or apologize. She wouldn't have expected the latter anyway. Technically speaking, though, she was right. He had been in the wrong. She made to speak but her phone rang and, pressing it to her ear with a final malevolent look at him, she strode off through the incident suite and into the corridor. Good, that got rid of her.

He crossed to the crime board in the deserted incident room. Even Trueman, who always seemed to be at work, had left. Emanating from the picture of Quintessa's bones in the centre of the board were three lines with the names of the three missing women at the end of each, and only brief details about them and their disappearance, which Trueman had already given him. The fact there wasn't more, nor that any of them had been eliminated, meant that Trueman and Marsden were still gathering information and uniformed officers were in the process of talking to the relatives to find any connection with Rat Island.

Now with this latest news from Brandon about the phone call being from Adele Goldsby, Horton thought it highly unlikely any of the missing women could be Quintessa — not unless Trueman unearthed a connection between one of them and Dudley Goldsby. Or, Horton mused, a connection between one of them and Peter Jarvis. But they wouldn't find one with the latter — not unless he told them to look for it. Was he hindering an investigation by not doing so? Maybe.

Tomorrow, Trueman would add Brandon's information to the board, which meant the sergeant would have to put Adele Goldsby's name on it and, by virtue of that, her late father. Uckfield would *have* to make a request for them to re-examine the Dudley Goldsby case, despite what he or his retired father-in-law wanted. He had no option but to do so.

Uckfield's door burst open. 'You still here?' he snapped, marching towards the corridor.

'Looks that way.'

'What is it? I'm late.'

'For what?'

'What do you want?' Uckfield strode towards the stairs.

Horton fell into step beside him. 'I want you to get the Dudley Goldsby case reopened and I want you to ask your father-in-law if he thought there was anything suspicious about it. It seems to have been a very hurried investigation.'

'You're saying Reg cocked up?' Uckfield rounded on him.

'No. I'm saying that pressure might have been put on him from on high to clear it up quickly, what with the general election looming. Maybe there was something that didn't quite make sense or there was evidence that on the surface looked to be good but he felt uncomfortable with, or, on reflection, he wondered about.'

'He's never mentioned it to me and we've discussed a few high-profile cases over the years.'

'Including Dudley Goldsby's death?'

'No.' Uckfield paused at the bottom of the stairs. 'I'll ask him *if* I get the opportunity.'

Which meant he wouldn't. Horton returned to the interview room where Brandon was about to sign his revised statement. Cantelli looked relieved, probably because he would soon be free of the sickly, fetid smell in the room. Despite this, Horton sat and began again to go over the questions he'd asked earlier, hoping to provoke or tease some new information out of the man. He didn't get it. Brandon stuck solidly to his story that he had never seen nor spoken to any female who could have fitted Adele's age and he hadn't given his mobile number to anyone. And he had no idea who the woman buried on Rat Island was or how she had got there.

There was no shifting him. Horton warned him not to talk to anyone — especially the media — about the phone call or the human remains and threatened him with enough charges to make it sound as though he'd be locked up in the Tower for treason if he so much as breathed a word. Brandon didn't look frightened. On the contrary, he looked smug. He refused a lift home, saying he needed some fresh air.

'Me too!' Cantelli said with feeling. 'I've had sweeter-smelling vagrants in here.'

'I suppose his nerves could have made him worse,' said Horton, leaving the door open behind him and heading back to CID.

'I thought that might be the case at first but the longer we questioned him, the more confident he grew. There's something he's not saying.'

'About Adele? You think he's recognized who she might be?'

'I'm not sure. It was as though he expected us to question him about something else. He looked almost relieved when we banged on about how Adele might have got hold of his mobile number. He just doesn't smell right, and I don't mean his body odour.'

Horton knew exactly what Cantelli meant. Sergeant Elkins had said the same. He relayed the gist of his meeting with Uckfield and Bliss, which took them to the CID operations room. Walters had already left, which wasn't surprising. It was gone nine.

Crossing to his desk, Cantelli said, 'The Explosion Museum is only open at weekends at this time of year. I'll talk to the curator at the National Museum of the Royal Navy tomorrow in the dockyard, but she won't know if anyone approached Brandon at the Explosion Museum or if anyone has given out his mobile number. She should be able to tell me where that information is held, though. I guess Adele or a confederate could have seen it on a database. Adele could be working for either of the museums and have access to it, or someone she's working with has given it to her.'

Cantelli had a point. 'She rang me and Mike Danby from the harbour railway station, which is just a couple of hundred yards from the dockyard. Maybe she called us before she went to work.'

'And then couldn't get away.'

'Or had no intention of getting away, or was prevented from doing so. I'll ask Elkins to find out how the Cruising Association keep their records and if they've had any new members lately or anyone helping them on the admin side.'

'It could be someone who assists them with the mailing list or the website, perhaps working on a freelance basis. Or it could be a hacker, or rather someone expert at hacking — either Adele herself or a colleague.'

Horton entered his office and grabbed his leather jacket and helmet, while Cantelli shut down his computer. Glancing out the window, Horton saw that Bliss's car had gone. He flicked off the light and he and Cantelli made their way to the rear entrance.

'Brandon's computer could have been hacked into and his mobile number retrieved from it, but I didn't see a computer in his house,' Horton said. 'I suppose it could have been in another room.'

'Well, he claims not to have one and says he doesn't access the internet on his phone, but that could be lies. Perhaps Uckfield will authorize a search warrant.'

'At the moment he's not even likely to authorize the ordering of a paperclip in this case, but I'll suggest it in the morning. And Walters might get something from the railway station CCTV footage.'

Horton made his way to his boat, mulling over what Cantelli had said about Brandon looking and acting relieved the longer the interview had progressed. Was that because they hadn't questioned him more closely over Dudley Goldsby's death? Had Brandon been instrumental in the politician's murder, if it had been murder? And how the blazes did that fit in with Peter Jarvis? Brandon was hardly in the same league as the wealthy entrepreneur and could never have been, even back in the eighties.

His thoughts switched to Catherine. Was she with Jarvis now on that super-slick luxury yacht? Was she taking Emma with her to Barbados on it? Horton knew he'd have to ask her. He also knew he couldn't prevent her from doing so. He had no right to — in fact, he seemed to have sod-all rights as far as his daughter's upbringing was concerned. But he needed to know more about the man who would be spending time with her.

After a scalding-hot shower in the marina, he fired up his laptop, and with the heating on the boat on full blast he looked up Peter Jarvis on the internet. Everything he read confirmed what Danby had told him. Jarvis was clever, successful, wealthy and charitable. *A veritable saint*, Horton thought with bitterness. Had he ever put a foot wrong in his life? He had one failed marriage behind him and a son of sixteen, but Horton could find no mention of an acrimonious divorce and no scandal connected with him.

It was just after eleven when he decided to call it a day. The wind was moaning through the masts and intermittent bursts of rain battered the coach roof.

His sleep was troubled by dreams of Emma turning against him and Catherine spouting poisonous lies to his daughter and colleagues. Several times he woke in a cold sweat and willed himself to think of something else, but his brain refused to play ball. At six o'clock, he gave up. There was nothing for it but a punishing run along the seafront, not halfway to South Parade Pier this time but all the way to the Square Tower at Old Portsmouth and back. Seven and a half miles. That would cure his sluggish head.

The sun was just rising, tinting the sky light orange. The wind was still in the north-west, making it cold, but it promised to be a fresh, bright March morning. It was quiet on the promenade with only the occasional early jogger and dog walker. The lights across the Solent on the Isle of Wight gradually faded as the weak sun rose higher. The hovercraft swung noisily out to sea.

Horton headed through the deserted funfair, spying a police car on the far side of the car park close to Spur Redoubt, an ancient ruined fort, built, he seemed to recall, in the seventeenth century. It was separated from the land to the north by Long Curtain Moat and a grassy bank. A small wooden bridge stretching over the moat from the promenade and the ruins led into a tunnel under the bank. PC Johnson was talking to a woman in her late thirties dressed in running gear, while in front of them standing in the ruins was PC Allen, who was on his radio. Allen looked up, saw Horton and hurried towards him.

'We've got a body, sir, in the moat.'

Horton rushed to where Allen indicated — the far eastern corner of the ruins. There in the shallow water, where the ground in the moat rose slightly, a man's body was lying face down.

'I was just calling it in, sir. The woman who found him is a doctor up at the hospital. She checked for a pulse, didn't find one and called us. We don't know who he is—'

'We do,' Horton interjected, taking a breath. 'I even know what he's wearing under that brown zip-up jacket — a grubby checked shirt with a frayed collar and a navy-blue jumper with beer and gravy stains on it.'

An astonished and puzzled look crossed Allen's lean face.

Horton continued, 'Less than twelve hours ago that man was sitting across the table from me in the interview room. His name is Neil Brandon.'

CHAPTER TWELVE

Friday

'For God's sake, Steve, this has to be connected with Dudley Goldsby's death,' Horton insisted to Uckfield as they both stared at the body, which Jim Clarke, the forensic photographer, was in the process of photographing.

Behind them, the promenade was sealed off in both directions, and the car park adjoining the ruins to the east had been cordoned off. Parked in it was Uckfield's BMW, two patrol cars, the undertaker's private black ambulance with darkened windows, the white SOCO van and Clarke's blue estate car. The small bridge to their left, which led over the moat into the tunnel, had also been sealed off and was being guarded by a uniformed officer, but that wouldn't stop people from crowding along the top of the bank opposite. In fact, some had already gathered there. Two uniformed officers were doing their best to keep them moving, but they couldn't patrol the whole of the rampart or prevent people from taking pictures on their mobile phones. Soon someone was bound to post something on social media and the reporters would arrive.

He wished they could erect a tent but there was nothing to fix it to. They needed to move the body as soon as possible but couldn't until Clarke had finished and the doctor had arrived. Even though the female medic jogger had confirmed life was extinct, they still needed the official police doctor to verify that.

'Brandon could have been attacked and killed by a druggie or a mugger,' Uckfield sullenly replied. His eyes were bloodshot and his rugged face sallow as though he'd had little sleep. Horton wondered if his own face mirrored Uckfield's. But whatever had kept Uckfield up half the night, Horton knew it wasn't anguish over not seeing his daughter. He had two, and a doting wife, and he still played the field. To Horton's trained eyes, he thought Uckfield was suffering from the mother of all hangovers.

'Bit of a coincidence, wouldn't you say?' Horton caustically replied.

'They happen,' grunted Uckfield.

'Not in this case,' insisted Horton. 'Brandon obviously knew a hell of a lot more than he told us and, as a result, he's been prevented from ever telling it.' As yet, Horton couldn't tell how Brandon had died. There was no stab wound, no blood on the back of his jacket and no head injury, but then the body was still lying face down in the moat.

Perhaps something would be found in Brandon's house which might lead them to Adele Goldsby and to his killer. Uckfield had already instigated a search of it, which he'd said that DI Dennings, back from his course, was overseeing. Horton hoped they'd find details of Brandon's next of kin, or his GP, who would have it on his medical records. Failing that, the neighbours might know, and they'd be interviewed in case Brandon had said anything to them about finding the skeleton and had mentioned Adele Goldsby, although Horton thought the latter highly unlikely.

He wondered how Brandon's colleagues at the National Museum of the Royal Navy would take the news of his death. He hadn't yet told Cantelli about it — he was due at the museum later that morning. It was only just after eight.

He said, 'Brandon must have called the killer shortly after leaving the station. Either that or his killer knew he was being interviewed, waited until he left, then persuaded him into his car.'

Uckfield rubbed his forehead and stared glumly at the moat.

Horton continued, 'Which means Brandon knew the killer and was comfortable getting into his car, but why come here? Why kill him here when there are far more private places to do so?'

'This could still be a mugging.'

Uckfield was determined not to give up the idea. Before Horton could answer, though, Uckfield exclaimed, 'About time!'

Horton looked up to see Dr Sharman's short, lean figure striding across the bridge to the inner cordon, where Beth Tremaine, one of the scene of crime officers, handed him a scene suit, which he donned.

Joining them, Sharman said, 'I suggest we get him out. I'm not getting my trousers and feet wet for anybody, including you, Detective Superintendent Uckfield.'

Clarke nodded to Uckfield to indicate that he had all he needed. Uckfield flapped an arm at two officers bedecked in crime scene suits and wellington boots — as was Phil Taylor, head of SOCO — to step into the moat to assist them. Brandon had been a big man and was now a dead and very wet weight. He'd take some moving.

The tide would slowly trickle into the moat during the morning with high water just before midday, but it rarely reached a very high point on this upward-slanting part of the moat. Horton suspected that Brandon had entered the water at low tide last night not long after leaving the station.

He steeled himself for what they might see as the four men hauled the corpse up onto the ruins and then turned it over. Suppressing his revulsion at the nauseating stench, Horton swiftly took in the deathly white face and staring, sightless eyes of Neil Brandon. Gravel and dirt were smeared on his face and in his beard and hair. There was no sign of a facial or head injury but there was a small area of discolouration on the brown jacket which could be blood, and that meant a stabbing or shooting.

Sharman made his brief examinations. Straightening up, he said, 'Rigor is present throughout the body. He's overweight and it was a cold night, both of which slow down the onset of rigor, but from what I can see of the exposed areas of skin, lividity looks to be well established. You'll need him undressed to find out if it is complete throughout the body — if it is, then you're looking at six to eight hours. However, pressing the skin where the lividity is evident, the stain is permanent, which indicates he's probably been dead for between ten to twelve hours.'

Horton said, 'More like ten. He was alive at 8.45 p.m. when he left the station.'

'Then you have the advantage of me. Want me to empty his pockets?' Sharman asked.

Uckfield nodded. Taylor stepped forward with an evidence bag and Horton watched as Sharman dropped the sodden contents into them: a large, dirty handkerchief, a wallet, a small pen, some coins, a packet of cigarettes, the small red plastic throwaway lighter and a mobile phone. He handed the bag to Uckfield, who extracted the phone and, with his latex-covered fingers, checked it. 'Dead, like him. Too wet to work.'

That meant they'd have to wait for the mobile phone company records to see if anyone had called him or if he called anyone after he'd left the station. Uckfield peered inside the wallet. 'Nothing except a few sodden bank notes, a debit card, and a few shop loyalty cards. No credit card. Any idea how he was killed, Doctor?'

Sharman pulled off his gloves. 'Possible knife wound to the thorax.'

As in Quintessa's death, thought Horton. But then that didn't necessarily mean anything. Sadly, many others were killed in a similar way.

Sharman took his leave. Uckfield nodded SOCO in and gave instructions to one of the police officers to tell the undertakers they could take the body to the mortuary. Stepping outside the inner cordon, Uckfield removed his crime scene suit, immediately reached into his jacket pocket and extracted a packet of painkillers. He swallowed a couple without water.

'Heavy night, Steve?' Horton asked, slipping out of his scene suit wondering what the onlookers would make of him in his running kit.

'Not as heavy as Brandon's,' grunted Uckfield.

'If Brandon came straight here on foot after being released then he'd have arrived at about 9.45 p.m., possibly even a bit later as he wasn't the fittest of men. But I'd be more inclined to believe he either caught a bus or taxi, which means someone will have seen and spoken to him. Or if he was driven here by the killer, then the car will have been parked close by, so we might pick him up on the street CCTV. But why here? I can't see how this place has any connection with Adele or Dudley Goldsby.'

'Precisely,' declared Uckfield almost triumphantly. 'For all we know, the man could be knee-deep in enemies. He could be peddling drugs or flogging stolen goods, and before you ask, I did speak to Reg last night. He says the Goldsby case was a straightforward investigation and he's never heard of Neil Brandon.'

'And Adele Goldsby?'

'We continue looking for her but without a song and dance about it.'

That wasn't quite what Horton had meant but he could see he wasn't going to get anything further from Uckfield on that score.

Uckfield said, 'Call Dr Clayton and tell her she's got a customer.'

Horton walked towards the promenade and punched in Gaye Clayton's number. A ferry was heading out towards Fishbourne. On his right, a motorboat was skirting the coastline of Gosport and a giant container ship was passing Spitbank Fort. The wind was picking up speed. Gusts of over forty miles an hour had been predicted for later that morning. Horton thought it would be a rough crossing to No Man's Fort for Jarvis and his guests.

'Andy, nice to hear from you. Or is it?' Gaye greeted him brightly.

His heart skipped a beat at the genuine warmth in her voice and he felt a momentary stab of guilt for not having called her. He had promised her dinner but hadn't got round to it. 'Depends on your viewpoint. But as we've got a body, it might be nice for you. Not so nice for us or the poor beggar's family, if he's got one.'

'You have an ID?'

'Neil Brandon. He was being questioned yesterday evening in connection with one of the skeletons found on Rat Island.'

'The more recent one — female, died sometime between 1980 and 1985?'

'You know about it?'

'John Lauder and I have been discussing her.'

'Has he got any more information on Quintessa?'

'Who?'

'It's what Cantelli christened her. The fifth skeleton.'

'Pretty name. No, not yet, but I agree with his analysis and I've asked him to keep me posted. I'll look at your more recent cadaver as soon as you get him to the mortuary.'

'There's something else I need you to do,' Horton hastily added before she could ring off. He glanced in Uckfield's direction. He was on his phone, no doubt giving instructions to Sergeant Trueman in the incident suite. 'The autopsy on a man called Dudley Goldsby, died on the twenty-second of April 2005. Can you review it?'

'Of course. Any connection with this recent death?'

'Possibly, and with Quintessa's. I'll tell you more when I see you.'

'Can't wait.'

He rang off, wondering if she meant she couldn't wait to see him or couldn't wait to hear about the case. *The latter probably*, he thought, though he hoped it was the former.

He gazed around the area. It would have been dark when Brandon had arrived, but the promenade and the ruins were lit up and someone might have seen him, his killer, or both heading here. Would a public appeal bring forth any late-night dog walkers, joggers or insomniacs? Possibly. But this killer would have made sure they weren't seen.

He watched as the undertakers zipped Brandon into a body bag, and reconsidered the interview with him the previous day. Both he and Cantelli had sensed that Brandon had been holding something back. He'd been too at ease in the station, too uncomplaining after the initial shock of being taken in. Had he known who Quintessa's killer was? Had he in fact been involved in the murder? Or had he made the connection with the killer while being questioned and had contacted him as soon as he'd left? Perhaps.

Uckfield appeared by his side. 'Trueman's organizing a mobile incident unit to be set up next to the statue of Nelson looking out to sea. Pity *he* can't tell us if he saw our killer last night. Bliss is getting officers into the funfair to ask if anyone saw anything and she's organizing a team for a house-to-house in the High Street, Grand Parade and Broad Street.'

But Horton knew, just as Uckfield did, that officers would have to return in the evening as many of the residents would be at work.

'I'll give out a press statement when I get back to the station and I've asked Trueman to organize a search of the moat for a possible murder weapon, even though it'll be a waste of time unless the killer was really stupid. Why chuck it in the moat when he's got the entire Solent at his disposal?'

Horton watched Uckfield stride off and climb into his car. He needed to get back to his boat and change out of his running gear. Uckfield could have given him a lift but it obviously hadn't crossed his mind to offer. Horton could get a patrol car to drop him off but he decided to run back. It wouldn't take him long anyway. Before he set off, though, he called Cantelli, relayed what had happened and asked him to pick him up from the marina in forty minutes.

He handed the crime scene over to the uniformed sergeant after briefing him about the arrival of the mobile incident unit and the search of the moat. They'd set up signs and posters in the area and put information out on social media, asking for anyone who might have been out walking or running last night to come forward if they had seen the victim or anyone else along the top of the ancient walls or along the promenade, and indeed in the square of Grand Parade below, either heading for the steps to the promenade or along to the tunnel under the mound.

He ran back the way he'd come eastwards, but at South Parade Pier he drew up as he'd done before on the Harley and stared across the road at the Solent Waves Hotel, where Dudley Goldsby had died. It was a large baroque building erected in the mid-1800s and had gone through many refurbishments and changes of ownership since, but it had always managed to hold on to its premier position as a luxury hotel. The Labour politician certainly hadn't chosen a seedy place to end his life, or a quiet one. On the contrary, the hotel was at the top end of the market, attracting high-profile conferences and posh weddings as well as coach parties of the more discerning type of clientele. Several suited men and women were climbing the steps to the entrance now, briefcases and computer cases clutched in their hands. So why choose such a prestigious and busy hotel if he'd been intent on killing himself, or taking a fix and risking the chances of someone recognizing him? The answer had to be because he'd had no idea that this was where his life would be so abruptly and cruelly cut short. Someone had suggested they meet in a bedroom in this hotel and it had been chosen because it *was* busy and select.

Horton ran on while his thoughts swung back to that night in April 2005. He tried to recall everything about the scene that had greeted him and Hans Olewbo when they had entered that room, but although his memory was good, it was coloured by what he had expected to see — Callum Durrant with a tart, not a dead Labour politician, naked, alone and sprawled on the bed.

He needed to reboot his memory, or rather open his mind to new possibilities in light of what had occurred over the last two days. Although he knew that much would have changed inside the hotel, and in the bedroom where he had discovered Goldsby, a fresh look was what he needed. It might throw up more ideas, not just for him but also for Cantelli. It was time they revisited the scene, and stopping off there for half an hour wasn't going to hurt anyone or delay the investigation into Brandon's death.

CHAPTER THIRTEEN

'There are over a hundred bedrooms in this hotel and most were booked that night,' Cantelli said as they stood in the lobby with its deep red carpet, gleaming brass rails, sparkling chandeliers, plush seats, expensively dressed guests, subdued conversations and silent waiters. The smell of coffee, polish and luxury filled the air. It was an oasis of calm and tranquillity, of order and efficiency in contrast to the roar of the increasingly strong wind and the tumultuous sea outside.

The lobby had been redecorated since Horton had been here on the night Goldsby had died in 2005. It had probably been redecorated many times since then, but he'd had no cause to visit it in the intervening years. It was still as swish and elegant as he remembered. Fleetingly he wondered if Jennifer had ever set foot inside it and what it had looked like in 1978 when she had worked just across the road. Now, as Horton surveyed the reception area, he could see exactly how someone could have entered the hotel, climbed the stairs, accessed Goldsby's room and killed him without drawing attention to himself, especially if his physical appearance blended with the expected clientele.

A phone rang. Horton heard the receptionist answer it in pleasant hushed tones as though she was in a select nursing home or hospital.

Cantelli continued, 'There was also a conference and a couple of other functions taking place that night, so it was particularly busy.'

'Precisely,' said Horton. 'If Goldsby had really wanted to commit suicide in a hotel bedroom, it would have been much better to do so in a small, nondescript hotel and way off his constituency patch and home town. I think he came here to meet the person who had reserved that room.'

'It was booked the day before in the name of Arthur Barberry. He paid cash and in person, although when the reception staff were questioned no one could remember him or what he looked like. And when we ran a check, there was no one of that name, so it was assumed Goldsby had made the reservation himself using a false name. We obtained a list of the guests and staff but it would have been a mammoth task to talk to them all and we were very quickly told it wasn't necessary. No one wanted a fuss or scandal, or rather the powers that be didn't. We asked Frieda Chillerton, Harry Belling and Prudence Goldsby if they recognized any of the names on the guest and staff lists but they claimed they didn't.'

Which, Horton thought, was probably the truth as far as Belling and Frieda Chillerton were concerned, but he wasn't so sure about Prudence Goldsby, even though he had no reason to suspect that, having never interviewed or even met her. He was only going by what he'd been told.

'Let's talk to the manager.'

Horton showed his ID to the receptionist and a couple of minutes later a petite blonde woman in a smart black suit and crisp white blouse, probably in her early forties, emerged with a troubled expression on her immaculately made-up round face. She introduced herself as Chantelle Blythe and led them to her office, where she offered them coffee, which they declined, and gestured them into seats in front of her desk.

'I hope it's nothing serious,' she said anxiously.

Horton answered, 'We're reinvestigating an incident that occurred on the night of the twenty-second of April 2005.'

'Before my time,' she answered with relief in her well-modulated voice.

'A man was found dead in one of your bedrooms. He was, at the time, a local Member of Parliament.'

Her well-shaped eyebrows rose a fraction.

'There are just one or two points we need to re-examine. I wonder if you could supply us with a list of those who attended any conferences and private functions that night.' Cantelli had said the staff and guest list were already on file.

'I'm sorry, but that's not possible. We don't keep a guest list of those who attend functions — that's the responsibility of the organizers.'

Would they still have that in their possession? wondered Horton. He asked for the contact details of the function organizers.

'It will take me a while to retrieve those for you. It's on the computer but I'll need to access the archives. Would you like to come back?'

'How long?'

'Thirty minutes, but I might be able to do it quicker.'

'Could we see room eighty-four while we wait?'

She logged on to her desktop computer. 'It's booked for tonight but the guests don't check in until after 2 p.m. so that will be fine.' She rose. 'It's been refurbished since then.'

'It's just the layout we need to see.'

They followed her back to reception, where she handed Cantelli the key and gave them directions to the room. Not that they needed them, Horton remembered the way and so too did Cantelli. It wasn't something you forgot. The room was on the fourth floor facing the seafront at the eastern end of the building. As they climbed the deep-pile red-carpeted stairs, Cantelli said, 'During the original investigations we didn't get a list of the function organizers. It sounds sloppy now when you think about it but the pressure was on to keep it contained and low key.'

'And anyone from one of those functions could have booked the room in a false name and slipped up and killed Goldsby. In fact, anyone suitably dressed could have walked in off the street, which is exactly why the killer chose this hotel. It was a busy Friday night. The staff were probably working flat out.'

'No one we spoke to, which was mainly the reception and waiting staff, said they saw Goldsby enter the hotel or walk up the stairs. And he wasn't given the key by anyone at reception, *if* they are to be believed. They were short-staffed and very busy.'

'Which means Goldsby could have collected the key himself and just wasn't noticed, or he was given it by his killer before arriving. Or the killer was already in the room.'

Horton recalled how he and Hans Olewbo had walked up these stairs in 2005. They hadn't met anyone on the way up or in the corridors. It had been deathly silent. The manager had given them a pass key and had been keen to escort them, but they'd managed to dissuade him by saying the less fuss, the better. He'd remained below wringing his hands and looking anxious until they had returned. Or rather until Olewbo had returned and told him there was a dead politician in one of his bedrooms. The manager had probably had kittens on the spot and had certainly been even more anxious when uniformed officers had arrived along with the scene of crime officers.

Cantelli, breathing a little heavily, from the exercise, said, 'I found my old notebooks last night. Goldsby came here directly from that meeting in Somerstown. He left the meeting at just after ten. All the statements agreed to that — although we didn't get one from the Reverend Pilbeam because, like I said, his name never came up. Goldsby must have arrived here at about ten thirty if he walked, which he must have done because none of the taxi drivers admitted to bringing him here. The bus drivers weren't questioned, but no one came forward to say he had caught a bus.'

Horton agreed with Cantelli's view, which prompted him to consider Neil Brandon's trip from the police station to Long Curtain Moat. It was only two and a half miles but as he'd said to Uckfield, he couldn't see Brandon walking that distance. For Goldsby, the journey from the church hall to here would have been about one and a half miles.

As they came out onto the corridor, Horton recalled how he and Olewbo had been keyed up expecting to find Durrant in the bedroom at the far end on their right. It had been silent and deserted then, but now two bedroom doors were open and there was a trolley between them containing bed linen and cleaning materials. A vacuum cleaner was humming inside one of the rooms.

Ahead was the fire exit but Horton stopped before they reached it at a door two rooms from it on their right. Cantelli followed his train of thought. 'The fire door was shut and no prints were taken from it because no one believed Goldsby had been murdered. Besides, it's alarmed, and anyone opening it would have alerted the manager.'

Horton remembered that he and Olewbo had wondered if Durrant would make a bolt for it using the fire escape; they'd had no backup but they did have the advantage of surprise. Durrant could hardly leap out of the window, and by the time he considered making an escape he would have been well and truly restrained. Even if there had been two occupants in the room, it was highly likely the other would be female and already shot up with cocaine. There had been no sign of Durrant's car in the hotel car park or on the promenade or in the side streets close by. They'd assumed Durrant had arrived in a girlfriend's car.

Horton recalled how he and Olewbo had stood and listened outside the door for a while. Only silence had greeted them. Then with a nod at Olewbo, Horton had inserted the pass key, slammed open the door and they'd crashed in, only to draw up smartly at the shocking sight that had greeted them.

He turned the key and stepped inside. Cantelli followed him. The layout of the spacious room was exactly as he remembered. In 2005 it had been sumptuously decorated in gold and red — now it was brightly decorated in a contemporary style in orange and yellow and kitted out with modern furniture. There was, as before, a king-size bed and opposite it a door to the en-suite bathroom. Ahead was a wide window with white net curtains swept back and heavy linen curtains embroidered with orange flowers.

Horton closed the door. 'I remember Olewbo saying, "Who the blazes is that?" and then, "Durrant's added murder to his repertoire." Olewbo called it in while I crossed to the body and felt for a pulse, although it was obvious that he was dead. His features didn't register that he'd died an agonizing death. I remember thinking he looked quite peaceful. If there had been sleeping pills, I'd have said he'd taken a massive overdose, but there was nothing beside his body or on the floor, no tablets or syringes around him. I didn't know then who he was. There was a briefcase on the table by the window. I crossed to it.'

He approached the table which, now as then, contained two bottles of water, two glasses and two large mugs, a tray with a small kettle, tea, coffee and sugar sachets, small plastic tubes of milk and two packets of biscuits. There was also some writing paper and a folder with details about the hotel.

'The bottles hadn't been opened?' asked Cantelli.

'No, the seals were unbroken. The glasses could have been used and rinsed out, though, and so could the cups.' He drummed his fingers on the table while he gazed out of the window. His mind went back to 2005. It had been dark and the glow from the lights on the promenade hadn't reached down the pebbled shore as far as the sea. There had just been a black expanse beyond. Now he could see the grey swollen waves rolling onto the shore and crashing in a spray of foam. The sky had grown heavy and dark since early morning. A handful of dog walkers, runners and a few pedestrians were battling along the prom into the wind. He turned back.

'There were some papers inside the briefcase with the House of Commons crest on them addressed to Dudley

Goldsby MP. His wallet was inside his suit jacket, which was lying on the floor confirming he was Goldsby. I remember thinking, "Durrant's gone up in the world, supplying a member of Her Majesty's Government with drugs," but that didn't feel right. It didn't look right. I wondered why Goldsby was naked. Had there been anyone else in this room? Had he undressed to be with a lover who had hastily beat it when he died?'

'According to SOCO there was no evidence of anyone, male or female, having been in this room with him. They found no prints, only Goldsby's — oh and a few smudged prints but couldn't get anything from them, and the autopsy showed no signs of sexual activity, or anything to suggest that he'd injected himself.'

'Gaye's reviewing the file.'

Cantelli raised his dark eyebrows. 'With Uckfield's knowledge? Obviously not,' he added, interpreting Horton's expression.

'Uckfield's refusing to even consider reopening the case or to discuss it with the Assistant Chief Constable, despite Brandon's murder.'

'Probably because it could cast a slur on his father-in-law's reputation if something obvious was missed.'

Horton's sentiments exactly. 'Dyer's no longer in the job, though. Would it matter to him?'

'Probably. You know how pompous and self-righteous he is. Might besmirch his name down the Lodge,' Cantelli said cynically.

'And Uckfield can't be seen to be backstabbing his father-in-law,' Horton acidly replied. 'His fellow Masons wouldn't like it. So they all close ranks now just as they did in 2005.' Horton didn't know if Mike Danby was a Lodge member. Probably. And Jarvis and his buddies on board his superyacht? He guessed so.

He stepped to the side of the bed closest to the window. 'Goldsby's clothes were on the floor here, and his body lying on the other side of the bed. Olewbo returned to say that he'd received a call that Durrant had been picked up in Guildhall Square. It was just before midnight. Olewbo left to question him, I stayed on for about another twenty minutes to hand over to Danby and volunteered to break the news to Goldsby's next of kin, who Danby said was his wife.' He frowned at the memory. 'A woman PC came with me. Prudence wasn't there. Adele answered the door. She hadn't been in bed — she was still dressed and looked anxious, but that was probably due to our unexpected appearance. She said her mother was out, she didn't know where, but she'd call her. She refused any help. I told her that the media would probably be doorstepping her in the morning. She didn't seem fazed by that. I detailed the PC to remain outside until relieved. I remember Adele politely thanking me. She took the news with a sort of coldness.'

'Shock?'

'Possibly. Or perhaps, judging by what I've heard about her, it was a defence mechanism she'd perfected over the years to stop herself from being hurt.' And he knew all about that.

Cantelli said, 'I only saw the photographs of the body. By the time I arrived the following morning, Goldsby and his belongings had been removed. He hadn't used the bathroom and he hadn't made a call on the internal phone or switched on the television. His prints were found on the door, the table in front of the window and the bedside table to the left, where he'd put the key.'

Horton remembered seeing it there. Briskly, he said, 'OK, Barney, let's see if we can work out how he ended up naked and lying the way he was, dead on that bed.'

CHAPTER FOURTEEN

'Scenario number one. Let's assume that Goldsby bought that cocaine and took it deliberately in order to kill himself. He books the room in a false name, collects the key maybe that night but probably earlier in the day so that he doesn't have to ask for it at reception later. He unlocks the door and enters.' Horton began to enact his words. 'He walks across the room to the window where he places his briefcase, unopened and facing upwards. He doesn't pull the curtains.'

'No, but the net curtains were drawn across the window.'

'They were, you're right. He turns, walks around the bed and puts the key on the bedside table nearest the door alongside the telephone. Why that side? Why not on the table closest to the window?'

'Force of habit? Maybe he always slept on the left-hand side of the bed at home. Or perhaps he placed the key there before walking to the table and depositing his briefcase.'

'He switches on the bedside light.'

'No. There were no prints on it. Both bedside lights were switched on from the main switch by the door, which he must have done immediately after he let himself in. There was a good print of his on that.'

'OK, so no one inside waiting for him unless they were sitting with the lights out. Say, though, he was alone. After putting on the lights and dumping his briefcase on the table, he undresses next to the bedside table closest to the window.' Horton paused. 'Barney, make as if you're undressing.'

Cantelli walked to the window side of the bed and obliged by removing his jacket.

Horton continued, 'I remember that his clothes weren't neatly folded but neither were they all over the place as though he'd ripped them off in a frenzy. They were just in a pile on the floor. Jacket and tie, shirt, trousers, then underpants and socks on top.'

Cantelli removed his tie and laid it down. 'I'll leave the rest to our imagination.'

Horton smiled. 'His shoes were just to the side of the clothes.'

'OK, off they come.' Cantelli slipped off his lace-up black shoes and placed them to the right of his tie just on the outside edge of the bedside cabinet. 'From the photographs taken I remember that they were lined up, not flicked off or placed any old how, and they were black lace-up brogues, good quality, like his clothes.'

'Was there any indentation on that side of the bed where he sat?'

Cantelli rapidly thought. 'I don't think so, but I'd need to check.'

'Let's say he sat.' Cantelli did so.

'And was suddenly taken ill when the drug took effect.' Cantelli clutched his heart, made a face and fell back.

'Quite,' said Horton. 'He'd have fallen backwards across that side of the bed where his clothes were placed or possibly forwards on to the floor. But his body was found on the other side. So he stands up, naked, and starts to feel bad.'

Cantelli reeled, clutching his stomach. Horton smiled although he knew it was no joke. 'I'm not sure you'll get an Oscar.'

'Pity. And there's me thinking I'd missed my vocation.'

'Goldsby makes to cross to the bathroom for a glass of water.'

'Why not the glasses and water on the table?'

'He's ill, not thinking straight. As he reaches the bathroom door, he feels dizzy and disorientated.' Cantelli staggered a little.

'There might be time for that Oscar, yet,' Horton joked. Then more seriously, he continued, 'He walks around the bed as though to get to the phone to summon help. Perhaps he's changed his mind and doesn't want to die after all. He sits on the bed.' Cantelli sat. 'He feels dreadful and falls back.'

'Sounds possible but my legs are dangling over the edge and Goldsby was about the same height as me and he was lying fully on the bed.'

'Maybe he climbed on the bed then reached across for the phone, couldn't find it, hauled himself up further onto the bed but fell back and died.'

Cantelli tried it. Horton eyed the sergeant's position. 'It's not quite right. Almost but not quite. The angle of the legs is slightly wrong.'

Cantelli sat up. 'He could have shifted about, feeling unwell.'

'Maybe.' But it still didn't look right. 'Goldsby's expression showed no sign of agony or anguish. Was he in the habit of checking into hotel bedrooms?'

'Not that I know of.'

'Right, second scenario. Goldsby came here to meet his killer not knowing what was in store. He's been passed the key beforehand by the killer, who booked the room in a false name and paid cash. Goldsby unlocks the door and enters. His killer is not here. He places his briefcase on the window table, sits in the chair there and waits.'

Cantelli obliged.

'The killer knocks and Goldsby lets him in. It's OK, Barney, let's take this one as read. They share a drink, which the killer has brought with him, only Goldsby's is laced with cocaine. Goldsby shows the killer to the door after they've discussed what it is they are here for. But on the way Goldsby feels the effects of the drug and falls. The killer stands and watches Goldsby die. He then needs to make it look like suicide. He stuffs the drink and glasses he's brought with him back in a bag, undresses Goldsby and—'

'But why leave his clothes on the other side of the bed and fairly neatly placed?'

'Maybe he thinks that's what Goldsby would have done.'

'Why undress him in the first place?'

'Because he wants to make it look seedy, as though Goldsby was here to meet a lover or a prostitute.'

Cantelli shrugged. 'OK.'

'After undressing Goldsby our killer runs out of strength and energy and has only sufficient of both to haul him up and lay him diagonally on the bed. He then straightens out the bedclothes, wipes the room clean of his prints but makes sure that Goldsby's are still around and leaves the way he came, by the stairs and through reception, or he returns to one of the functions being held below. No one would have noticed him slip out and, even if they did, he could have said he was going to the toilet.'

'It would have taken quite an effort to undress a dead man and shift the body onto the bed.'

'Yes, so we're looking for someone physically quite strong.'

'And clever.'

Horton considered this. 'Scenario three then could be that Goldsby was given the cocaine earlier and died in this room before the killer got here. The killer saw Goldsby enter the hotel, waited for the drug to take effect and then came up here to dress the set. In order to do that, either Goldsby would have made sure the room was unlocked, as instructed by the killer, or the killer had a pass key, which means he was a member of staff or knew a way to access the key.'

'But why kill him?'

Horton frowned. After a moment, he said, 'Was he killed because of Quintessa? There has to be a link between them.

Adele Goldsby made that phone call to Brandon and now he's dead and Adele seems to have gone missing.' Horton sincerely hoped nothing had happened to her but he was worried it might have done. Brandon's death meant this killer would not hesitate to murder to cover his tracks.

Cantelli said, 'But Quintessa was killed twenty years before Goldsby, and if Dudley Goldsby was involved in her death, then his daughter would hardly point the finger at her late father.'

'I agree, but she could be telling us that her father's killer and Quintessa's are one and the same. God knows how she discovered it, but seeing as she's not shown up to tell us who it is, we need to find out for ourselves before . . .' But his words trailed off. He could see by Cantelli's worried expression that he was thinking along the same lines.

Quietly Cantelli said, 'She could already be dead.'

'Yes, which was why she didn't show on the ferry.' He left a moment's pause. 'Let's see if Ms Blythe has got that list for us.'

She had. 'I've managed to access everything you might need, Inspector.' She locked eyes with him and in them, he thought he read an invitation to get closer. She reached across her desk and handed him the list. Her hand brushed his for a moment. 'I've also pulled off a list of the staff at that time. I've put an asterisk beside those members of staff who are still working here.'

Horton noted there weren't many. The hotel and catering industry had a high turnover.

'If you need to speak to them, I'd be happy to arrange that for you. They're all shift workers, as you'd expect, so you might need to return at different times of the day and night.'

She sounded as though she might welcome that, but perhaps he was imagining things. He admired her efficiency and that was all.

'I also thought you might like the guest list for the night of the twenty-second of April 2005.'

It would be useful to compare it with the one on file, if Uckfield ever agreed to reopen the case. Horton was certain that at some point he would have to. Again, she reached over, only Cantelli took it.

'There are four names on there that I recognize,' she continued. 'They are regular guests, who come every year, not always at that particular time but usually in the spring. Some of the guests were block booked — a holiday coach party from Leeds, another from Norwich. And some were booked in with the conference that was being held in the Southwick Suite, which brings me on to the list of functions held that night. I have the details of the company and individual who booked the function rooms but, as I said earlier, not their guests. There were four functions in total. The largest, which was held in the Southwick Suite, was a two-day conference on Allergens, Food, Health and Nutrition on the twenty-second and twenty-third of April. Refreshments and lunch were ordered for 120 people and there were eighty guests for dinner on Friday night, not all of whom stayed here. You'll find the names of those who stayed overnight on the hotel guest list.

'There was also a charity auction with a dinner in aid of those serving in the armed forces and veterans. There were no overnight bookings for any of those guests and the same for the other two smaller private parties. One was held in the Collingwood Room, the other in the Nelson Room. I've pulled off the details of the organizers but they could easily have changed by now.'

She handed over the piece of paper. As Horton stared down at it, his heart leaped into his throat. The organizer of one of the private functions was none other than Peter Jarvis.

CHAPTER FIFTEEN

'There must be more than one Peter Jarvis in the country,' Cantelli said, pushing a piece of fresh gum in his mouth as they made their way through reception.

'But not one whose billing address was a factory in Gosport. That was where Jarvis's food processing company was based.'

'But what motive could he have for killing Goldsby, an old school friend?'

'Quintessa.' Horton halted on the steps to the hotel and peered out at the stormy weather and the pier opposite. 'Perhaps they had both been in love with her and Jarvis killed her when he discovered she had betrayed him with Goldsby.'

'He took a long time to seek revenge on Goldsby,' Cantelli quipped.

Horton frowned. 'Yes, doesn't quite fit, does it?' But he'd like it to. 'Perhaps Goldsby killed Quintessa in the eighties and Jarvis didn't discover this until 2005 and then killed him.'

'If that's the case then I'll repeat what I said before — Adele couldn't have known that her father was a killer, because she'd hardly draw our attention to the fact.'

'No, and neither does Goldsby sound like a killer according to what I've heard of him.' Horton sighed. 'But maybe there was a dark side to him.'

'And Jarvis? What's he like?'

Horton returned Cantelli's steady gaze, seeing the concern in the sergeant's dark eyes and appreciating it. He stepped out into the teeth of the wind. Cantelli followed. The sea was an angry dark grey with waves like a rollercoaster. Horton dashed a glance at the granite fort and thought, *Good* — the crossing was rough enough to make Jarvis and his guests sick.

He had to raise his voice above the howling gale. 'I've only met him once, yesterday, on board his superyacht at Oyster Quays. I didn't take to him. OK, Barney, so I'm prejudiced.' He quickly added, 'Not because he's Catherine's new boyfriend but because of Emma.'

'Why, what's happened?' Cantelli asked, alarmed and concerned.

'Nothing as far as I know, but I just find it hard to stomach that he can see more of her than me and yes, all right, I'm worried that she'll want to be with him more than me because he's rich. Barney, he can give her far more than I ever can.'

'Except love.'

'Why not? He could love her too.'

'But not like a father. And Emma will know that.'

'Will she?'

'Yes,' Cantelli firmly replied, 'if you continue to be there for her when you can and when you're needed. Besides, this relationship between Catherine and Jarvis might fizzle out.'

'Then there'll be someone else.'

There was moment's silence before Cantelli said, 'Even more reason for you to always be there. The one consistent male in her life. Kids can be very resilient.'

And didn't Horton know it. He'd had to be during the years following his mother's desertion, but that didn't mean it didn't hurt or affect you or that you didn't get angry. Maybe he could provide Emma with more stability than Catherine could, especially if he changed jobs. There was Mike Danby's offer. But who was to say he wouldn't have relationships himself? He hoped he would.

His mind flicked to Gaye, then quickly he pushed it away. He liked her a great deal and they got on well, but was it more than that? He doubted it. Especially on her part. And he couldn't see any judge giving him custody. He had to try for greater access, though. He had a phone call to make, to his lawyer, which he vowed he would do later that day.

Cantelli's solemn voice broke through his thoughts. 'Just hang on in there, Andy. Emma won't leave you. She knows how much she means to you.'

'Despite Catherine.'

'Yes.' Cantelli replied stoutly as he zapped open the car door.

Horton hoped Cantelli was right. He stretched the seat belt across him. 'I asked Jarvis about Dudley Goldsby and he said nothing about being in that hotel the night of his murder. Why didn't he?'

'Maybe he didn't think it relevant.'

'Jarvis is clever and possibly ruthless to have run such a successful business, which, according to Danby and the media, he sold for millions.' And perhaps that was why he needed security from Danby, because there were people he'd trodden on, who he'd used and abused on his way to making his multimillions.

'Doesn't make him a killer.'

'He didn't come forward at the time — don't you think that suspicious?' But Horton didn't wait for an answer. 'Why did Adele get in touch with me now, when Jarvis's yacht is moored up at Oyster Quays? And why call Danby with the phoney name and use Jarvis as the fake client? It's all pointing to him.'

Cantelli started the engine.

'I'd like to know where Jarvis was last night between ten and midnight.'

'You think he killed Brandon?' Cantelli said, surprised.

Did he? No. He couldn't see the wealthy entrepreneur slipping off his warm luxury yacht in the dark hours and sticking a knife in Brandon. But perhaps he knew someone who would oblige. That fit, thirty-something crew member who had greeted Horton on board yesterday? Horton consulted his watch. It was just after midday. Jarvis should still be at Oyster Quays.

'I think it's about time I asked him why he wasn't concerned enough about his school friend's death to come forward. Not you, Barney. I'll go alone.'

Cantelli threw him a concerned look.

'It's all right, I'm not going to do anything stupid. And you're due at the Royal Navy Museum in the dockyard to talk to the curator about Neil Brandon. Drop me off at the entrance to the shopping centre. I'll meet you in St George's Square opposite in about an hour.'

'Think it will take you that long?'

'No. I think he'll say as little as possible given my last encounter with him, and he might already have left for the fort. If he has, I'll meet you at the museum.'

Cantelli reluctantly agreed. As he pulled up by the church in the square, he urged Horton to take it easy.

'Would you be happy if you thought one of your daughters was spending time in the company of a killer?' Horton retorted.

'We don't know that he is one. But, no, you're right, Andy.' Cantelli sighed. 'I'd probably be doing the same as you.'

Horton nodded and climbed out. He was pleased to see that Jarvis's boat was still on the pontoon. With his pulse beating a little faster, he made his way towards it. The wind was wailing and whistling around him, and the pontoon was lifting and falling with the movement of the sea even in the shelter of the harbour. The small green-and-white Gosport ferry looked as though it was having a tough time crossing the short distance from Portsmouth.

There was no one on the deck of Jarvis's boat. Horton climbed on board and saw through the wide glass doors to

125

the salon that Jarvis had company, which included Catherine. He'd have preferred it if she hadn't been there. Their last meeting hadn't exactly been cordial, but then that was the norm. It had been after a particularly disturbing investigation that had involved the death of a child the same age as Emma. He had rushed up to the house they had once shared together when married. All he'd wanted was to see Emma. To hold her. To tell her how much he loved her. But Catherine had refused to let him in on the grounds it wasn't his contact day. A bitter row had ensued.

He steeled himself to keep a check on his emotions, urging himself to recall his police training and to consider this case like any other investigation, but he knew it would be difficult.

He noted that with Jarvis was Dominic Keats and the short man he had seen boarding with Keats yesterday, called Alex. The lean, bespectacled man he had seen in the salon on the previous day was also present, along with the very skinny blonde woman. But it was the tall, upright, balding man that aroused Horton's interest. It was the former Chief Constable Reginald Dyer, Uckfield's father-in-law. Horton had never liked Dyer and Dyer had never cared for him. Dyer hadn't believed he was innocent of those rape charges and, even when he'd been exonerated, Dyer had refused to believe it.

But it was interesting that Dyer was a guest of Jarvis. Horton hadn't known that any relationship between them existed. Had they been close friends in 2005? If so, that made things more intriguing. Was Uckfield aware of his father-in-law's friendship with Jarvis? Of course he was. And it was the reason why he was reluctant to get the case reopened, or even re-examined. Horton's suspicions about Jarvis's involvement in Goldsby's death deepened, along with the fact that Dyer could have supressed evidence that his buddy had been at the hotel on the night in question.

Jarvis saw him. There was no turning back. Not that he would have ducked out, but he knew Dyer would get on the phone to Uckfield to tell him he was there. Horton pushed open the door and stepped inside.

The conversation immediately ceased as all eyes swung to him. In an instant, Horton rapidly assimilated their response: Dyer was eyeing him as though he'd like to fry him slowly over a fire, Keats as though he was a rather nasty insect that had crawled in, the bespectacled man with the curiosity of a scientist discovering a new breed, the short, muscular man with suspicion and arrogance, while the thin blonde woman beside him on one of the leather sofas turned her anxious light-brown eyes on him. He also registered Catherine's blue ones filled with fury and Jarvis's flush of anger.

'Can I help you, Detective Inspector Horton?' he asked crisply.

'I'd like a word in private.' He was dammed if he was going to say 'sir' — not unless he injected the word with a sneer, and this wasn't the time for that.

Catherine, who was looking daggers at him, made to speak, but Jarvis forestalled her. 'Come through to my study.'

'Peter, if you need me—'

Jarvis interrupted Dyer. 'I don't, but thank you, Reg.' Jarvis turned, as though expecting Horton to follow, which he did. He felt the other guests' eyes boring into his back. Jarvis addressed an auburn-haired, slender woman in the galley. 'We won't be long, Ruby. No need to delay lunch.'

That was Jarvis's way of making it quite clear he would only give him limited time. But Horton would take all the time he needed. He followed Jarvis into a cabin just beyond the galley on the right. It was, as he anticipated, luxuriously fitted, with bookshelves on two sides and a leather bench seat on the third, in front of which was a coffee table. There was also a desk and on it a laptop computer. Jarvis didn't invite him to sit. Horton hadn't expected him to.

'I trust you don't intend going over the same ground as yesterday because I've said all there is to say on the subject of Dudley Goldsby,' Jarvis said, his tone businesslike with an edge of ice.

Not quite all. 'You hosted a private dinner at the Solent Waves Hotel on the twenty-second of April 2005. Who were your guests?'

Jarvis looked momentarily stunned. He clearly hadn't anticipated that question and there was no reason why he should have. Rapidly recovering himself, he said, 'That was years ago. Why do you want to know about that?'

'Just answer the question, please.'

'Not unless you give me a good enough reason to do so.'

'Dudley Goldsby.'

Jarvis's pale grey eyes hardened. 'Is this really necessary?'

'I would say so, wouldn't you, when it involves a man's death?'

'I don't see what my private dinner party has to do with Dudley's suicide.'

'The coroner didn't say it was suicide.'

Jarvis looked irritated. 'Misadventure then. And besides, the case is closed.'

'Is that what Mr Dyer told you?' Before Jarvis could answer, Horton continued, 'Did you see Dudley Goldsby that night?'

'No. I didn't even know he was in the hotel.'

'But you knew he died there.'

'Only afterwards. I heard the news on the radio the following morning.'

'Why did you choose that hotel for your event?' Horton asked.

Jarvis assumed a world-weary expression that to Horton smacked of condescending superiority, as though he'd decided to humour a tiresome child or idiot employee, or perhaps that was just his interpretation of it. 'It's an excellent hotel. I was entertaining clients.'

'Why didn't you tell the police that you were in the hotel?'

'Why should I have?'

'Because Dudley Goldsby died there that night and he was very well known to you.'

The condescending look vanished and in its place came a coldness, which was reflected in his voice. 'That sounds as though you are implying something, and if so, then I'd like to know what authority you have to do so.'

'It would be helpful to have your guest list,' persisted Horton.

'I shouldn't think for one moment I still have it.'

'Might it be on your computer archive?'

'It might, but until I know the reason why you want it, and until you, or your superiors, show me they have good reason to request it, and confirm that the police are officially reinvestigating Dudley's death, then I see no reason to ask my PA to spend time trying to find it.'

Horton knew that he was on difficult ground. He had no authority to insist. 'I would have thought you'd want to help us with our inquiries.'

'I will once those inquiries have been fully explained to me and I am reassured that it is an official investigation. Until then I have nothing to say to you. I'll show you out.'

Horton held his steely gaze. Why was Jarvis being so obstructive? The only reason Horton could think of was that he had something to hide. The interview hadn't quite gone the way he had expected but Jarvis's hostile reaction was interesting and perhaps more revealing than if he had simply answered the questions and been cooperative. Why hadn't he been more concerned about the death of his old school friend?

As they stepped outside the cabin, Horton said, 'Where were you last night between ten and midnight?'

Jarvis flashed him a look of fury. 'That is none of your business.'

'Murder is, though.'

Jarvis's mouth tightened. 'If you have any accusations to make, or wish to question me further, then you must do so formally with my lawyer present.'

He strode off through the main cabin. Once again, the conversation ceased as Horton followed him. He caught Catherine's hard expression. Dyer was glaring at him and had his mobile phone in his hand. No doubt he had already called Uckfield to let him know he was here. A crew member appeared as though by magic, and while Jarvis returned to his guests without a by-your-leave, the crew member waited until Horton alighted. Before he had gone a few paces he felt the pontoon rock and turned back to see Catherine storming towards him. Her coat was wrapped around her slim body, her arms folded against her chest, the wind whipping her shoulder-length blonde hair around her scowling fair face. Horton had half a mind to ignore her and walk away but he didn't. After all, he had a critical question to ask her about Emma.

'How dare you embarrass me like that,' Catherine raged. 'Just because you can't bear the thought of me being with another man you have to persecute me and go after anyone I care to have a relationship with. What I do with my life and with whom I do it is nothing to do with you.'

'You're right, it isn't,' he said earnestly, taking her by surprise. 'But my daughter has everything to do with me. Is she with you on the fort this weekend for your boyfriend's party?'

'It's business,' she snarled. She pushed her hair off her livid face. 'If you must know, Peter is trying to encourage a younger generation of entrepreneurs by setting up a venture capital trust for start-up companies specializing in scientific research, and the last thing he needs is PC plod barging in, treating him like a criminal and embarrassing him. Have you any idea who those men on Peter's boat are? No,' she said without waiting for his answer. 'Jonathan Sloane is a world-renowned chemist and founder of Grendon Biotechnology. Alex Cummings is one of the most revered international luxury yacht designers in the world—'

'Design that floating gin palace for Jarvis, did he?'

Catherine ignored the barb. 'Dominic Keats is the owner of—'

'I know who Keats is,' Horton crisply interjected.

'Then you know that not only is he highly successful but he has very wealthy contacts worldwide, as do Alex Cummings and Jonathan Sloane, people who are extremely influential and important.'

'Depends how you look at it.'

'Well, Peter looks at it as being vital,' she snapped. 'You could have made them doubt his integrity if they didn't already all know one another. At least he's trying to give something back and encourage others, which is more than I can say for some,' she hissed, eyeing him malevolently.

'Catherine, he's not doing it out of the goodness of his heart and neither are Sloane, Cummings and Keats. It's about money, making more of it and saving tax.'

But she didn't hear him. 'You had no right to come on board and take Peter aside like that just to warn him off me.'

'Don't flatter yourself,' Horton said scathingly. 'I'm here on business.'

'Oh, yes, what kind?' she hissed.

'That's between me and Jarvis.'

'That's it, hide behind the job, use it as an excuse, just like you always do,' she scoffed.

He ignored the taunt. 'Ask your boyfriend, maybe he'll tell you why I'm here.'

'I wouldn't demean myself.'

'No? And while you're acting as hostess where will our daughter be?'

Catherine looked as though she was about to say, 'That's none of your business,' but briskly said, 'Staying with friends.'

He badly wanted to say, 'She could have stayed with me,' but how could he when he was working on an investigation? And that point had been made by his lawyer in January when he'd consulted her about increasing his access to his daughter. He didn't always work, he'd insisted — except he did. Catherine was right, he worked a great deal, but now only because there was little else in his life.

Sick of her, he said harshly, 'Is Emma going with you and Jarvis to Barbados at Easter?'

'How do you know about that?' she asked sharply, her blue eyes narrowing with suspicion.

Coldly he said, 'When were you going to tell me that my two days' access during her school holidays were to be revoked?'

She pursued her lips. 'It's only just been finalized.'

'Without consulting me,' he said stiffly. 'It's not safe for her.'

'Don't talk rot. You can't stop me taking her there.'

She was right, blast her. Curtly, with anger churning inside him, he said, 'Then I'll have Emma for two days over a weekend before she goes, in addition to the two days a month I get.'

'She's got things arranged.'

'Then rearrange them, Catherine.' He took a silent breath and steeled himself to remain calm, though his body was so tense he thought it might snap in two.

'I haven't got time to stand here arguing with you.' She turned towards the boat.

He wanted to reach out and grab her arm to prevent her, but with a supreme effort he restrained himself, knowing it would only play into her hands. She wanted him to become violent. And wouldn't that give her an excellent excuse to go back to the lawyers and restrict his access even further, or deny it completely, especially as he could see they had witnesses. Jarvis was on deck with Dyer and a member of his crew.

In a strained voice, Horton said, 'If that's the way you want it, Catherine, we'll do it through the lawyers.'

She turned back and, with heavy sarcasm said, 'I've heard that all before.'

And she was right. He'd threatened many times to go back to the courts to apply for greater access to Emma and he'd never done it — he'd been too wrapped up in his work and his search for the truth behind his mother's disappearance. But was that just an excuse? He was desperate to avoid having a public tussle through the family law courts, not because of the cost but because of the humiliation he felt at having to declare publicly that his marriage had failed. That *he* had failed. And he abhorred the thought of having his background exposed because he knew that Catherine, through her lawyer, would throw up his troubled childhood, the false rape allegation, the demands of his job and the fact that he lived on a small boat, which all demonstrated how unstable he was. Well, he could counter it with the unsuitability of her boyfriend, except that this boyfriend looked highly suitable, as opposed to the previous one, who Horton had discovered had been into hardcore porn and sadomasochism. This one was a respectable, successful, wealthy entrepreneur, an upright citizen. Or was he? Could he be a killer? Horton noted that Jarvis hadn't asked who had been murdered last night. Was that because he already knew? That didn't make him a killer, though. Uckfield could have told Dyer and Dyer could have told Jarvis.

On the boardwalk Horton turned to look at Jarvis's superyacht as it slipped away from the pontoon. The skinny blonde woman was on the deck and she was looking directly at him. He was troubled by her anxious expression. Perhaps she got seasick like Cantelli. Then she turned as though she'd been called and vanished from view.

Horton made his way out of the waterfront shopping centre to St George's Square wondering what he'd achieved. The answer was nothing except a bollocking from Uckfield. And he knew that was coming just as he knew the rhythm of the tides.

CHAPTER SIXTEEN

'What the devil did you think you were playing at storming
onto that boat and demanding to know Jarvis's movements?'
Uckfield demanded in a low voice with his mouth full of
steak and kidney pie. Horton had stopped off in the canteen
to buy some sandwiches, while Cantelli had headed back to
CID to eat his homemade ones. As soon as Uckfield had
seen him enter he'd directed a podgy finger at the vacant seat
in front of him, indicating for Horton to join him. His headache seemed to have disappeared, although he still looked
haggard and his eyes were bloodshot.

'I didn't storm on and I'm not playing,' Horton said
coolly.

'Then you'd better have a damn good reason for what
you did.'

'I simply asked Peter Jarvis why he was at the same hotel
at the same time Dudley Goldsby's body was found and why
he didn't tell the police that.'

Uckfield paused in chewing.

'Didn't Jarvis mention that when he complained?' asked
Horton loftily, knowing full well it wasn't Jarvis who had
phoned Uckfield. A fact that Uckfield bore out.

'It wasn't him.' Uckfield resumed eating but there was a frown etched on his rugged forehead.

'No, it was Dyer. What was your father-in-law doing on Jarvis's boat?'

'That's hardly any of your business.'

Was Dyer there because Jarvis, learning that Quintessa had been found, had called in a favour from the man who had headed the criminal investigation into Goldsby's death? Although on a good pension, Dyer didn't have the sort of money Jarvis was looking for to invest in any venture capital trust fund. Again, Horton considered whether Dyer had done Jarvis a favour in 2005 by keeping his name out of the investigation.

Uckfield said, 'How do you know Jarvis was at that hotel?'

Horton told him about his and Cantelli's visit there. Uckfield listened while finishing his meal. Pushing away his plate, he said with exasperation, 'For Christ's sake, Andy, we're not investigating Goldsby's death but Neil Brandon's. Yes, I know you think they're connected — and they might be — but I need more than thoughts to go on before requesting the Goldsby investigation to be reopened. His having been a politician makes it extra sensitive. Questions will be asked at the highest level.'

'So?'

Uckfield removed a wooden toothpick from his suit jacket pocket and began to manoeuvre it around his mouth while keeping a steady gaze on Horton. 'It'll be plastered all over the newspapers. The integrity and competency of the officers involved in the original investigation will be questioned, and that includes you. You weren't on the case but you and Olewbo found the body.'

Nice, thought Horton with bitterness. A cop with a dubious past. Exonerated, but what the hell did that matter to the hierarchy? He'd be fair game to hang out as a scapegoat even though he'd had nothing to do with the ensuing investigation nor any previous connection with Dudley Goldsby. But if the fact that Adele had approached him became public knowledge then the newspapers and the trolls and goons on social media would assume that there was some connection and put two and two together to make the usual half a dozen and more. Is this what Dyer had told his son-in-law to say? Was Dyer threatening him?

Tersely Horton said, 'Not forgetting that your father-in-law was the detective chief superintendent in charge of criminal investigations at the time. He's told you to make sure the Dudley Goldsby investigation stays where it is, hasn't he? Filed under no further action. Case signed off. Archived.'

Uckfield squirmed a little. 'Reg was only marginally involved. He took up the assistant chief constable position in Avon in May that year.'

'Yeah, so he didn't want to rock the boat by asking too many awkward questions.'

'He'd already been appointed. He had no reason to cover up anything.'

But Uckfield knew as well as Horton that Dyer would have done as he was told if given instructions to close down the investigation. And those instructions could have come from the government via Special Branch, but for what reason? Because it was during a general election and there was something that the politicians didn't want coming out? Or had Dyer covered up for his pal, Jarvis? Dyer had returned to Hampshire after being promoted to chief constable three years later. Horton knew that without Uckfield's backing to take this higher and get it reopened, he'd never be able to get his hands on Jarvis's guest list.

Uckfield threw the used toothpick on his plate and sat forward. 'The fact that your ex-wife is in a relationship with Jarvis doesn't exactly mean you're unbiased. Keep away from him and his guests.'

'Is that a threat?'

'No, it's an order.' He scraped back his chair and rose. Horton followed suit. Uckfield continued, 'We concentrate on Neil Brandon's murder because it might just lead us to more information on Quintessa's death.'

'So we ignore the fact that Adele Goldsby telephoned Brandon and told him about those human remains.'

'No. We still try to find her but without a bloody song and dance about her father and his fate.'

'I'm permitted to talk to her mother, then? Prudence. She lives in Old Portsmouth, not far from where Brandon's body was found.'

Uckfield scowled as they headed up the stairs to his office and the incident suite. 'You can ask her when she last saw or heard from her daughter and that's it. Not a word about phone calls, skeletons or Dudley Goldsby. Has Cantelli spoken to the curator at the museum?'

'Yes.' Horton relayed what Cantelli had told him in the car on the way back to the station after Horton had given him the edited highlights of his conversation on Jarvis's boat, which didn't take long. He'd omitted his conversation with Catherine. 'Cantelli said that the curator, Ms Montrose, was very reticent at first to talk about Brandon, but when he told her that his death was being treated as suspicious, she opened up. Brandon was overbearing and patronizing. He wasn't popular among the staff or the volunteers, and she'd suspected for some time that he had been stealing from the museum. Items had gone missing after his shifts. It started with small things: pens, pencils, key rings, fridge magnets, but over the last six months there were hats, clothing, books.'

That hadn't surprised Horton or Cantelli, because just as some people could smell a copper, they could smell a thief, which made Horton think of Keith Harnley in Somerstown and the robberies at business premises in that area.

He continued, 'Ms Montrose reported her suspicions to the director. They were due to have a word with Brandon, which was probably why she looked relieved and then a little guilty according to Cantelli when he broke the news to her that he was dead. Her files show that Brandon's next of kin was named as his mother at the same address. She didn't know his mother had died. And she didn't know of anyone who had paid particular attention to him, or who seemed keen to talk to him, but she admitted that she could easily have missed them as she wasn't there all the time. Her time is split between the Explosion Museum where Brandon volunteered and the National Museum of the Royal Navy in the dockyard. We'll need to speak to the staff and volunteers at the Gosport Museum.'

Uckfield nodded agreement as he pushed open the door to the incident suite. It was humming with activity and packed with personnel, somewhat different from when it was discovered Quintessa had been murdered, thought Horton.

He continued, 'Ms Montrose said they hadn't given Brandon's phone number to anyone and as far as she was aware their databases hadn't been compromised. Elkins has spoken to a few people at the Cruising Association and discovered that Brandon was tolerated rather than liked.' And Horton knew that Elkins was now wading through the moat, it being ninety minutes off low tide, and had told him on the phone earlier that he had bugger all to show for it, except probably a cold tomorrow.

Cantelli was writing the brief points from his interview with Ms Montrose on the crime board. Bliss, who was in the office she commandeered on these major investigations next to Uckfield's, diverted her eyes from her computer and sprang up, hurrying out to them. There was no sign of DI Dennings so Horton assumed he must still be overseeing the search at Brandon's house. Walters was studying his computer screen. The phones were constantly ringing.

Trueman addressed Uckfield. 'From the press statement you put out earlier, guv, half the population of Portsmouth has seen someone loitering about the Spur Redoubt. All the descriptions are way off the mark unless you believe the killer looks like a cross between Captain Hook and the Elephant Man, and that's discounting sightings of the ghosts of Admiral Lord Nelson, Henry VII and Henry VIII. All we need now is for someone to say the killer was an alien from outer space.'

'And we'll probably get it,' grunted Uckfield.

'Aside from that, we've got the know-it-alls who are demanding to know why we haven't caught the killer, charged him, had him convicted and banged up like they do on the telly. After all, if they can do it in an hour why can't we? They've even gone so far as to offer us advice on how to conduct the investigation. Next they'll be performing the autopsy.'

Horton smiled and asked if the forensic team on Rat Island had found anything.

'A buckle and some buttons. They could have come from Quintessa's clothing, but no personal items.'

Trueman's phone rang. Bliss asked Walters, who had been studying the CCTV images that the British Transport Police had sent over earlier, if he had picked up anything.

'There's no sign of a woman in her mid-thirties at the payphone, just some guy.'

'Show us,' Uckfield demanded.

Walters tapped his keyboard and the images came up on the wide-screen TV in front of them, next to the crime scene board. The figure at the payphone was wearing grey trousers and a grey hooded jacket with the hood up obscuring the face. It had its back to the camera and its head well down. The time on the coverage corresponded to the time Adele Goldsby had called Horton. He wondered if she was on camera at the time she called Danby too. He hadn't asked Walters to check that because he hadn't told anyone about Danby's mystery caller, except Cantelli, and he'd said nothing. The caller hung up and turned away. It was impossible to see any features.

'It's not a man,' Horton said adamantly.

'Walks like one to me.'

'Maybe she put that on to fool the cameras,' suggested Cantelli.

'You think she knew she was being filmed?' Walters asked.

Horton did. She wasn't taking any chances. But where had she gone after that? He knew it would be impossible to pick her up on any of the street CCTVs. Besides, she might have discarded the trousers and the hooded jacket in the ladies' toilet at the far end of the railway station. She wasn't carrying a rucksack but the clothes looked bulky enough to have hidden another pair of trousers underneath and a different jacket or top. Or perhaps she'd left a bag in the toilets, made the telephone call and returned to the cubicle where she changed. There was also the possibility that she could have used the toilets in the Wightlink Fast Cat ferry terminal, the entrance to which was just behind the payphone. Horton said as much.

Crisply Bliss addressed Walters. 'Get the Transport Police to ask the station staff if they remember seeing that person—' she waved her scrawny arm at the TV — 'and if any clothes were found in the ladies' toilets.'

'Or on a train,' Horton added. 'She could have boarded a train and changed in the toilet or simply got on a train that wasn't due to depart for a while, changed and then stepped off and walked away.'

Bliss looked peeved she hadn't thought of it. To Walters, she said, 'Check which trains were on the platforms at the time the call was made and for how long, and if anything was left behind on them.'

Dennings barged in looking flustered and irritated. 'Brandon's house is a tip. It'll take ages to sift through it all. There's tons of paperwork, bills, receipts, mail order catalogues, circulars and anything else he felt like keeping, all of it a lot of old dross dating back years. From the most recent bank and building society statements we managed to find, it seems his mother left him several thousand pounds. The house is in his name, left to him by his mother. Her clothes, jewellery, toiletries and make-up are still in her bedroom.'

Too painful for him to get rid of or too lazy? wondered Horton. He'd never been given anything of his mother's to take with him when they had carted him off to the children's home. But he had come across a brooch that he was certain had once belonged to her in the ownership of the widowed and late PC Adrian Stanley, who had cursorily investigated her disappearance. He'd seen it in a photograph pinned on the chest of Stanley's wife when her husband had received the Queen's Medal for Bravery. He'd visited the former copper's flat in April to ask him what he remembered about his investigation into Jennifer's disappearance. Nothing was the answer, but on Stanley's death shortly after his visit, the brooch, along with all photographs of it, had vanished. It had been shaped like a flower with a large blue oval gem in the centre, a small, square pink gem underneath it, and diamonds that mimicked leaves around the outside. A highly distinctive piece, but he'd found no record of it on the internet or on the database of stolen arts, antiques and jewellery, perhaps because it had been merely cheap costume jewellery.

'There's also a lot of stuff from the museum in the house and in the shed: pens, pencils, notebooks, sweatshirts and hats,' Dennings said.

Cantelli swiftly relayed what Ms Montrose had told him about the museum's suspicions of Brandon's stealing.

'That figures,' Dennings added. 'We also found boating equipment, life jackets and fishing rods in the shed, all probably stolen.'

Horton said, 'And I bet some will be from the boats broken into on the Cruising Association pontoons the night before last, which Brandon claimed was the work of hooligans.'

'An inside job. Brandon vandalizes his own boat to cover his tracks,' Bliss suggested.

'Yes. To make it look as though he was a victim instead of a crook, and to claim on the insurance.'

Dennings continued, 'One of the neighbours says that Brandon regularly did the marine jumble sales and car boot sales. It sounds as though he supplemented his pension with a bit of pilfering and selling.'

Uckfield addressed Trueman. 'What was Brandon's last paid job? I'd like to know how long it lasted and if he was sacked from that or any previous jobs.'

'We're still waiting for his employment record to come through.'

Horton said, 'We know that he worked at the Royal Clarence Victualling Yard in the eighties when Quintessa was killed. He told us that.'

Uckfield replied, 'I've already asked in my press statement for anyone who worked there with Brandon to come forward. If they do, they might know if Brandon had a girlfriend then or was particularly friendly with any women.'

They all knew that would be a long shot.

'Any relatives?' Horton asked Dennings.

'Can't find one. There's not even a Christmas card, and believe me, he would have kept them. There's no evidence of him having had any girlfriends from the photographs we found in the house. Lots of pictures of him and his mum, none of his dad.'

Horton knew Trueman could get details of Brandon's father from the General Register Office, unless his birth certificate specified 'father unknown', as his own did. But Horton was damn sure that Jennifer had known who her child's father was, she just hadn't been encouraged or permitted to say. In the case of Brandon, Horton didn't think it signified very much unless his father was still alive and could formally identify his son, but that seemed unlikely if he hadn't seen him for years. Perhaps he had deserted the family when Brandon was a child.

'Did you find a computer?'

'No. The neighbours we've questioned claim never to have seen anyone visit the house and Brandon never talked about relations or much else to them except to give them lectures on local history. Not all the neighbours are at home, though.'

Trueman said, 'I'll get some officers from Gosport round there tonight.'

Horton addressed him. 'Any sightings of him after he left here yesterday?'

'Not so far. We've checked out the most likely bus route from here to Old Portsmouth but none of the drivers report seeing him. We've circulated his picture to all the taxi companies too — none of them picked him up outside the station or nearby.'

Dennings said, 'Maybe he was a blackmailer and he knows who killed Quintessa. After being released from here, he called the killer and threatened to tell unless he coughed up.'

Horton recalled his interview with Brandon and relayed what he and Cantelli had discussed earlier. 'It's possible that the idea of who was behind Quintessa's death began to dawn on him during his interview here. He was nervous and defensive when first brought in, then he seemed to relax. Or he could have remembered something Adele told him on the phone, which he held back from us. He could have been lying when he claimed not to have heard of Dudley Goldsby. Maybe after her phone call he did some research on the name, found details of the politician's death and something clicked with him. She singled Brandon out for a reason. There must be a link with Dudley Goldsby and hence him with Quintessa.' Horton looked at Uckfield, who simply glowered at him before turning to Trueman.

'Give us an update on the inquiries into the women reported missing who fit with what Dr Lauder told us about Quintessa.'

'The circumstances behind the disappearance of two of the women tends to indicate suicide. They were being treated for depression. First, Margaret Telham, aged thirty-four, from Reading. She'd recently divorced, no children, and her mother, her only sole surviving relative, had died during her divorce. She was last seen in 1982 catching a train to London. Second, Kathryn Cutler, aged thirty, from Luton. She was being treated for postnatal depression. She drove off in the family car on Boxing Day in 1983 without explanation. The vehicle was found abandoned near Brighton two days later. Her husband died four years ago. Her son is working for a finance company in Germany. Her mother is still alive, so if Dr Lauder manages to extract some maternal DNA, we can check that out. The third woman, not diagnosed as suffering from depression or any other medical problems according to the file, is Karen Klixby. Aged twenty-eight, married, with three children — two boys, aged ten and eight, and a girl aged seven. She disappeared from Basingstoke in 1984 while walking to pick her kids up from school.'

Marsden picked up the conversation. 'Her husband, Stuart Klixby, was interviewed several times. There was no hard evidence that he did away with her but friends claimed they were going through a difficult time since he'd come out of the army and couldn't settle to a job. He saw service in the Falklands War in 1982. He was found dead two years after his wife went missing. Walked in front of a train.'

'Guilty conscience?' ventured Dennings.

'Or maybe desperately cut up over his wife's disappearance,' Horton said more charitably. 'Provisions for the Falklands War were despatched from the Royal Navy Victualling Yard. Could he have been there during or after the conflict, or at the armaments depot nearby?'

Dennings again. 'Maybe he knew Quintessa. They had an affair or she was a prostitute and he had a violent temper and one night he lost it and killed her. Being a fit squaddie, he could have transported her body to the island over the spit and then buried her. He confessed to his wife, who said she was going to report it to the police, so he also kills and buries her. Then, unable to live with what he'd done, he kills himself.'

Trueman said, 'I'll request his service record but I might not get it. The army don't have to release it to us.'

'Is Karen Klixby's mother still alive?' Horton asked.

'Haven't got that far yet.'

If she was, then DNA could provide her with the answer to the question that must have tormented her for years. Jennifer had no living relatives except him, maternal or otherwise, so there was no mitochondrial DNA for him to be matched with if the body was hers. He could instigate a test to see if his DNA matched with Quintessa's but he'd have to say why, and that was the last thing he wanted.

Horton said, 'If Klixby is our killer then why would Adele Goldsby call Brandon and tell him about the skeleton buried on Rat Island?'

'Perhaps Klixby was under orders to kill Quintessa,' Marsden suggested.

'Why?'

Marsden looked blankly at Horton, who thought of his mother's disappearance and what he'd recently learned. Had someone been under orders to kill Jennifer? Antony Dormand, for example — one of those six men in that photograph from 1967 that Andrew Ducale had left on Horton's boat. Horton had found Dormand at Northwood Abbey on the Isle of Wight in October and Dormand had confessed to him on the shores of the abbey that he was an assassin before taking off on a dinghy into a dark stormy sea, never to be seen again. But why kill Jennifer? The reason had to be because she knew something that was dangerous to someone. Could the same be said for Quintessa?

Marsden enthusiastically continued as an idea obviously struck him. 'Maybe she knew something that could expose a government minister.'

Horton felt a jolt at his words. Was that why Jennifer had been killed? Andrew Ducale and Lord Richard Ames had both worked for the Foreign Office, although Horton secretly believed that was a euphemism for the intelligence services. Had one of them confided in Jennifer about a government minister, and for that she had to be killed? Then Ducale had experienced a pang of conscience, rescued him from the children's home and placed him with his twin sister, Eileen and her policeman husband, Bernard. Or perhaps the order for Jennifer to be silenced had come from Richard Ames because he knew Jennifer had a powerful secret in her possession. Maybe that secret had been told to her by Richard Ames's brother, Gordon.

Horton swiftly brought his mind back to Marsden, who was speaking. 'Adele Goldsby could have discovered some documentary evidence in her father's papers relating to the orders to kill Quintessa. He was spokesman for the Ministry of Defence, so perhaps Quintessa's death had something to do with secrets that threatened the government or the defence of the realm.'

'You mean as in spy novels?' scoffed Uckfield.

Marsden flushed.

Horton came to his rescue. 'Quintessa was found on Ministry of Defence land, so perhaps Marsden's idea isn't that wide of the mark. We know nothing about her, who she worked for, her friends, lovers, not even where she came from, so anything is feasible.'

Marsden threw him a grateful look.

It was Dennings who spoke next. 'If that's the case then Adele Goldsby could be—'

'Dead, yes,' Horton interjected. But where did that leave him with Jarvis? Nowhere was the answer.

Uckfield's mobile phone rang. He retrieved it from his suit jacket pocket and listened for a few minutes, then rang off. 'Dr Clayton says she'll be over with her preliminary findings in an hour — meanwhile, we've got plenty to get on with. We'll look for sightings of Brandon after he left here and dig further into his background.'

Horton returned to his office, where he called his solicitors, Framptons, and asked for the earliest possible appointment with Frances Greywell to discuss a family matter. This time he was determined to see what progress he could make in getting greater access to Emma. Yes, Monday at three thirty would suit him fine. Then he turned to his paperwork, thinking over what Marsden had said but in respect of Jennifer. Was there the possibility that Richard Ames had ordered her disappearance and Antony Dormand had taken her out? He had claimed not to be her killer but Horton couldn't believe the word of an assassin. Jennifer's death had been covered up for over thirty years and Ames had every intention of keeping it that way, whereas Ducale had left that photograph in the hope that Horton would start to ask questions and maybe even discover the truth, if he'd be allowed to. No one had tried to take him out yet, but then maybe that was because he wasn't anywhere near finding out what had really happened in November 1978.

He was almost certain that Quintessa was not Jennifer. Were they any closer to finding out what had happened to Quintessa in the eighties? It seemed not. As to finding Brandon's killer, well, perhaps Dr Clayton would hold the key to that.

CHAPTER SEVENTEEN

'Death was caused by drowning,' Gaye announced in the incident suite a few hours later.

'Then what's that on his chest?' Uckfield asked cynically, pointing to the photograph of the victim Gaye was pinning on the board.

'That, Detective Superintendent Uckfield, is a stab wound, but it is not what killed him. However, it was the primary contributory factor that led to his death. He was stabbed with a narrow-bladed knife with a single cutting edge. See the single, clean-cut, pointed incision.' She pinned up an enlarged picture of the wound. 'The wound resembles a fishtail.'

It was remarkably small, thought Horton. The telephones behind them were ringing incessantly and noisily. Horton caught the murmur of voices but focused his concentration on the pictures and what Gaye was relaying. It was late and dark outside.

'It's difficult to say the exact length of the blade because of the elasticity of skin shrinking slightly on the withdrawal of the knife, but you're looking for a weapon of between six to eight inches and an expensive one rather than a cheap run-of-the-mill blade. It didn't break on impact and there are no foreign objects embedded in the bone or in the surrounding organs and body parts. X-rays prove that.'

'How much force would have been needed?' Horton asked. 'Brandon was a big man.'

'Yes, but once the skin was penetrated, the knife would have passed through the body fairly easily. It's the sharpness of the knife that matters, not the force, and this one was very sharp indeed and used in an area of the body where the skin is at its thinnest — the chest, not the stomach, where there is greater protection. It would only have needed moderate force.' She pinned more pictures of the victim's chest on the board.

Cantelli, chewing his gum, said, 'So someone who knew what they were doing rather than just striking lucky, or unlucky in Brandon's case?'

'Or someone intelligent enough to reason or research how and where to stab.'

'Premeditated and cold-blooded, though, not done in anger or in a sudden passion or a fight,' said Horton.

'Correct. Usually in the case of a stabbing in a fight, the assailant and victim are moving around in a highly charged altercation, so the pattern of the knife wound would reflect that. It is often irregularly shaped or sometimes V-shaped, but it's neither in this instance, as you can see. As I said, the wound is also small, which backs this up. If both the assailant and the victim had been moving then the wound would be much larger. The knife was plunged in and then withdrawn with remarkable precision and coolness.'

'Would the killer have been covered in blood? There was nothing at the scene.'

'There wouldn't have been because there was very little exterior bleeding and only on the victim's clothes, which of course have been sent to the lab for analysis.'

Cantelli said, 'His killer must have got pretty close to him. Could it be the same or similar weapon as that used on Quintessa?'

'If it's the same one then it's been kept sharp all these years. I'll compare notes with Dr Lauder.'

'Did Brandon face his killer?' asked Horton.

'Yes, and he didn't put up any kind of resistance. There was no sign of bruising to his back or on his arms where he might have been held or pushed or thrust into the water, and nothing on his hands or wrists to show he defended himself against an attack.'

'So Brandon knew his killer,' mused Uckfield.

'Which means this wasn't a mugging,' Horton quickly chipped in, drawing a black look from Uckfield.

'And Brandon agreed to meet the killer there,' Dennings added.

Gaye continued, 'You'll have to wait for the full toxicology tests, but I can confirm that the victim had drunk alcohol and eaten. The food hadn't entered the small intestine, so his last meal was about two hours before he died.'

'He stopped at a pub,' declared Uckfield. 'Trueman, check out all the pubs around the Spur Redoubt and Old Portsmouth. Get officers into the key ones tonight.'

Trueman looked as though he was about to protest and Horton knew why. Where the devil was he going to get enough officers on a Friday night when they would be tied up with the usual pub brawls, drunks and nightclub crowd? Horton had a better idea. 'Two hours before his death means he could have stopped at a pub closer to here to recover following his interview. Walters could take one of the routes that Brandon might have taken, and at about the same time as when he left here at 8.45 p.m. and call in at the pubs on the way.'

At first Walters looked peeved at having to work so late, but his expression brightened when it became clear he could go on a pub crawl on expenses.

Horton continued, 'We've got two probable routes. Brandon turned south down the main drags of Kingston Road and Fratton Road heading for the seafront, or he cut through the side streets, Gamble Road, Malins Road and through the city centre. I think he'd more than likely have chosen the first major and more direct route. There are more places to eat and drink along it. Walters could take that route and I'll do the second one.'

'Sergeant Cantelli can do that,' Bliss smartly rejoined, indicating that Horton was far too senior an officer to get involved in such matters.

Horton had been hoping to spare Cantelli a late night. He'd also thought he could look for Billy Jago en route to see if he had any intelligence on the Somerstown robberies and find out why the lorry thieves hadn't shown at Farlington Marshes as he'd declared they would. Thankfully there hadn't been any thefts from lorries in the last couple of days, but give them time.

Gaye continued, 'Several studies have shown that stab wound victims can be capable of quite strenuous activity after being stabbed. Victims can survive for more than five minutes even if drugged or drunk. There is no clear evidence that your man was drugged but you'll have to wait for confirmation of that from the toxicology tests. However, unless the stab wound involves the brainstem, death is not instantaneous, and victims of stabbing are capable of energetic actions, such as running and climbing stairs before they collapse.'

Uckfield groaned. 'Don't tell me he was stabbed in the street, ran up the steps to Battery Row along the promenade and then staggered down on to the Spur Redoubt where he fell into the water?'

Horton broke in, 'Why should he run that way, though? He'd stand much more chance of surviving if he'd approached the houses in the square or even staggered back to one of the pubs in the area for help. How long would he have lived?' he asked Gaye.

'Up to thirty minutes, but do not fret, he didn't,' she quickly added with a smile. 'As I said earlier, he drowned, and that indicates his killer pushed him into the moat after stabbing him. And, studying Clarke's photographs—' she waved a hand at the crime board — 'and the grit under the victim's fingernails, I'd say that he fell into the moat on his back, tried to get up, staggered, fell down again — this time face forward — and made another attempt to get up but was already weakening. Being a big man and very unfit, he'd have needed to find extra strength to haul himself up, which he didn't have. He scrabbled in the water, hence the grit under his nails, and swallowed mouthfuls of water as the tide was coming up, and the water level was rising slightly in the moat. He drowned. I found evidence of foam in the mouth and nose to indicate he was still alive when he went face down into the water and there was no water in the stomach, which shows his death then was rapid. I also found diatoms — microscopic algae — which again confirm he was alive when he entered the water, unless those diatoms were in his system beforehand as a result of contamination from eating shellfish, salads or watercress.'

Walters shuddered at the thought that anyone could eat such 'rabbit food', as he always called it.

Gaye said, 'But, like DC Walters, the victim doesn't look much of a salad man to me.'

Walters grinned and said optimistically, 'Maybe he grabbed a takeaway.'

Horton could already see Walters mentally totting up how many takeaway eating places there were along the route he was to take that night. He wondered if the killer had watched Brandon struggle to stay alive.

'Time of death?' asked Bliss.

'Between ten and midnight, possibly a little later. I'd like to visit the scene of the crime. I need to take a sample from the moat to match what I discovered in the victim's system. Although it's dark there are lights around that area, and I take it you still have the moat sealed off?'

Uckfield confirmed they did. Elkins had already called in to say he and Ripley hadn't found anything resembling a weapon even though they hadn't known it was a knife they had been looking for at that stage. 'No dead cats, no shopping trolleys, not even a beer can,' Elkins had commented. The SOCO team had also reported that they had found little with the exception of some cigarette ends that had been bagged up and which could be Brandon's. There were a few fingerprints on the railings, which had been lifted and would be checked.

Horton rose. 'I'll go with you.'

Bliss wasn't sure whether she should protest. She threw a glance at Uckfield but before the Super could speak, Horton added, 'I'll call into the mobile incident suite while I'm there and see if Prudence Goldsby is at home. She lives very close by.'

Uckfield gave a curt nod. Horton said he'd meet Gaye at the mobile incident unit unless she'd like a lift on his Harley.

'Tempting, but it's raining and it will play havoc with my hair.'

He smiled as he eyed her cropped auburn hair.

Fifteen minutes later he pulled up outside the unit in the partly cobbled square that was called Grand Parade. Brandon could easily have asked for help from the occupants of the houses bordering the square to the north and south if he had been stabbed here. The road to the east led round to the Garrison Church and to the moat, while to the west it gave onto the High Street of Old Portsmouth, and just beyond that, Prudence Goldsby's residence.

Two uniformed officers greeted him in the mobile unit with the news that several people had called in but their information wasn't relevant — the timing was wrong. They had taken names and contact details, though. Horton wondered if they'd get more later from the night-time dog walkers, shift workers and insomniacs.

He watched Gaye park her red Mini and retrieve a silver square case from the passenger seat. She was wearing a green sailing jacket and made no attempt to put the hood up in the invidious cold drizzle. *Not so bothered about her hair now*, he thought with a smile. But at least the wind had dropped. He offered to take the case.

'I should refuse according to the feminists,' she answered brightly. 'And I would if I didn't know you because it would mean surrendering part of myself to you, therefore making me vulnerable, even possibly putting me in danger if you were a psychopath. But as you're not, as far as I am aware, be my guest.' She handed it over with a smile.

They made for the tunnel under the grassy bank. It was still cordoned off with police tape and an officer was mounting guard. He admitted them. There was a very heavy old iron door at the entrance, but Horton had no idea when that had last been closed.

'Why not kill him inside this tunnel where there's less likelihood of it being witnessed?' Gaye asked.

It was lit, short and narrow, and was where Lord Nelson had walked in 1805 on his last departure from England. 'Perhaps there wasn't enough room. And maybe the killer thought asking Brandon to meet him in the tunnel might have looked odd.'

'It's still an unusual location to meet, though, in the ruins.'

'Perhaps the killer intended to push Brandon in the moat and let him drown because he wasn't sure the stabbing would kill him,' Horton said.

They came out onto the small wooden bridge. It was still some hours off high tide and the moat water was low. The promenade in both directions was cordoned off and an officer was standing at either end, not just to prevent people from entering the Spur Redoubt or to ogle over the railings at Long Curtain Moat, but to ask passers-by if they recalled seeing anything unusual the previous night.

Gaye said, 'By the way, I managed to have a cursory look at the autopsy report for Dudley Goldsby before your victim arrived in the mortuary. I need to study it in more detail but my initial thought is that it looks to have been very thorough. Heart failure following an overdose of cocaine but no evidence that it was inhaled or that he was a regular user. The fatal dose was therefore taken orally and willingly, because from what I've read, there was no bruising to the mouth to indicate he was forced to drink it. Unusual way to ingest cocaine if he had been a regular user but not necessarily if he wanted to end his life, although there are other easier ways to do so, if taking your own life can ever be termed easy.'

'How quickly would it have taken effect?' asked Horton.

'Depending on how much was ingested, it could have taken minutes, or anything up to three hours.'

Horton was surprised. That meant Goldsby could have taken it, or been given it, either at the hotel, as he and Cantelli had re-enacted, or some time before he'd arrived at the public meeting. 'What would the symptoms have been?'

'Hyperactivity, hallucinations, abdominal pain, convulsions, coma and heart failure.'

Horton threw her a startled look. Interpreting it, Gaye said, 'No, not the most pleasant of ways to end one's life and, judging by your expression, you don't think that sounds right.'

'Have you seen the photographs of the body?'

'No. Why?'

'I'll let you see for yourself.'

'Is it connected with this case? Only I didn't see anything on the crime board about it.'

'It could be. In fact, I'm sure it is — and that it's linked with Quintessa's death, but at the moment Uckfield refuses to believe that.' He told her about the calls made by Adele Goldsby.

'I'll take a more thorough look at the autopsy report tomorrow, and the photographs.'

Horton handed over her case. Her description of the way Goldsby could have died didn't sound like the scene he and Cantelli had played out in that hotel room. If Goldsby had been hallucinating and hyperactive then surely he'd have made a much greater mess of that room, unless the killer had tidied it up after Goldsby died. But Horton thought the body would have been hunched over, not lying spreadeagled on the bed. He supposed the killer could have repositioned the body after death and before rigor set in, but if Goldsby had died in agony and had convulsions surely that would have been reflected on his face, and the killer couldn't have altered that.

As Gaye took her samples his thoughts returned to the death of another man allegedly by a drug overdose, Gordon Ames. Was Gordon really dead? Richard Ames had formally identified his brother's body when it had been found on Town Beach in Nhulunbuy, off the Arafura Sea in the Northern Territory of Australia on the Gove Peninsula in 1973, but that could have been a charade. OK, so there must have been a body on that Australian beach, but was it a stranger who was buried in the Ames family vault? Why would Richard Ames have wanted to cover up his brother's death by falsely identifying him? Because Gordon had already been dead by then? Or because he was protecting his brother for some reason and wanted everyone to believe he was dead?

Horton recalled what a former work colleague of Jennifer's had told him shortly before her disappearance. At the casino Jennifer had seen someone enter who had caused her to go as white as a sheet, as though she'd seen a ghost. Had that ghost been Gordon Ames, who Jennifer had believed was dead? Was that the secret she held that had led to her death? But why? How could it have?

'OK, so I'm your killer.' Straightening up, Gaye put the samples in her case and turned to face him. 'You're standing in front of me with your back to the moat. I chat to you. You're not agitated and moving about so you feel quite safe with me. You probably know me. I bring out a knife.'

'From where?'

'Inside my jacket or pushed up my sleeve. You stare at it, alarmed and not quite believing what you're seeing. Before you can do anything, though, I thrust it in your chest.' She pushed her hand against Horton's chest. He felt like reaching down and holding it, but before he could she quickly continued, 'I pull back my hand and then I push you in.' She again pushed her hand against his chest.

He lifted it, smiling. 'I'm not taking a swim for anyone, not even you.'

'Where's your spirit of adventure?'

He released her hand and picked up her case. 'You need to dispose of the knife.'

'Right. So I head for the promenade.'

They turned towards it. Horton nodded at the wet and cold uniformed officer stalking the pavement. Ahead was the entrance to Portsmouth Harbour and opposite it the shores of Gosport.

'Does this place have some significance in the case?' Gaye said.

'Not that I know of. Perhaps it was just a convenient location for the killer, this being somewhere he could easily reach.'

'From where?'

'One of the pubs at the harbour entrance, the Camber—'

'Where he might have been on board a boat.'

Or from Oyster Quays, thought Horton. Jarvis's yacht also had a tender, which he could have motored to the Camber. Or he could have walked the short distance through the Wightlink car ferry terminal to here. Jarvis hadn't answered his question on his whereabouts at the time of the murder. But, as he'd previously considered, Horton just couldn't see Jarvis coming here to kill Brandon in cold blood. He'd have chosen a subtler method and a more private place, such as ditching the body at sea, or making it look like accidental drowning.

They descended the steps. Horton halted and stared across the road to the alleyway that ran around the Camber. 'Have you got rid of the knife yet?'

'No. I didn't want to risk throwing it in the sea from the top of the fortifications because someone in those houses there might see me.'

Horton eyed them. They were a mixture of two and three storeys with the latter overlooking the ancient walls out across the Solent. He saw Marsden and Somerfield emerge from one house and, after quickly comparing notes, knock on the adjoining property.

Gaye said, 'I'd stroll along here as though making for the pubs at the end of the road, but I'd dive into the hole in the wall onto the small beach and simply toss the knife into the sea. No one would see me, and even if they did, they'd think I just wanted to look at the sea and was throwing some stones at it.'

They turned right in the opposite direction and walked slowly back towards Grand Parade, where Gaye's Mini was parked. After a moment, she said, 'You still owe me that dinner.'

He'd promised it to her so many times but work had intervened. That and a slight hesitation on his part, not because he didn't want to have dinner with her — on the contrary, he could think of nothing better — but there was a nagging, annoying voice in the back of his head that warned him against getting involved with a colleague, albeit someone not directly employed in the police service. He decided to ignore that voice. 'Sunday, seven o'clock, if you're not doing anything.'

'Great, but I'll pick you up.'

'Where's *your* spirit of adventure?'

'In my taste of food, not on your Harley, on this occasion. I'll find somewhere exotic and book us a table.'

'Just as long as it's not one of Walters's favourite places.'

'That won't be difficult. Fast-food restaurants and takeaways are not my usual cup of tea.'

With a wave of her hand, he watched her drive away, feeling cheered, before turning back and making for Oyster Street and Prudence Goldsby.

CHAPTER EIGHTEEN

'I have no idea where she is and I don't want to know,' Prudence Goldsby declared after Horton had introduced himself and shown his ID. Judging by her harsh words and the sour expression on her lean, lined and sallow-complexioned face, she was not at all pleased to have been asked. She also had no intention of letting him in; she kept him standing at the door.

Horton had noted the fancy new car in front of the garage with a personalized number plate. Her clothes were fashionable and to his trained eye looked to be expensive, as was her jewellery. She certainly seemed to have benefited from her husband's death, unless she had a successful career or business, or a private income. He hadn't checked her background. Neither did he know how much Goldsby had been worth on his death. It was possible that Prudence had been wealthy before they had married, or perhaps the late politician had been heavily insured. The coroner's verdict hadn't been suicide, but even if it had been Goldsby's insurance company could still have paid out depending on his policy. Did it matter?

He hadn't thought Prudence Goldsby had killed her husband, but maybe he should consider it. Although, he recalled that Cantelli had said she'd had a cast-iron alibi. She'd been at a dinner party. Perhaps she had got a boyfriend to do it and her daughter knew who that boyfriend was. Perhaps Adele had revealed the name to Brandon and he had tried to blackmail him as well as Prudence.

Horton couldn't see Prudence Goldsby venturing out on a wet and windy night to stab Neil Brandon, but her house was just a stone's throw from where his body had been found. She could have enlisted the help of this lover, the same man who had obliged her the first time round by giving her husband that cocaine. If that was the case, then he was wrong about Peter Jarvis — unless Jarvis had been her lover. But why would Adele have told Brandon this? And why single out Brandon to be the messenger boy?

Horton made a move towards her. 'If I could just step inside for a moment.'

She glanced at her watch.

'I won't keep you long.' He was keen to know why she was so hostile towards her daughter.

'Oh, very well,' she said with ill grace and stepped back to allow him into the narrow, tiled hallway. Ahead he could see a kitchen. There was a door to his left which was the cloakroom and another door to his right, which, judging by the layout of the house, led into the garage. She made no effort to show him through to the kitchen but stood squarely in front of him, blocking his way. Was that because she had something to hide or to make it clear that she expected him to leave as soon as possible?

'When did you last see your daughter?' he asked.

'The day of my husband's funeral. He was a Member of Parliament, Dudley Goldsby,' she explained in case he didn't know. He hadn't mentioned Dudley but had simply asked if she knew where he could find Adele. And Prudence Goldsby hadn't asked him why he wanted Adele. 'He committed suicide in 2005. She packed her bags just after the wake and said to write to her care of our solicitor. Her father left her a small sum of money.'

How small? he wondered. Enough for her to live off for some years? Or enough to get away and start afresh somewhere, which was clearly what she had done.

'Weren't you concerned about her?'

Prudence Goldsby's light brown eyes narrowed but she showed no discomfort or guilt. 'Why should I have been? She was over eighteen and quite capable of looking after herself. She made that perfectly clear. If she didn't want to keep in touch, then why should I?'

He refrained from saying, 'Because you're her mother'. He knew from his job that not all mothers loved their children and not all children loved their mothers. 'Was your relationship always strained?'

'What has that got to do with you or finding her and why do you want her anyway?' she finally asked. 'What's she done?'

'I thought you weren't concerned.'

She flashed him a spiteful look. 'I'm not, I'm just surprised because knowing Miss Goody-Two-Shoes, I can't think she'd have done anything wrong and certainly nothing to warrant police interest. I can't help you.' She made to move forward but Horton held his ground.

'Just a couple more questions, Mrs Goldsby,' he said firmly. 'Is it possible your daughter could have killed herself in distress over her father's untimely death?'

She snorted, and Horton cared for her even less than he had on first sight, although he made sure not to show it.

'Not bloody likely. She didn't believe in suicide. When Dudley killed himself it was a huge blow to her.'

'But not to you.'

'Of course I was upset.'

I bet, thought Horton. The woman in front of him would have been more upset if she'd broken a fingernail.

'But then he was always highly strung, very nervy. How he ever became a politician I don't know. He wasn't thick-skinned enough. But he did have such an overdeveloped sense of community and Christian charity, which was where

Adele got it from — him and those nuns.' She made it sound as though it was a sin rather than a quality.

'Nuns?'

'The ones who used to live opposite us, brainwashing her with all that religious rubbish. Looking down their noses at me.'

'You think they turned her against you.'

'You bet they did. They had no idea what I had to put up with — a husband who thought more of penniless down-and-outs, wasters, moaners and criminals in his constituency than me. He'd do anything to help them and nothing to help me, or Adele come to that, only she couldn't see it like that. She was always striving to get his attention.'

'And you weren't.'

'I gave up long before he died. He thought more of his agent and that secretary of his than he did of his family.'

'Frieda Chillerton.'

'You know her?' She studied him suspiciously. He'd just let on that he knew more about her husband's death than she had believed. That didn't bother him.

'I wondered if she might know where Adele was.'

'I doubt it. After Dudley died, Frieda's interest in her ended.'

'Were they having an affair?'

'She'd have liked one, but Dudley wouldn't have had time for that when he barely had time for me. A woman doesn't like coming second to her husband's job, but in my case, I was even lower down the pecking order than that. I'd got to the stage where I'd had enough. But neither Dudley nor Adele could understand that.'

'She blamed you for her father's death.'

'I don't know and I don't care. Why don't you ask that vicar who was so pally with him?'

'The Reverend Simon Pilbeam.'

'If Adele talked to anyone then it would have been to him or those bloody nuns.'

'Would the solicitor know where she is?' *Perhaps they forwarded Adele's correspondence*, thought Horton, cursing the fact he hadn't considered that before. Their offices would be closed now until Monday.

'No idea. It's Belmonts in Landport Terrace. Now, if you've finished, I've got to go out.'

'Of course. I'm sorry to have bothered you, especially as you must have had a visit from the police already today,' Horton said smoothly, knowing that Marsden's team hadn't called on this road because it was tucked away from the High Street.

'Why should I have had a visit from the police?'

He noted a slight flush under her sallow skin. 'A man's body was found in Long Curtain Moat in suspicious circumstances this morning.'

She looked away. 'Really?'

'You must have seen the mobile incident unit and police officers.'

'I don't walk that way.'

No, thought Horton, eyeing her stiletto shoes. He doubted she walked anywhere.

'And I don't listen to the news,' she added, as though to pre-empt him. 'It bores me rigid, it's always the same old tripe. I had enough of that as a politician's wife with Harry Belling telling Dudley he must do this and say that to keep the media happy.'

And keep you under control, thought Horton, *which neither Dudley Goldsby nor Harry Belling had managed to do.* She didn't ask about the death nearby. Horton could see she didn't care.

She said, '*If* you find Adele don't bother coming back to tell me because I don't want to know. And neither do I want her turning up here, so I'd appreciate it if you didn't tell her where I live.'

Horton held her cold gaze. This time there was no slight flush, no softening of expression. Whatever Adele had done or said to her mother it had drawn the shutters down for ever. It must have been one hell of a row.

He returned to the Harley. Maybe Pilbeam did know where Adele was and he was protecting her. Or perhaps she had joined a convent after her father's death. But how had she come to discover Quintessa's death and why had she selected Neil Brandon to find the remains?

He didn't think much of Prudence, a bitter, callous woman. Had her marriage with Dudley made her like that after she realized that her husband was more devoted to his work and his constituents than keen to climb the greasy, backstabbing pole to the top of the political ladder? Or had she always been hard? What had made her hate her daughter so much? Was it because Adele had taken her father's side and Prudence resented that? Enough to kill her husband, and Adele knew what she had done? Prudence could have done very well for herself out of her husband's death. He wouldn't mind checking the probate records to see just how well.

On his return to the station, Horton reported back on his interview. Uckfield grunted and Bliss frowned. Walters and Cantelli had started on the routes Brandon could have taken on leaving the police station. Trueman had Brandon's employment record, though. He'd had several jobs over the years, rarely staying anywhere for long. Probably, Horton thought, because he was light-fingered. He'd worked at the Royal Clarence Victualling Yard from 1980 to 1986, the period that matched with when Quintessa was killed.

So far no one had come forward to say they had worked with Brandon. But Horton, looking over Trueman's shoulder at the computer screen displaying Brandon's employment details, was interested to see that Brandon had also worked at Jarvis's packaging and food processing company from 1988 to 1990. Not that that meant much — Jarvis employed a lot of people. It was another link, though he made no mention of it. It wouldn't get him anywhere if he did.

He grabbed something to eat in the canteen and returned to his office where he unfurled the list of functions that Chantelle Blythe at the Solent Waves Hotel had given him. Aside from Jarvis's party there was the conference on allergens, food and health and Wellbelove's armed services and veterans' charity auction and dinner. If Adele hadn't been pointing him to Peter Jarvis then maybe it was Dominic Keats she wanted to draw his attention to. Keats was clearly a close friend of Jarvis's and he was a former Royal Navy commander. Could he have been at Wellbelove's dinner and auction?

He recalled what he and Cantelli had discovered about Keats during a previous investigation. On leaving the services, Keats had become a skipper on a private yacht for three years before starting up the Superyacht Training Academy. He was divorced with three children, had an apartment at Oyster Quays, a yacht on the Hamble, and was keen on yacht racing. Nothing there to connect him with Dudley Goldsby, except for that link with Goldsby being spokesman for the Ministry of Defence and Rat Island being owned by them. Keats was on No Man's Fort with Jarvis's other guests. Did that include Dyer, the former chief constable? Horton was curious to know. He sent Elkins an email asking him to get a guest list from the fort manager.

It was almost 10 p.m. and there was nothing from Walters or Cantelli. Horton returned to the incident suite, where Dennings reported that, amid the chaos of paperwork in Brandon's house, they had found details of a relative, a woman who lived in Hull. The local police were contacting her now. Marsden and Somerfield returned from the house-to-house inquiries, wet and weary. No one they had spoken to had seen anything or anyone suspicious on Thursday night and none of those questioned had been out and about between the hours of nine and midnight.

The incident suite had been wound down for the night. Horton made for the coffee machine and had just grabbed a coffee when his mobile phone rang. It was Walters.

'I've got a positive ID, guv,' he said excitedly. 'Brandon was in The George and Dragon, on the corner of Kingston Road and Washington Street just after 9 p.m., where he had a pint.'

'Did he eat there?'

'No. He took his pint to a table in the corner and checked his watch several times as though he was either expecting someone or had to leave to meet someone. He left the pub at 10.10 p.m.'

'He made that beer last a long time.'

'That's what the landlord said. Brandon then bought a kebab in the takeaway further down the road.'

And the stomach contents would confirm that, thought Horton with a wave of nausea. 'Any idea where he went after that?'

'Yep. He caught the bus.'

'How do you know that?'

'Because it's what I would have done.'

Of course, it took one to know one. 'But the bus drivers don't remember him.'

'That's because Sergeant Trueman was looking at the wrong buses. This one does. I'm on it now. It's the number one. It goes all round the houses but it ends up at Clarence Pier. That's where Brandon got off, according to the driver. I'll do the same and time it to the Spur Redoubt, then I'll call in to the mobile unit.'

'You've excelled yourself, Walters. I'll buy you a dough-nut tomorrow.'

'Only one?'

'A bag of them then.'

'Cheers, guv. Can I claim the kebab on expenses?'

'Of course.'

'Good, because I had two. Well, I had to while I waited for the bus. And of course the pint of beer. All in the line of duty.'

Horton rang off and punched in Cantelli's number. 'You can call it off now, Barney. Walters has traced Brandon's movements. No, go home. There's enough of us here, no need for you to come back.'

Horton relayed the news to Uckfield, Bliss and Dennings. Walters called again to say he had arrived at the Spur Redoubt within four minutes of leaving the bus. There was nothing more they could do that night but at least they now knew that Brandon had arranged to meet his killer at the Spur Redoubt, because there could be no other reason for him to go there. And, as Horton said to Uckfield, he didn't go there for a blast of sea air.

'Brandon knew who Quintessa's killer was when he was sitting in the interview room. He was keeping that knowledge to himself, ready for his spot of blackmail, only it backfired.'

Horton played back the tape, looking for something he or Cantelli might have said that had triggered Brandon's memory or stimulated his thoughts, but he couldn't identify anything, and neither could the others. It was agreed that tomorrow Horton would talk to the Reverend Simon Pilbeam and the nuns to see if they knew where Adele was.

CHAPTER NINETEEN

Saturday

'How the bleeding hell can I stay calm when I don't know where he is?' A woman in her late thirties was haranguing Pilbeam as Horton entered the church hall.

'You should go to the police,' came Pilbeam's somewhat weary reply.

'Oh, yeah, and what would they do? Sod all, that's what.'

'Then maybe the police can come to you,' Horton said.

They spun round.

'Who are the hell are you?' the woman demanded.

'Detective Inspector Horton.'

'Don't look much of a cop to me.' She eyed his leather gear through the slits of her overly made-up eyes. Horton didn't recognize her, but he did the child in the pushchair. It was Keith Harnley's grandson, the boy who had been trying to bash another child over the head with a plastic sword the last time he was here.

'He *is* a policeman,' Pilbeam confirmed in a tired voice. Horton thought he looked dreadful, as though he hadn't slept in days.

The woman's eyes narrowed further and her thin lips tightened. 'I don't want the pigs involved.'

'Is your partner in trouble?' Horton enquired, noting no wedding ring, but that didn't mean anything. Her look of derision and the snort that accompanied it told him there wasn't one. 'Then it's your father, Keith, you're talking about.'

'See, what did I tell you?' she flashed triumphantly at Pilbeam. 'Just because Dad's got a record, the police will assume the worst.'

'Inspector Horton is assuming nothing, Bethany. How can he when he doesn't know what's happened?' Pilbeam said with patient resignation.

The child in the pushchair began to grizzle. She shouted at him to shut up. Pilbeam winced. Horton noted the dark circles under his bloodshot eyes.

Horton addressed the sullen, dark-haired woman, whose ponytail was scraped back off of her sharp-featured face, which reminded him of DCI Bliss. 'Let's try again. Your father, Keith Harnley, is missing.'

'He was meant to be looking after Riley this morning and I've lost wages because he's not at home and won't answer his phone.'

Horton wondered if that was the real source of her anger — not that her father was missing but the fact that she had been lumbered with her child and had lost money as a result. 'Where do you work?'

'What's that got to do with you? This is useless.' She turned her hard, angry gaze on Pilbeam. 'If you see him, tell him not to bother calling me.' She swung the pushchair round and marched off down the hall with the child's grizzling rising to a crescendo of cries, earning him a few choice swear words in return.

Pilbeam let out a heavy sigh. 'Not the most charming of young ladies but she is anxious about her father. So am I. She's right — Keith wouldn't miss looking after his grandson.'

'Perhaps he's sleeping off a hangover somewhere.' *Or a late night occupied on a spate of robberies*, he thought, although, as far as he was aware, none had been reported in the area for last night.

'Bethany phoned him at home just after seven o'clock this morning and he answered then. He said he'd look after Riley for the morning. She's managed to get some additional hours' work because someone has gone sick and she was looking forward to having the extra money. She went to drop Riley off at Keith's flat an hour later as agreed, but, when she let herself in with her key, he wasn't there. She waited around thinking he might have popped out to get a newspaper, but when he didn't return, she called him on his mobile. There was no answer. She's been trying ever since. I tried calling his mobile just before you arrived and just got his voicemail. I left a message, no doubt after several from Bethany.'

'Have you tried the hospital or the police station?'

'No, should I?' he asked, somewhat alarmed.

Horton retrieved his mobile. 'I'll call the station.' He wondered if uniformed officers had paid a visit to Harnley on information received and had taken him in. Maybe Harnley hadn't thought to call his daughter to tell her. 'You try A&E.' He stepped away from Pilbeam.

A few minutes later he returned to the vicar, who shook his head. 'He hasn't been taken to hospital.'

'And he's not been detained.' Horton had also asked if there had been any break-ins the previous night. 'Not in the Somerstown area,' had been the reply. 'Did Bethany ask her father's neighbours if they'd seen him?'

'I don't think so. Keith lives in a flat in one of the tower blocks. He might not even know his neighbours. Sadly, quite often you don't.'

Horton knew that all too well not only from the job but as a child living in one with his mother.

Pilbeam said, 'Bethany probably wouldn't even think to ask the neighbours if they'd seen him. She came here because she wondered if she'd made a mistake and Keith had said he'd pick up Riley here. Or that I'd phoned Keith and asked him to come and help me. It's the senior citizens' lunch club. But that's not Keith's scene.'

So what had put the wind up him? Maybe Harnley was involved with some crooks and he'd seen them approaching and done a runner. He said as much, earning a concerned frown from Pilbeam.

'Keith told me he's stayed clean for years. And I believe him. I can't see why he'd resort to stealing again.'

'Maybe the temptation was too great.' And a vicar would know all about that. Horton wondered if Harnley had taken clothes or anything else with him. 'Do you know where Bethany works?'

'She cleans for a contract company, offices and shops in the city centre mainly.'

'And Keith?'

'He's on incapacity benefit. What do you suggest we do? He can't simply have disappeared.' Pilbeam asked, worried.

Oh, but he can, Horton thought. *People do — Jennifer for one and Quintessa another. No one had missed her or rather reported her missing. Why? Did she have no family or friends?*

'Give me his mobile number and I'll call him and leave a message in case he picks it up.'

But Pilbeam hesitated.

Horton added, 'You won't be betraying a confidence.'

Pilbeam somewhat reluctantly relayed the number and Horton punched it into his phone. He'd call later when he was away from the vicar, although he didn't think for one moment that Harnley would answer it or return a copper's call. Then again it might put the wind up him enough to come in, especially if he was being hounded by bigger crooks than himself. He might want the sanctuary of the police station.

'You didn't come here about Keith, though, Inspector. Is it about Dudley again?' Pilbeam looked anxious.

'His daughter, Adele. We're keen to find her. I've spoken to Prudence and she said that if Adele had confided in

171

anyone it would have been you or the nuns who used to live opposite them.'

'She never confided in me. I suppose she might have confided in the nuns. She was very close to them. They've moved from the convent opposite to where the Goldsbys used to live, though. They're now in a convent not far from here, close to the railway station at Fratton.'

Horton would call in there. 'You told me that you hadn't seen or heard from her. Are you quite sure?' He held Pilbeam's gaze.

'Absolutely. She's never made contact with me, and, as I told you before, the last I saw of her was at her father's funeral.'

'I believe she's in Portsmouth and that she visited her father's grave.'

'That's no crime.'

'No, but perhaps she believes her father's death was. That's strictly between us, vicar. The investigation is not being reopened. Did she say anything to you about it at the time that made you wonder? You said before that you believe Mr Goldsby could have taken that drug accidentally. Perhaps she witnessed something.'

'If she did, she never confided it to me. I know nothing more about Dudley's death than I've already told you.'

But Horton wasn't so sure this time round. Pilbeam's eye contact wavered and he ran a hand through his fine, limp hair. Perhaps Dudley Goldsby or Adele had confided something to the vicar. 'Do you know a man called Neil Brandon?'

Pilbeam looked taken aback at the change of tactic. It took him a few moments to answer. 'I don't think so, although the name does sound familiar.'

'Perhaps you heard it in connection with Dudley Goldsby or Adele mentioned it to you?'

'No, I don't think so.'

He was looking frazzled. Horton showed him a printed photograph of Brandon, which Dennings had got from the house. They'd cropped out Brandon's mother beside him. 'Do you recognize him?'

'I'm not sure. I see so many people.'

'Of course.' Horton put the photograph back in the inside pocket of his leather jacket. 'Do you recall Dudley Goldsby talking to anyone before the meeting?'

'No, he was late. He went straight onto the stage and exchanged a few words with Harry Belling, who then introduced him. Mrs Chillerton and Adele were already seated, as were the rest of the audience.'

'And you were where?'

'Me?' He hesitated. 'I was in the lobby.'

'So you met him there?'

'Yes.'

'Anyone with you?'

'No.'

Horton wondered why Pilbeam was looking so uneasy. 'Did Dudley say why he was late?'

'He said he'd mislaid some papers and had been looking for them. He seemed flustered.'

Horton left a short pause as he considered this. Had Goldsby really been flustered? Were the missing papers an excuse? Had he been delayed because he'd had to meet the killer, who had handed him the key to the hotel room, or was Pilbeam making this up?

Pilbeam wrapped his bony arms around his chest. The wind was rising and whistling around the building. It felt cold inside the church hall and Pilbeam looked it. Horton hoped they'd turn the heating on before the pensioners' lunch.

'Why did you meet Mr Goldsby in the lobby?'

Pilbeam delved under his cassock and took a handkerchief from the pocket of his trousers. 'Mr Belling was getting worried. He asked me to look out for Dudley. If he didn't show in five minutes, Mr Belling said to come back in and he'd start the meeting, hoping Dudley would arrive before he ran out of things to say. But Dudley arrived after a couple of minutes.'

'Didn't you or anyone try to get hold of Mr Goldsby?'

'Mr Belling called but there was no answer. I'm not sure if he left a message.'

'What was Mr Goldsby carrying when he arrived?'

'His briefcase.'

'Nothing else?'

'No. And no bottled drink if that's what you're wondering, Inspector.'

'Was he wearing an overcoat?'

'No. Just a suit — it was a mild night for April.'

'And he came straight in here? He didn't go to the gents' beforehand?'

'No. We walked in here together. He made for the stage without stopping to speak to anyone.'

'Did Mr Goldsby ever mention a man called Peter Jarvis?'

'No.'

Horton studied the vicar closely as he blew his nose.

'Or Dominic Keats?

'No.' Pilbeam pushed the handkerchief back in his pocket.

He had no reason to lie, but he was clearly edgy. Perhaps it was Harnley's disappearance, maybe it was the pensioners' lunch, or perhaps he was ill. He looked unwell. His skin was grey.

Horton said, 'I'd prefer it if you didn't mention to anyone that we're interested in finding Adele. We don't want the media picking up on it.'

'Of course. I understand.'

'But if she does get in touch, would you let me know?' Horton gave Pilbeam his card and together they walked to the door. Did he sense relief in the vicar or was that just his imagination?

He made for the convent, mulling over what Pilbeam had told him. The fact that Goldsby had been late for that meeting could be significant. His delay could have been caused by a rendezvous with his killer, who could have handed him not only the key to the hotel bedroom but a drink containing the cocaine, which he'd drunk before entering the church hall. There was an alternative. Pilbeam admitted that he had been alone in the lobby waiting for Goldsby. Pilbeam could have slipped him the key, but probably not the contaminated bottle. That wouldn't have fitted into the briefcase or into Goldsby's suit jacket pocket — not unless Goldsby had drunk it before entering the hall and Pilbeam had dispensed with it.

But why would Pilbeam want to kill Dudley Goldsby? And could a man of the cloth have lived with that all these years? Perhaps it had slowly eaten away at him and when he had shown up on Thursday asking questions about Goldsby, Pilbeam realized his secret could soon be exposed, hence his nervous disposition and his haunted appearance.

At the convent, Horton asked to speak to the Mother Superior. Forty minutes later he was no further forward in trying to locate Adele Goldsby, but he did have another person's view of her personality. He'd have to treat it lightly because the Mother Superior wouldn't speak ill of anyone or betray a confidence. He'd had the same experience with the Benedictine Monks at Northwood Abbey when he'd been trying to discover more about Antony Dormand's time there, when he had gone by the name of Brother Norman. The abbot, Dom Daniel Briar, had given him nothing except that Brother Norman had been a very private man, and had come from a monastery in Italy, where he had been for two years, which Horton had confirmed. Under his real name, Antony Dormand, Horton had found no trace of his movements after 1971. In Adele's case he'd learned she was painfully shy but desperate to be what her father wanted her to be — confident, assertive and charismatic. Horton secretly questioned whether that was what Dudley Goldsby really wanted or whether it was what Adele thought he wanted.

He thought of Emma as he weaved his way through the traffic towards the police station. He just wanted his daughter to be happy, to feel safe, secure and loved, all the things he had missed out on. Did that mean stepping back from her life and allowing her to be with Peter Jarvis? Not if he was a killer, it didn't.

He stopped off at a bakery to buy the bag of doughnuts he'd promised Walters. The Mother Superior had said that she hadn't seen or heard from Adele since her father had died. Horton believed that was the truth. They'd offered her comfort and help, which she'd politely but firmly declined. 'It was as though she closed the door on us,' the Mother Superior had told him. 'Adele wouldn't let anyone get close to her. It could have been her way of dealing with her bereavement. It affects people in many different ways.' Horton knew that all too well having seen death so many times in his job. Cantelli also knew that, not only on a professional level but also personally from losing his much-loved father just over a year ago.

In the station, Horton tried Keith Harnley's mobile as he made his way to his office. He got his voicemail. He left a message saying he'd like to talk to him. He didn't say that it was connected with the Somerstown robberies. He had no real hope that Harnley would oblige either by returning his call or by giving him any inside information on the thefts or even a confession. He bought a coffee at the machine outside CID and, seeing Cantelli heading towards him, pressed the button for tea for him. Bliss hadn't been in her office, but as her car was in its allotted space, Horton guessed she was in the incident suite with Uckfield. Cantelli confirmed this, and that Walters was also there.

'He's still writing up his report from last night in between frequent visits to the toilet after a double dose of kebabs.' Cantelli took the plastic cup from Horton. 'I told him that takeaway has been raided twice by the health inspectors and will probably be closed down any day now — not sure that made him feel any better.' Cantelli crossed to his desk. 'The wicked witch in the wardrobe only let me out because I said I wanted to fetch my sandwiches. I recognized the sound of your Harley coming into the car park.' Which meant Bliss might also have done.

Cantelli sat at his desk. 'We've got a witness who saw Brandon walking past Clarence Pier into the funfair on

Thursday night, but after that, nothing. The witness was walking in the opposite direction towards his car, which was parked on the seafront outside Isabella's café.'

Isabella was Cantelli's sister.

'She was closed by the time Brandon reached that area so she wouldn't have seen him. Walters's bus driver says that Brandon was the last to alight from the bus and didn't tell him where he was going or say goodnight. The bus driver didn't think Brandon looked worried or nervous and neither was he looking as though he'd won the lottery, but then the driver hadn't taken that much notice of him. He was concentrating on the road and looking forward to going home.'

Horton pulled off his jacket and took Walters's seat. He put the bag of doughnuts on Walters's desk and gestured at Cantelli to help himself. Horton took one and, in between bites and sips of coffee, he brought Cantelli up to speed with his interviews with Pilbeam, the nuns and Prudence Goldsby, which caused Cantelli's dark eyebrows to knit and his face to assume a sorrowful expression.

Horton said, 'When you were on the investigation did you see Goldsby's mobile phone records?'

'No. And no one told us he was late for the meeting. I don't think anything was mentioned about the jug of water on the stage either. We didn't visit the church hall. There was no need with Goldsby dead at the hotel, and Harry Belling and Frieda Chillerton were interviewed independently in Goldsby's constituency office.'

Horton's phone rang. With amazement he recognized the number that flashed up as being the one Pilbeam had given him and which, not long ago, he'd tried. It was Keith Harnley.

'I need to talk to you, copper. And I ain't going anywhere near a police station.'

'If it's to do with the thefts—'

'What bloody thefts? I want a meet, and alone. You don't tell no one where you're going, especially those in that shithole of yours.'

Horton caught the fear in Harnley's voice. What had spooked him? 'You'll have to give me more.'

There was a fraction's pause, then a breath. 'Neil Brandon. I'll meet you at Lumps Fort in ten minutes.' He rang off.

CHAPTER TWENTY

'You alone?' Harnley growled at Horton, who had managed to escape the station before Bliss asked him to report in. Cantelli would cover for him if needed. Harnley gazed anxiously around as though he expected armed police to suddenly appear.

'Yes.' Horton had left the Harley in the adjacent car park and walked the short distance to Lumps Fort, which had become the Southsea Rose Gardens years ago. Built in the mid to late 1800s, it was just off the seafront, with only the ruined fortified walls and a few gun mounts to show it had once formed part of the city's defences. In summer the gardens were a riot of colours and scents. Now the bare rose twigs sprouted tentatively above the well-cultivated brown earth. It was just after one o'clock, but the gardens were deserted thanks to the almost gale-force wind gusting off the sea and accompanied by fitful showers.

Harnley was huddled in the far left-hand corner under the covered shelter that ran along part of the walls. Horton took a seat beside the fidgety, fretful man, whose eyes were constantly moving. Harnley, like Pilbeam, looked drawn and ill.

'Christ, I can't believe this — I must be mad. It can't be right . . . only . . .' He gulped and pushed his straggly grey hair off his lined face.

'Let's take it step by step,' Horton said evenly.

But it was as if Harnley hadn't heard him. 'I can't trust any of the other filth. Not sure I can trust you, but Pilbeam says you're OK.' He dashed a semi-hostile glance at Horton.

'You've spoken to him today?'

Harnley nodded. 'Just after you called me and left that message. He said he'd given you my number.'

'Did you tell him you were going to contact me?'

'I've told no one. But I know why you've been questioning him. He told me when you came sniffing around the first time. It's about that politician who died, Goldsby.'

Horton didn't much like the sound of that. It meant Pilbeam might also be telling others the same. 'Go on.'

'I saw that fat copper on the telly this morning. He said the guy they fished out of the moat at the Spur Redoubt was Neil Brandon, is that right?'

Horton took the 'fat copper' to be Uckfield. 'Yes. You knew Brandon?'

Harnley reached into his jacket pocket and retrieved a packet of cigarettes. His hands were shaking as he took one out and attempted to light it from a box of matches, some of which spilled on to the concrete. Horton could see he was genuinely shaken. He said nothing, but waited. Harnley lit his cigarette and took a long drag at it, his yellowing eyes darted to Horton.

'I didn't really *know* him,' he stressed. 'But I'd done business with him, if you know what I mean. But it was years ago. Now Brandon is dead like the others.'

'Others?' Horton picked up, puzzled. He could guess what kind of 'business' Harnley was referring to.

'It's some copper's doing. That's why I wanted to meet here. I don't want to be next.'

Horton's mind was racing. 'You think a police officer killed Brandon?'

'Yeah, and the others, including Goldsby. Don't look so bleeding shocked. Some of you lot are more bent than the villains.'

Horton knew there were some corrupt officers — he'd met them in the past. And he'd known coppers who had killed and covered it up. DCI Ingham was dead, so Harnley couldn't be referring to him. Besides, Horton had worked with Ingham, a clever, honest police officer, and nothing would induce him to believe he had been corrupt and a killer. The same went for Mike Danby. And for Dyer? Yes, in respect of murder, but Dyer could have been party to a cover-up. Would he have protected a murderer though and a fellow police officer? Possibly, if the stakes were high enough.

Harnley was saying, 'That's why you won't get me anywhere near an interview room because you buggers will probably stitch me up for Brandon's murder. And I don't want no coppers coming after me. You catch the bastard who is doing this, then I'll go home, but do it quick, for Christ's sake.'

'Where are you staying?'

Harnley scoffed. 'I'm not telling you that!'

'OK. You said "others", what do you mean?'

Harnley took a deep breath, scoured the area and drew on his cigarette before replying. 'We was doing a job, see — me, Vic Fisher and Frank Bray. Frank had the boat.'

Horton rapidly recalled that Pilbeam had mentioned Vic Fisher. He had been the man Pilbeam said had been making a beeline for Goldsby after the public meeting on the night the politician had died. Knowing of Brandon's light fingers, Horton was already ahead of Harnley. 'Brandon was your inside man at the Royal Clarence Victualling Yard in Gosport in the early eighties.'

Harnley looked stunned that Horton knew about it. Then he nodded and sniffed. 'We'd been doing it, no trouble, a few times. Frank would take the boat round to the western side of the island closest to the victualling yard and pick up a buoy. He'd tow a tender. There wasn't any fancy marina there then, so no one to be nosy. It was dark too. I'd take the tender over to the yard. I'd row quiet like if the weather was still, but if it was windy, I'd chance the engine because no one would hear that above the noise. Brandon would meet me on the quayside with the goods. He knew Frank Bray. They both had boats. Brandon said there were a lot of easy pickings in the stores. Nobody noticed small things missing just so long as we didn't get greedy. We didn't, but after we found the body, we didn't go back.'

Horton's heart skipped a beat and his mind raced. 'When was this?'

'October 1985.'

Although he'd already ruled out Jennifer, a little part of his mind had still wondered. Quintessa definitely wasn't Jennifer, thank God. Harnley had said 'body' not 'skeleton', so it couldn't have lain there for long. 'You're certain of the date?'

'It's not a thing you can forget.'

'You've managed to over the years,' Horton said acidly.

'I thought it better that way, and I would have kept quiet now if it hadn't been for you sniffing around, Brandon ending up dead and them skeletons being found. I thought all them skeletons was convicts from years ago. I didn't think it had anything to do with the woman we found.'

'You got scared.'

'Yeah, and so would you when everyone on that job except me is dead.' Harnley threw down his smouldering cigarette and ground it out with the toe of his shabby trainer. He shook another out of the packet. The wind was swirling and howling around them and the rain was sweeping in from the south-west, but they were sheltered from the worst of it. And they were alone.

Horton said nothing. Harnley lit up. This time his lined and bony hands were steadier. 'Frank kept his boat in the harbour close to Whale Island. We'd tell anyone who got nosy, although they never did, that we were going out for a night's fishing. Sometimes we did, other times, when Brandon gave Frank the nod, we'd slip over to Rat Island. On this particular night — our last because of what we found — Frank dropped anchor on the western side of the island as usual, out of sight of the main harbour. I went across to meet Brandon. He was late.' He drew on his cigarette. 'I had to hang around. I was about to give up on him when he showed.'

'Did Brandon say why he was late?'

'No, but he'd got the gear — food, clothes, electrical equipment, odds and sods. We loaded it up. I paid him off and rowed back to the boat, only when I got there, I could see by Frank's and Vic's faces that something had happened. I thought the Ministry of Defence Police had twigged us, or someone had reported seeing us, but Vic said they'd seen someone arrive on the island in a small boat. Frank's boat wasn't showing any lights because we didn't want to draw any attention to it. They'd seen this small dinghy run up onto the shore.'

Horton studied him keenly. Was that the truth? Possibly, because Harnley was alive and according to him, Bray and Fisher were dead. Horton didn't know how they'd died, or how Dudley Goldsby was implicated, but they'd come to that soon.

'A bloke climbed out of the boat and began heaving the dinghy up on to the shingle as though there was something heavy in it.'

Horton thought the man must have been young, strong and fit.

'Then he tipped the dinghy over and dragged what they thought looked like a body into the bushes. I said, "Don't be daft." They were seeing things, the island being haunted, or so the local legend claims, because of the convicts on those prison ships in the harbour. But it weren't no ghost. He was gone for about ten, fifteen minutes at the most.'

So had the killer already prepared a grave for Quintessa? Horton again wondered why he hadn't simply tossed her body into sea. But then she might have been found and identified. If that was the case the trail could have led back to the killer, and he couldn't take that risk. The fact that he went to Rat Island on a small boat also meant that he didn't have a vessel suitable enough to go out into the Solent but had to stay in the sheltered waters of the harbour. Burying her on a small, disused island had seemed a far better option.

Could the same have happened to Jennifer? Not on Rat Island but on another piece of land, remote, protected by the Ministry of Defence, which Lord Ames could have had access to. Or perhaps on his own private land. He had enough of it around the country. Had he owned that Isle of Wight estate in 1978? Maybe. Perhaps that was where Jennifer lay.

Harnley was saying, 'We decided to take a look. We took the tender onto the shore and a couple of torches.' His hand shook as he recalled the incident. Horton found himself imagining the three of them uncovering the remains, only they hadn't been remains then. Eagerly he waited for Harnley to continue.

'We could see where the earth had been dug over and some branches and shingle piled up. It didn't take long for us to clear some of it. I wish to God we hadn't. She had short, curly blonde hair, staring blue eyes. In her twenties, I'd say.' Harnley gulped. His expression paled. 'We was all pretty shocked.'

'Not shocked enough to report it,' Horton said coldly.

'How the hell could we without admitting what we were doing there?'

'You could have stuck to your story about fishing.'

'Oh, yeah, and you lot would have tried to pin her murder on us. We got the hell out of there as quickly as we could and said nothing.'

'Did you tell Brandon about it?'

'No. Leastways, I didn't. I never said a word to anyone. Frank told Brandon we didn't want any more stuff from that victualling yard. Maybe he gave a reason, maybe he didn't.' A shadow crossed his narrow face. Horton could see that he was remembering something but he fell silent.

'Did you see how the woman had died?'

'No, we only saw her face, but her throat hadn't been cut or anything like that and she wasn't disfigured or bashed about.'

'Do you know who she was?'

'We didn't stop to search her!' he said cuttingly.

'Haven't you wondered about her over the years or felt bad about leaving her there to rot?'

'Why should I? I didn't kill her and shove her in that grave. We just bunged the earth and shingle back over her and got the hell out of there.'

'And Fisher and Bray knew who had put her there?'

Harnley took a breath, stubbed out his cigarette. 'I didn't think so at the time. They said it was just some bloke. But they must have seen who it was, because they both died not long after that politician, Goldsby, killed himself, only the vicar says he didn't kill himself — someone else did, and you were asking questions about it. It made me wonder about the way Frank and Vic died.'

'But what makes you think Goldsby's deaths and those of Bray, Fisher and Brandon are linked to what you found on Rat Island?'

His brow furrowed. 'I've been thinking back to when that politician died. It was two days before Vic and Frank were killed. Vic had been buoyed up about something. Flashing his money about too, and so was Frank. I asked Vic if he'd struck lucky, but he said it was none of my business. He had a political meeting to attend. The bugger had never been interested in politics in his life. Then I saw Vic the day after Goldsby had died and he looked dreadful. Cut me dead. Next thing I heard, he and Frank had been killed in an explosion on Frank's boat. It was an old boat but sturdy. It could get across the channel and back if needs be. They said it was an accident, gas cylinder exploded, rotten pipe or something. They were killed outright, don't think there was much left of them.' He drew a shaky breath. 'I had no idea that it was anything to do with what we found on Rat Island in 1985. How could it be? That had been twenty years before. I thought that perhaps Vic and Frank had been involved in smuggling with some big-time villain, got greedy and been taken out. I put it out of my head until you showed up. Then . . .' He hesitated.

185

'Go on.'

'Look, it might have nothing to do with this, but I also got to remembering how a couple of years ago Vic's daughter showed up. She said Vic had told her mother just before he died that he was scared someone was after him because of what he'd seen on Rat Island years ago. She asked if I knew what it was. She'd been told that I was friends with Vic and Frank.'

'Who told her that?' Horton was vastly interested in this new information. He didn't believe for one minute that the woman who had come to talk to Harnley was Fisher's daughter.

'I don't know.'

'You didn't ask?' Horton asked incredulously.

'No — maybe — I can't remember. She didn't answer me if I did. I told her I knew nothing about it. I just wanted to get rid of her. I hadn't thought about it for years and I didn't want to start thinking about it then. She said that she'd heard from her mother that the three of us often went out on Frank's boat. She insisted that the explosion was no accident. I told her not to rake things up, that Frank's boat was a disaster waiting to happen and that she'd do well to keep her suspicions to herself. We never saw nothing.'

'But you mentioned Brandon?'

'I don't know, maybe. Look, I can't remember. I was going through chemo. I wasn't thinking straight and I felt like shit. Anyway, Brandon never approached me.'

'Did you see her again?'

'No.'

'What did she look like?'

'I don't know, she was just some woman,' he said, exasperated.

'But you must have recognized her. You knew Fisher.'

'Yeah, but his wife walked out on him when the kids were little. He never saw them again and neither did I. She moved up north somewhere.'

Which to the likes of Harnley could be just twenty miles away. And maybe Adele knew this or simply took a chance on it, because he was certain it was Adele who had been posing as Vic's daughter. He was beginning to think that Adele didn't take a chance on anything. It had all been cleverly planned. Her conversation with Harnley had given her all she needed — a link to Brandon. Harnley *must* have mentioned him. And perhaps she had got more out of Harnley than he was now relaying.

Horton eyed the nervous man shifting beside him. Maybe Harnley had told her they'd discovered a body. But if he had and he'd mentioned Brandon, it had taken her two years to approach the man — why? Because she needed time to track him down or because she was still searching for her father's killer and the link between him and Quintessa?

But she *had* found Brandon and learned he was a volunteer at the museum. Then, feigning an interest in local military history, she'd got hold of his mobile phone number and had called him just over two weeks ago. She hadn't used Harnley as her messenger because having met him when she'd pumped him for information, she had realized he wasn't suitable and as he was ill, there was every chance he could have been dead by the time she was ready to put her plan into action.

Harnley continued, 'Then you come along asking the vicar questions about that politician and next thing I hear is that Brandon's dead. And if this killer's worked out that Brandon was in on that job in 1985 then he'll have worked out I was there too, or Brandon told him, and I'm not taking any chances.'

'And you think Dudley Goldsby was involved in burying that woman in 1985?'

Hanley squirmed. 'I don't know, but why else would Vic say he had a political meeting to attend, and after that meeting Goldsby was dead and Vic looked like shit?'

If, as now seemed likely, Vic Fisher had known who had buried Quintessa, why had he waited twenty years to use that information?

'Where did this boat explosion happen?' he asked.

187

Harnley took the last cigarette from the packet which he tossed on the ground. His cheeks were sunken in his grey face. 'Somewhere off the Isle of Wight.' Horton could easily get the information from the marine accident investigation report. Harnley rose. 'You'd better find this ruthless bastard and quick. I don't want to end up on a mortuary slab with me throat cut.'

Horton watched him shuffle away with the rain beating against his thin, inadequate clothes. That Harnley was petrified was obvious. As soon as he'd seen Uckfield's appeal on the morning news, he'd left his flat without even taking a coat.

Under the cover of the veranda, Horton called Cantelli. 'I need you to look up a marine accident investigation report for the twenty-fourth of April 2005 or around that time,' he said. 'A boat explosion that killed Frank Bray and Vic Fisher. Is Walters there?'

'He's tucking into his doughnuts. Bliss has let him escape the incident suite as nothing seems to be happening on the Brandon investigation.'

'It might now. Get Walters to run Vic Fisher, Frank Bray and Keith Harnley through the database. I'll explain everything when I get back.'

He picked up Harnley's discarded cigarette packet and was about to head for the Harley when Elkins rang.

'I've spoken to Craig, the manager at No Man's Fort, and got the guest list for Jarvis's bash this weekend. I'll email it over.'

'Any names familiar to you aside from my ex-wife?'

'Quite a few. The former chief constable, Dyer, his missus, former DCI Mike Danby, Dominic Keats, Alex Cummings—'

'How do you know him? I didn't think you were in the market for a superyacht?'

'Met him at Cowes a few times and at Oyster Quays. He's got a yacht about the same size as Jarvis's. Keeps it on the South of France. Has a house at the Hamble but is rarely there. Bit of a playboy, always seems to have a different woman with him, been married four times. He's with future wife number five, Sarah Lemont. She was his PA, might still be. At least twenty years younger than him, I'd say.'

'How do you know all this?'

'It's my job to fraternize with the yachting crowd and those working in and around the marinas and harbours. They're a hotbed of gossip. We get all sorts of intelligence. Cummings is a local boy, did his naval architect apprenticeship at Camper and Nicholsons in Gosport.'

Did he indeed. The same place as Goldsby had done his, according to Frieda Chillerton. Horton asked Elkins for a description of Alex Cummings, which confirmed he was the barrel-shaped man he'd seen on Jarvis's yacht, as Catherine had already told him, but he wanted to be certain. And Sarah Lemont was the very thin, anxious-looking blonde woman.

'Anything dodgy about Cummings?'

'Not that I know of. He's said to be designing a boat for Jonathan Sloane, another regular at Cowes who's also on the fort. He's a successful entrepreneur, runs a biotechnology business in Guildford. Something to do with agriculture and pesticides, I think.'

Horton recalled what Catherine had said. Sloane, then, was the lean, bespectacled man on Jarvis's boat.

'Sloane's single,' Elkins continued. 'Not short of female company but cleverer than Cummings in that he manages to escape getting entangled.'

'And Peter Jarvis? What do you know about him? Aside from the fact my ex-wife is his girlfriend.'

'Probably about as much as you know, Andy,' Elkins answered diplomatically. 'Local boy made good, built up a food processing and packaging business from 1986 in Gosport and sold it for a fortune. Now he's got his fingers in several new business pies that are bound to be successful because he seems to have the golden touch.'

'And the gossip about his character?' probed Horton.

'Pleasant, takes time to talk to the staff, not showy.'

'Not unless you count his latest acquisition, that boat.'

'Guess he's got to spend his money on something. Dominic Keats both you and I know. Thinks more of himself than others do. The rest of the guests, ten in total — which include your former in-laws — are due over at midday today. The Solent Forts launch is picking them up from Oyster Quays. But I'm not sure they'll all make it. One of them in particular might be rather busy on a murder investigation,' Elkins said with something like malicious glee.

Horton quickly caught on. 'Uckfield's on the guest list.'

'Yep, along with his wife. Of course, Alison might go without him or he might hand the investigation over to DCI Bliss.'

And wouldn't she just love that. But Horton thought Uckfield could arrange to travel over for the night and return to Portsmouth and the investigation tomorrow morning.

'A gourmet dinner is planned for tonight — not sure the Super would want to miss out on that,' Elkins added with delight. 'They've even brought their own chef, a woman called Ruby Masters.'

Horton recalled that Jarvis had called the auburn-haired woman in his galley Ruby.

'Put Craig's chef's nose out of joint a bit, but then Jarvis is paying for it so he can't go against it. There's no entertainment but plenty of champagne. Craig's staff has ordered in extra crateloads.'

A lot of business would be conducted after that gourmet dinner and on the Sunday. Dyer had obviously wangled Uckfield an invitation because the Super was hardly wealthy enough to put money into a venture capital trust. And neither was Dyer.

'There's another dinner on Sunday night. The guests leave on Monday morning.'

'Hope the weather holds for them,' Horton muttered, eyeing the slanting rain. He rang off and made for his Harley, dropping Harnley's cigarette packet in the bin as he went and ringing Dr Clayton on the way. The long grey waves were rolling in and bursting in a torrent of white spray on the shingle and onto the promenade. He was the only idiot out in it. He couldn't see the Isle of Wight or the fort. In fact, he couldn't see anything but a grey blur beyond the shore.

'My God, Andy, where are you?' Gaye cried. 'Out at sea?'

'No, on the seafront just heading back to the station. Have you had a chance to look more deeply into the autopsy on Dudley Goldsby?' he bellowed.

'Yes, but it's just as I thought on my first reading of it — everything seems in order. Although I see what you meant about the photographs of the body. It doesn't look as though he died in agony. Have you got some new evidence?'

'Yes. But proving he was killed is going to be very difficult, maybe impossible. Is there anything the pathologist could have missed that could show Goldsby was deliberately killed with that cocaine overdose?'

'I could re-examine the toxicology reports.'

'Thanks.'

He rang off and headed for the station feeling that, although there were many questions still to answer, the twisted tale of Quintessa's death was slowly beginning to unravel.

CHAPTER TWENTY-ONE

After peeling off his waterproof leggings and jacket in his office, and listening to what Walters and Cantelli had unearthed, the three of them made for the incident suite.

As they entered Bliss sprang up as though someone had lit a firework under her. She flung open her office door looking ready to demand where he had been, but stalled as Uckfield marched out to join them.

Horton dropped his bombshell. 'We have a witness who saw Quintessa being buried and we have two more deaths connected with her murder that also link to the death of Dudley Goldsby.'

Uckfield looked stunned while Bliss eyed Horton with her customary suspicion.

'I've just come from interviewing this witness.'

'Where?' demanded Bliss.

'At a place of his choosing.'

'Where is he now?' asked Uckfield.

'No idea.'

Uckfield rolled his eyes. 'That is not the way it's done.'

'Sometimes it's the *only* way it's done,' Horton stressed. Bliss would never understand that, but Uckfield would. Horton saw Bliss flick a glance at Uckfield to see which way the wind was blowing. Horton pressed on. 'Now do you want to hear what this witness had to say?'

Uckfield nodded. He called over Dennings and threw himself down in one of the seats at the front of the room next to Trueman. Dennings perched on the edge of Trueman's desk while Walters sat at the one next to it, which he had previously occupied. Bliss hovered, tense and keen. Horton took up position between the two crime boards, one for Quintessa, the other for Brandon, with Cantelli beside him. They'd need another one now for Dudley Goldsby. Behind them the rest of the staff continued with their jobs, but Horton knew their ears were strained to bursting point to pick up this latest development. There was no sign of DC Jake Marsden or DC Kate Somerfield, who must be continuing with the house-to-house.

Succinctly and crisply, without speculation, comment or raising the questions that had buzzed around his head throughout Harnley's interview, and on his way back to the station, Horton relayed what Harnley had told him. He watched the expressions cross both Bliss and Uckfield's faces. They ranged from scepticism to interest and surprise, while Trueman's dark features remained stoic as ever. Dennings was eyeing him with hostility which had its roots in jealousy and an inferiority complex — he was constantly afraid of his position in the team because he knew he wasn't up to the job. When Horton had finished he nodded at Cantelli who, with the report of the boat accident he'd printed off the computer in his hand, began his briefing.

'The *Louisa May* was a fishing vessel.' He pinned a picture of it on Quintessa's crime board. Horton had expected a smaller motorboat. This could indeed easily have sailed across the English Channel and had probably been used for smuggling under the guise of fishing trips. 'It was an inshore crabber built of wood.'

'Which means it would have gone up like the clappers,' Uckfield broke in.

'Yes. It was built in 1973 and went down on the twenty-fourth of April 2005 just off Ventnor on the Isle of Wight.

The cause of the explosion was a ruptured hot water storage cylinder, which overheated, generating steam, causing over-pressure.' Cantelli glanced at his notes. 'The rupture probably occurred at about 3.4 bar, four times working pressure of the cylinder.' He looked up. 'The investigation findings say that the pressure-relief valve must have been set at this pressure or above, or it was seized in the closed position.'

'Deliberately so, according to Harnley,' added Horton. 'He believes Fisher and Bray were killed.'

Cantelli continued, 'The cylinder overheated when the immersion heater thermostat failed to shut off the electrical supply. There were no safety devices fitted to the system to prevent overheating or overpressure as a result of thermostat failure.'

Uckfield said, 'So our killer knows about boilers on boats.'

'Or boilers in general,' ventured Trueman.

'Any plumbers involved in the case?' Uckfield joked.

Trueman answered. 'Doesn't have to be a plumber. Anyone with a knowledge of electrics or boats, or who has a mechanical mind or is clever enough to research it, could have known what to do.'

'Yes, thank you, Sergeant. I think I could have worked that out.'

Trueman took no notice of Uckfield's sarcasm. He, like them all, was well used to it. But Horton's mind flicked to someone who was clever and had a first-class honours degree in science from Bristol University. Peter Jarvis.

Cantelli continued, 'Fisher and Bray couldn't radio for help because the radio batteries were destroyed in the explo-sion and the resulting flooding. The life jackets were old and stored inside the vessel too. If they'd been stored on deck, they might have stood a chance.'

Horton broke in, 'Did the killer get on board and move both the radio and life jackets out of reach? Or perhaps Bray was sloppy — he'd got away without having any accidents so had become blasé about safety. And I doubt whether either man ever bothered to undergo sea survival courses. But this killer didn't want to take a chance on that. He wanted to make sure they died.'

Cantelli said, 'There is no suggestion from the marine investigation accident report of it being anything other than an accident,'

'Just as in Dudley Goldsby's death. There was no hint of it being anything but suicide or an accidental overdose.' Horton looked pointedly at Uckfield, who glared back.

Walters chipped in. 'Harnley, Fisher and Bray all have criminal records Harnley was last convicted for theft six years ago and got a custodial sentence of two years, out in one. He hasn't reoffended, or if he has, he's not been caught.'

Horton said, 'That might be something to do with the fact that he was diagnosed with cancer and has been undergoing treatment.'

Walters nodded. 'Fisher and Bray had convictions for theft and receiving stolen goods. They'd both served short prison terms with the last being in July 2003 when they were sentenced for theft from Hamble Marina.'

Elkins had told Horton that Alex Cummings lived at Hamble. Had he lived there in 2003 and kept a boat in the marina then — or perhaps, more importantly, in 2005? Dominic Keats also kept a boat at Hamble Marina.

'Was Harnley on that job with them?' asked Horton.

'Yes. They were released in March 2005.'

'Any family?' queried Bliss.

'Fisher was married, two sons and a daughter, all in their mid to late thirties now.'

'Which fits with Adele's age,' Horton said. 'I believe she claimed to be Fisher's daughter.'

Walters said, 'Harnley is divorced, one daughter and a son. Bray was widowed in 1999. He had five kids, most with a criminal record. The youngest, at twenty-six, is inside for aggravated assault.'

Cantelli continued, 'The report concludes that the *Louisa May* sank because of damage to her hull caused by the violent rupture of the hot water storage cylinder. And there are no regulations for adequate standards for the construction, installation and maintenance of unvented hot water systems in fishing vessels.'

Horton studied the picture on the board. 'In order for it to have been sabotage, the killer must have known what vessel Frank Bray owned and where it was moored. He managed to get on board and below decks. Maybe he broke in and Bray didn't report it because he didn't want the police sniffing around. He'd have had a natural aversion to us, and perhaps the boat was being used to store stolen goods, so he just kept quiet about a break-in. Or maybe the killer was clever enough to gain access without it looking like a break-in or the boat wasn't terribly secure, it being old and probably not that well maintained.'

Bliss frowned. 'But why wait twenty years to blackmail Quintessa's killer?'

It was one of the questions that had occupied Horton on his way back to the station. He had one answer. 'Because it was only in April 2005 that one or both of them, Bray or Fisher, recognized the man they'd seen burying Quintessa.'

Uckfield shifted in his seat. 'Couldn't have changed much then,' he muttered.

'Perhaps there was something about his manner or his face that was distinctive,' Walters suggested.

Uckfield sniffed loudly. 'Like what? A camel hump? A huge wart on the end of his nose?'

'I'm not sure they would have seen that, it being dark,' ventured Horton.

'Unless he flashed a torch around,' volunteered Walters.

'Possibly,' Horton answered. 'It would have been difficult to see where he was going without one, and Harnley says it was a windy, wet night with no moon. The killer could have taken the chance that no one was in the harbour to see the light.'

Uckfield drew in an irritable breath. 'Or maybe he had a wooden leg, a hook for a hand and a ruddy great parrot on his shoulder.'

Bliss pursed her lips. 'The scar is a possibility, as is an artificial limb. He could have a stoop or walked with a limp.'

'Christ, is everyone going to take everything I say literally!'

Nobody answered. With exasperation, Uckfield continued, 'We can't even find Adele Goldsby, let alone this alleged killer.'

But there was nothing 'alleged' about Quintessa's killer. She had been brutally murdered and callously buried. Horton began to espouse the ideas that had occurred to him. 'You're right, though. How *would* Fisher and Bray have recognized the killer? Maybe the killer returned to the scene of the crime in 2005 to check Quintessa was still buried there and Fisher or Bray happened to be there at the same time. OK, so unlikely,' he quickly added when Uckfield looked at him as though he'd just suggested they'd beamed down to Rat Island from the Starship *Enterprise*. 'Maybe they recognized the boat used in 1985, although again that sounds unlikely given that Harnley said it was a small dinghy with an outboard engine and therefore not distinctive enough. There are hundreds of them around, and even if Fisher and Bray saw the name of it, it could have been sold several times since then and the name changed, or there could be more than one dinghy with the same name. But whatever Harnley says, Bray and Fisher *must* have seen the killer's face in 1985 and twenty years later recognized him as the man who had buried Quintessa. And that means either one or both of them came across this man in the course of their work, which was stealing and smuggling and avoiding being caught. But they were caught and sentenced in July 2003 and didn't get out until March 2005. So it's possible that they recognized this killer earlier but couldn't act upon it until they were released from prison.'

He dashed a look at Uckfield to see if he was following his train of thought. By his scowl he was. Dyer had been working in Portsmouth CID from 2003 to 2005 before leaving for Avon on his promotion to assistant chief constable that May.

Horton continued, 'Harnley is convinced a police officer is involved but he could be prejudiced. We should check the names of the officers involved in their arrest in 2003.'

Uckfield's eyes narrowed. He scratched his groin but made no comment.

Horton pressed on, 'Sergeant Elkins also told me that Alex Cummings, one of Peter Jarvis's guests at the fort this weekend, lives at Hamble. Walters, check how long Cummings has lived there, if he kept a boat in the marina in 2003 and the name of the boat owners Fisher and Bray stole from.'

Walters nodded. Uckfield couldn't very well refuse, though he looked as if he'd like to.

'There's also the fact that Cummings is as wide as he is short — distinctively short,' Horton added. 'Perhaps Fisher and Bray remarked on that to themselves at the time and in 2003 came across him and recognized him from his height and manner of walking. He walks like a sailor who's been at sea for a very long time. Plus, they could have seen his face, and maybe he hadn't changed much in the intervening years. It might be worthwhile getting hold of a picture of him from 1985 and one from 2005 and comparing them.'

Trueman made a note. Uckfield looked about to rise but Horton stalled him. 'Whoever the killer is, though, Fisher and Bray made a connection between him and Dudley Goldsby. There would have been a lot of news coverage of Goldsby around that time because he was campaigning for the general election. The killer could have been photographed *with* Goldsby.' Dyer would also have been in the news at that time with his promotion to assistant chief constable, and there was every chance he'd been photographed with the politician at an event. Or been asked by a journalist for comment in response to a statement made by Goldsby or someone in his party about law and order, which was always a political hot potato.

'They saw that Quintessa's killer either had a position to protect, or wealth, or both. They didn't know how to get hold of the killer with a view to blackmailing him, but they knew how to get hold of Dudley Goldsby. He was their Member of Parliament. Pilbeam claims to have seen Fisher making a beeline for Goldsby on the night of the public meeting and before that, Harnley says Fisher was flash with his money and smug, so we can assume that the night Pilbeam saw Fisher in action wasn't the first time he'd approached Goldsby. He'd already got money from the killer and was going back for more. And we know that Goldsby can't be the killer because he died two days before Fisher and Bray and he didn't come back from the dead to kill Brandon.'

Trueman said, 'We'll check the local media coverage for 2005 around that time.'

Horton nodded. 'The killer pays up, perhaps a few times, while he thinks of a way to get out of it. He has to kill all three of them — Goldsby, Fisher and Bray — to avoid his crime being exposed. Brandon and Harnley didn't see the killer, not that it would have prevented him from killing them. He simply didn't know they had been on that job that night. But Adele knows. And she knows who the killer is. The fact that she called me and asked to meet on the ferry, and that she made a hoax call to Danby naming Peter Jarvis means he or one of his guests could be the man we're looking for.'

Bliss sharply piped up. 'What's this about a hoax call to Danby? Who's he?' She hadn't worked in Portsmouth when Danby had been here.

Horton explained.

'And what else haven't you told us, Inspector?' she snapped.

Horton had no intention of mentioning Catherine being Jarvis's girlfriend. Maybe Uckfield would. Horton ignored the question. 'The fact that Adele has disappeared and Brandon is dead means she could have been made to tell the killer about Brandon. She might also have told the killer about her visit to Keith Harnley. Harnley's not taking any chances and has gone into hiding.'

Uckfield, looking thoughtful, waggled a finger in his right ear. 'So, after her father's death, she takes off and over the years amasses or discovers the evidence.'

Bliss flicked her ponytail, frowning. 'But how would she know where to start?'

Horton answered. 'Perhaps she knew the identity of her father's killer right from the beginning but couldn't prove anything, and she knew that if she did point the finger at him without evidence, it would be hushed up. Nobody wanted a scandal before the general election and there was a chance that Goldsby could have been involved with Quintessa and her death. Adele was in that hall at that public meeting and she must have seen Fisher with her father. Nobody really noticed her — she was quiet, mousey, always faded into the background. She could easily have overheard, or was able to lipread enough to get the gist of what was being said. Maybe she'd overheard them before. Then her father dies and Fisher and Bray die two days later. By then she's too frightened to speak out. There's no one she can tell who she trusts, or who she thinks will believe her. She leaves Portsmouth immediately after her father's funeral.'

'And comes back now, ready with her evidence,' added Cantelli.

'Yes, and that was why she went to Harnley under the pretence of being Vic Fisher's daughter about two years ago, maybe less, and pumped him for information about what he'd seen on Rat Island. It would have been easy enough for her to trawl through the local newspaper archives and discover Fisher and Bray's criminal involvement with Harnley. She tracked him down, got confirmation from him that he had been on that job and got Brandon's name out of him.'

Bliss again. 'She then pumped Brandon for information.'

'Yes, and discovered that he knew a hell of a lot about the history of Rat Island but nothing at all about Quintessa being buried there. But he could be useful. She arranged for him to find the skeleton.'

'Hang on — how did she know where exactly on that island Quintessa was buried?' protested Uckfield.

'She worked out where Fisher and Bray were anchored while waiting for Harnley to return with the stolen goods and, from that, where the dinghy had come ashore. She'd have guessed it was buried somewhere in among the clump of trees. I think she went there herself first at night in a small tender and discovered it. She needed to be certain she was right, and once she was, left it partially uncovered for Brandon to find. She followed the news of the discovery of the remains in the media and on the internet, perhaps puzzled and shocked there had been four other skeletons found on that island that were ancient bones. Maybe she even had doubts for a while that she was right and that it was Quintessa. Maybe she thought she'd been fooled and had found the convict remains. Or perhaps she surmised that the news of the more recent remains is being kept quiet. She knows who the killer is. She waits and watches to see what he does. Is he worried about Quintessa being found and being traced back to him? Does he approach someone who can tell him what's going on?'

'She called you because she was desperate for more information,' said Uckfield.

'But when I was on the ferry, I had no idea that one of those skeletons was recent and neither did anyone here, only Dr Lauder.'

'Check he told no one,' Uckfield tossed at Dennings.

Horton knew he hadn't. 'She said she wanted to meet me on the ferry because she had something to *show* me. And she wanted Danby there because he was one of the original investigating officers. She knew he ran a private close protection and security company. That's public knowledge. She gave Danby Jarvis's name because he could either be the man involved in Quintessa's death — there's still the fact that he had a factory in Gosport, he was friendly with Goldsby, and he had booked the hotel for a private dinner, giving him access to Goldsby's room and at the same time providing himself with an alibi. Or she knew it was someone else who would be on Jarvis's boat — Dominic Keats, Jonathan Sloane or Alex Cummings.'

He left off Dyer, but Uckfield would know that. And maybe Adele had known that Dyer would also be on Jarvis's boat.

Bliss frowned. 'If it was easy for Adele to trace Harnley and then Brandon, why didn't the killer do so and eliminate them in 2005 after disposing of Fisher and Bray?'

That was the bit that didn't make sense and that Horton had also considered. 'Perhaps the killer thought he had dealt with everyone who could identify him. In a way, he had. The other two hadn't seen him and, after monitoring the investigation into the boat explosion, he was satisfied it was being treated as an accident. Maybe someone inside the force told him there was nothing suspicious about it.' Again, Horton threw a glance at Uckfield, who grunted. 'Or perhaps he went to work abroad and thought he was safely out of sight.' That fitted more with Alex Cummings from what Elkins had told him, but also Keats, who had been in the navy. Keats had no distinguishing features, but he could have been in naval uniform when he'd dumped Quintessa. And perhaps he had worked at the victualling yard or had been detailed to do something in connection with it and either Fisher or Bray had recognized him. Bray might have come across Keats in the harbour. Keats might even have worked on the fishery patrols and stopped Bray on his boat sometime. Then, when Bray learned in 2003 or 2005 that Keats had made it good with his Superyacht Academy, he was ripe for the plucking.

Horton kept these thoughts to himself for the moment. 'When the killer found out that Brandon had been taken in for interview for finding those remains and then released, he knew he had to take action.'

'How did he know?' asked Walters. Uckfield shifted in his seat.

'Maybe Brandon had twigged who the killer was and called him immediately after he was released to blackmail him, as we surmised.'

Stubbornly Dennings said, 'Goldsby's death could still be suicide. He decided to take his own life because he couldn't hack the general election. That boat explosion could still be accidental and Brandon's death could have been a mugging gone wrong, or a drunken assault.'

'And that's what we would have assumed if Brandon hadn't told us his phone call had come from Adele, something the killer doesn't know.' Or did he? Horton's eyes flicked to Uckfield. Had Uckfield told Dyer? From his expression, Horton was damn sure he had. 'In order to expose the killer, we had to find Quintessa. Adele knew that Brandon would eventually tell us about that phone call coming from her.' He eyed Uckfield steadily. 'We need to find out who Jarvis's guests were at that hotel the night Goldsby died.'

'But this killer could simply have walked in off the street,' Dennings put in. 'He could have looked and acted like he was meant to be in that hotel and then slipped out.'

Which was what Horton had originally thought. 'He could, but there is also the fact that the drug squad received the anonymous tip-off about Callum Durrant being in that hotel room. Olewbo and I were despatched to follow it up, which backs up Harnley's claim that the killer could be connected with someone in the police force, and that would make him a very suitable blackmail victim.'

By Uckfield's expression, he didn't much like this. Neither did Horton.

Solemnly he said, 'In 1985, Quintessa's killer could have been a young copper but as the years progressed, so did he. He moved around Hampshire on various promotions and maybe even left Hampshire Constabulary to go to another force. Then on promotion he returned and was in a very senior position in 2005, when Fisher and Bray recognized him.'

Uckfield shuffled uncomfortably. The pattern fitted Dyer's career.

Horton added, 'Whoever called in with that anonymous tip-off to the drug squad — the call was traced to a public payphone — knew about Durrant being a wanted dealer.'

'Did the killer buy the cocaine from Durrant?' mused Bliss.

'Durrant was adamant he hadn't sold any coke to Goldsby, but he wasn't asked if he had sold it to anyone who could have been a friend or associate of Goldsby, because no one was looking at murder. And even if we had asked him, Durrant would have kept quiet. If, however, the killer is, or was, someone inside the force, he could have taken cocaine that had been seized. The killer then wanted Goldsby found, so he arranged for the tip-off.'

There was a moment's silence while they all considered this. The phones continued to ring.

'According to Harnley, Bray's boat was usually moored up in the harbour.' Horton looked to Cantelli to confirm this.

Cantelli studied the report. 'It was.'

'Which means the killer would have needed to reach it by boat. We know he can handle a boat, because, again according to Harnley, he arrived and left Rat Island in one. He sabotaged the boiler on Fisher's boat and then it was just a case of waiting for the next time they went on a fishing or smuggling trip, and *boom*!

'There are four men associated with Goldsby who not only know a great deal about boats but were guests on Jarvis's boat in Oyster Quays.' Horton didn't say, 'Five if you count Dyer.' Uckfield would know he was thinking it. There might be more suspects on the list of fort guests that Elkins had emailed over to him, he hadn't had the chance to look at, but, as far as he was aware, none of them had been on Jarvis's boat in Oyster Quays. He couldn't rule out anyone completely but he thought it best to concentrate on what Adele must have been pointing him to.

'There's Alex Cummings, a yacht designer, who did his apprenticeship at the same place as Dudley Goldsby — Camper and Nicholsons — and possibly at the same time.

He'd know all about sabotaging a fishing boat. Then there's Jonathan Sloane, an experienced sailor like Cummings, a chemist who runs a highly successful biotechnology company that Elkins claims has something to do with agriculture and pesticides. Sloane and Goldsby's paths could easily have crossed because Goldsby was the government spokesperson for the Department for Environment, Food and Rural Affairs, and a chemist would make it his business to know how to rig an explosion on a boat. Peter Jarvis was at school with Goldsby and remained a friend, but he didn't come forward to say he was in that hotel when his chum died. He's also an experienced sailor and has a science degree, so fixing a boiler on a boat wouldn't be rocket science for him. And there's Dominic Keats, again an experienced sailor with a lucrative yachting business, who'd know all about boilers and boats.'

'I've known Keats for years,' Uckfield declared.

'But not in 1985.'

'No.'

'Keats was in the Royal Navy and Goldsby was a member of the Defence Committee. Maybe they met at a conference or a seminar or worked together on a military project. Keats would know all about Rat Island, it being Ministry of Defence property, and he'd know about the Royal Clarence Victualling Yard.'

Uckfield looked as though he was sitting on a hot seat and suffering from piles.

Horton pressed on. 'And there is someone else I think who knows a great deal more about this than he's saying. The Reverend Simon Pilbeam.'

Uckfield's eyes widened but, before he could comment, Horton swiftly continued, 'Pilbeam was a very close friend of Goldsby's. If Goldsby was involved in Quintessa's killing, or knew the man who was, there's a strong chance he confided in Pilbeam, even though Pilbeam denies it. But it would explain why Adele didn't seek any comfort from the vicar after her father's death or from the nuns, she was afraid they'd tell Pilbeam. And there's something else I'm not entirely happy with.'

This time Uckfield rolled his eyes, while Bliss narrowed hers.

'Goldsby was late arriving at the public meeting and Pilbeam met him alone in the lobby — everyone else was in the hall. Pilbeam could have given Goldsby a drink that contained the cocaine, and he could have slipped him the hotel key and said he'd see him there after the meeting.'

'Now you think the vicar's the killer!' Uckfield said incredulously.

'Why not? Just because he wears his collar the wrong way round doesn't mean he's without sin. And Fisher and Bray might well have recognized him from a press photograph in 2005. He doesn't look as though he'd have enough money to be a blackmail victim, but how do we know that for sure? He could have a fortune stashed away.'

Walters looked puzzled. 'Wouldn't he have lied about being the only person in the lobby when Goldsby arrived if he's guilty?'

Horton shrugged. 'Perhaps he knew we'd be able to check that with Frieda Chillerton. All I'm saying is that we shouldn't discount him. There is something troubling him and there's been a noticeable change in his manner since I first interviewed him. It's possible that after giving Goldsby the drink laced with cocaine and saying he'd meet him at the hotel, Pilbeam made an anonymous call to us with the tip-off that Durrant would be at the hotel. Durrant lived and dealt on Pilbeam's parish. Pilbeam also knows Hans Olewbo. He attends one of Pilbeam's parish churches. Pilbeam wanted Goldsby's body found.'

Bliss said, 'And the boat? Does he know how to sabotage one?'

'No idea. But I'd like to ask him, and here in a formal environment.'

Uckfield looked at his watch. Horton knew why. Not only had he missed his day on the fort but he'd most probably miss his gourmet dinner there tonight, unless he could postpone the interview of Pilbeam until tomorrow, but Horton quickly cut in before Uckfield could suggest that. 'It has to be tonight. Sunday's the vicar's big day. He'll be preaching.'

With ill grace Uckfield acquiesced.

CHAPTER TWENTY-TWO

Pilbeam made no protest at accompanying them to the police station in relation to Dudley Goldsby's death. To Horton, it was as though he had been expecting it. He didn't even protest that he'd already told Horton everything he could.

Horton had introduced Cantelli but had made no mention of the sergeant being on the original investigation. Pilbeam meekly went to fetch his jacket after apologizing for the cluttered and untidy state of the shabby vicarage — an Edwardian terraced house sandwiched between similarly styled properties now given over to student accommodation — saying that he lived alone and that his wife had died not long before he'd been given the ministry in 1985. That was no excuse not to keep it clean and tidy, but if Pilbeam proffered it as one, who was Horton to argue.

While they waited for the vicar to return, Horton studied the only photograph on the overcrowded bookshelves. It was of a much younger Pilbeam with his arm around a young woman's waist. Pilbeam sported a moustache and his light brown hair was touching the collar of his shirt. He was dressed scruffily in trousers that hung low off a non-existent waist, while the woman beside him was wearing a white summer dress that buttoned down the centre, was gathered at the waist and had puffed sleeves. Her shoulder-length, fair wavy hair was unkempt and she was frowning into the camera as though the sun was in her eyes. It was difficult to see her full expression, because her eyes were masked by a pair of large square spectacles that covered much of her diamond-shaped face. They were standing on a shingle beach with a small boat to their right and behind them, some trees. Pilbeam's wife, Horton surmised. He wondered how she had died.

As they climbed into Cantelli's car, Horton thought Pilbeam looked exhausted. He also seemed to have shrunk since that morning. Perhaps that was because he was no longer wearing the long black robe favoured by vicars in the Church of England. His trousers were old and worn, and the shabby brown corduroy jacket hung off his scrawny shoulders. His pullover beneath it looked to be hand knitted, possibly by one of his parishioners. He seemed far more weighed down with worry and fatigue than on Horton's previous encounters with him.

Horton knew he should suspend asking any questions until they were in the interview room, but there was one he was particularly curious about and didn't think it concerned the investigation.

'Why did you tell Keith Harnley he could trust me?' he asked as Cantelli negotiated the dark, wet Saturday evening streets to the station.

'Because he can.'

'But how do you know that? I was the officer who found Dudley Goldsby's body. I could have been involved in his death.'

'But you weren't.'

'You know that for a fact?' Horton caught a glimpse of Cantelli's dark eyes and worried expression in the rear-view mirror. He wondered if he should postpone asking any more questions until they were in the police station. If it looked as though Pilbeam was about to make a confession, Horton would need to caution him and wait until they were safely ensconced in the interview room before questioning him further.

'No, Inspector, but I know people. You would never have done that and been able to live with yourself.'

'I could be a very good actor.'

'Your conscience wouldn't have permitted you to keep silent.'

'You seem so sure,' Horton continued suspiciously.

Pilbeam swivelled to study Horton. 'Like you, I have seen a great deal of human nature. I know what men and women are capable of, and yes, it has shocked and hurt me many times. I also know that it is impossible to tell just by looking at and talking to someone whether they are capable of murder, but sometimes there are some individuals where you can look in their eyes and see pain and hurt, anger and bewilderment, but never murder and not evil.'

Horton felt uncomfortable under his gaze. It was as though Pilbeam could see the anguish of his childhood and teens. As if he knew what he had suffered. But how could he?

He didn't press him further but sat in silence listening to the swish of the windscreen wipers and the rain beating against the windows.

* * *

As soon as they were seated in the interview room and Pilbeam had a cup of weak tea, one sugar, in front of him, Horton began. He didn't really think Pilbeam a killer but he did believe he knew more about Goldsby's death than he'd said.

'Has Adele Goldsby contacted you?' Horton asked.

'As I told you before, Inspector, I haven't seen or spoken to her since the day of her father's funeral.' Pilbeam held their gaze but his voice sounded weary and defeated. Horton wondered if he was ill. His face seemed to be growing more hollow with every passing minute.

Cantelli slid photographs of Fisher and Bray across the desk. 'Did you know, or have you ever seen either of these two men?'

Pilbeam studied them. 'I knew him.' He stabbed a finger at the picture of a man with thinning, overlong fair hair, a lined and pockmarked face and dark eyes. 'It's Vic Fisher. He's the man who I told you, Inspector, was at the public meeting the night Dudley died. But I can't remember seeing the other man.'

'How did you know Vic Fisher?' Horton asked.

'He lived in my parish. He wasn't a churchgoer, but his wife was. He was always in trouble with the police and in and out of prison. Mary Fisher had a hard time of it. She was often left extremely short of money, struggling to bring up their three children. The church helped her out on many occasions until she could stand it no longer. She left him. I don't know where she went or where she is now. Vic didn't seem bothered. He stayed in the area when he wasn't in prison. He was killed in a boat explosion along with another man.'

Horton looked to see if Pilbeam thought that was suspicious or if he knew more about it than he was saying, but his expression was bland, almost vacant. It was as though he was on autopilot.

'Did his wife return when he was killed?'

'I don't know. If she did, she never came to see me.'

'Did you tell Vic Fisher's daughter where to find Keith Harnley?'

Pilbeam looked confused at the questions. 'I haven't spoken to Fisher's daughter. Where is Keith? Have you seen him?'

'You said that on the night of the public meeting, you saw Fisher making a beeline for Dudley Goldsby. Why was Fisher so keen to speak to Mr Goldsby?'

'I don't know.'

Is that the truth? wondered Horton.

Cantelli broke in. 'Was it usual for Vic Fisher to be at a political meeting?'

'No.'

'Did they appear to have met before?' Cantelli again.

Pilbeam looked confused, not at the question, but because they were asking it. But he wasn't a stupid man — far from it, thought Horton.

Pilbeam said, 'You think Vic Fisher gave or sold the cocaine to Dudley?'

'Do you?' asked Horton.

Pilbeam took a breath and sipped his tea. After a moment he carefully put down the plastic beaker, placed his hands palms down on the table, thin fingers spread, and straightened up as though he'd made a decision.

Horton's pulse raced a little faster as the vicar eyed him steadily. He began in an even yet sorrowful tone, 'Vic Fisher dealt in drugs, or rather, he smuggled them into the country by boat. I had no proof of this, only what his wife told me. I didn't think much of it when I saw him making for Dudley, but when I learned that Dudley had taken cocaine I wondered if Vic Fisher had given it to him or sold it to him. It was clear from Dudley's manner, and I knew him well, Inspector, that he was under considerable stress, but I still find it hard to believe he would have resorted to taking illegal substances. It just didn't ring true, but there was always the possibility that, finding the electioneering campaign trail tough, and with Prudence clearly flouting her sexual proclivities in front of him and not caring what the media dredged up to ruin her husband, he became desperate for something to help him.'

'Did Fisher smuggle in drugs for Callum Durrant?' asked Horton.

'I don't know.'

'But you knew Durrant and that he was a drug dealer?'

Pilbeam nodded. 'Parents came to me desperate for help to get their sons and daughters out of his clutches. Any information I had I passed on to Hans.'

'Did Dudley Goldsby know Callum Durrant?'

'I don't know if he actually knew him, but he would certainly have heard the name because his constituents were very concerned about the drug problem on the estate, which you know as well as I do fuels crime.'

Horton left a short pause before continuing. 'How did Fisher look when he approached Dudley? Was he angry? Elated?'

Pilbeam considered this for a moment. 'Determined.'

Horton knew there was more and so too would Cantelli. Horton said, 'Did it also cross your mind that if the drugs weren't for Dudley, they could have been for someone connected with him?'

Pilbeam flushed and stared at his hands.

'Adele or Prudence?' prompted Horton.

Pilbeam's head came up. His eyes flashed with a spark of life — the first Horton had registered since they'd brought him in.

'Not Adele, but I did wonder if Fisher might have sold drugs to Prudence in the past, or to someone she associated with, and that Fisher was blackmailing Dudley with that knowledge.'

'Did you tell anyone about this?'

'No.'

'Not even his agent or secretary?'

'Of course not. I decided that I'd tackle Dudley about it the next day, only by then he was dead.'

'Why didn't you tell us this at the time?' Cantelli said stiffly.

'How could I? I didn't want his personal circumstances dragged through the mud of the media circus.'

Sternly Cantelli said, 'You withheld information that might have helped us with our investigation.'

'Really!' Pilbeam's thin eyebrows shot up. His voice was acid when he said, 'I thought you'd made up your mind Dudley killed himself.'

In the silence that followed Horton could hear a man shouting and swearing in the corridor. Obviously, he wasn't very keen to be interviewed. 'Did you tackle Prudence over it?'

'No.'

'Or speak to Fisher?'

'No. He died two days afterwards in a boat explosion, so there was no need. I thought it best to leave it. Raising my suspicions wasn't going to do anyone any good. And, well, I thought God had seen fit to punish Vic Fisher.' He spoke wearily, without conviction, as though it was an automatic response, and Horton wondered if Pilbeam had stopped believing in God. Perhaps he'd even given up on his fellow man.

'But you did mention Vic Fisher to me,' Horton said. 'Why?'

'Because you seem to be the only person I've met who believes Dudley didn't kill himself deliberately or accidentally. You are reopening the case, aren't you?'

'You're not concerned now that it could take us to Prudence Goldsby?'

'She can't hurt Dudley, and Adele has made it quite clear by staying away that she doesn't want anything more to do with her mother.'

'Did you mention Vic Fisher to anyone else either then or recently?'

'No.'

'Did you hear anything of the conversation between Fisher and Goldsby?'

'No.'

'Was anyone else within earshot?'

'I don't think so. I don't know. I got waylaid by a parishioner. I didn't see Vic or Dudley leave. When I heard that Dudley was dead, I tried to contact Prudence, but she wasn't taking any calls and there was a police officer on the door to her house. I finally managed to get hold of Adele but even she was non-committal. They had to see me, though, both of them, for the funeral. I conducted it but not from the church in Somerstown or the Anglican Cathedral, which his political masters wanted, but from All Saints Church, close to where Dudley lived. It was what he would have wanted.'

And in a poorer part of the city, thought Horton. He looked hard at Pilbeam. 'Did you give Dudley a drink when you met him in the lobby?'

'No.'

It sounded like the truth. 'Do you know who Prudence associated with at that time?'

'No. I had no contact with her. She'd given up long ago on Dudley being a leading light on the national political scene, so she'd lost interest in him and his career.'

Cantelli took up the questioning. Pilbeam confirmed that after the meeting he'd returned home and had stayed there. He had seen no one and spoken to no one. He had read and retired to bed after a sketchy meal.

Horton terminated the interview and asked Pilbeam if he'd wait a few moments longer. He looked as though he didn't care how long he waited. At the door, Horton turned and in classic police officer style asked one last question. 'Have you ever owned a boat?' He recalled the small craft in the photograph on the vicarage bookshelf.

'Yes, years ago. It was my father's.' He made to say more, then his lips tightened and he stared down at his hands.

Horton reported back to Uckfield, Bliss and Dennings.

'There's the fact that Pilbeam's father had once owned a boat, that he knew Callum Durrant and that he believed Fisher had brought in drugs. He was also alone with Goldsby in the lobby, where he could have given him a drugged drink. In addition to this, he has no alibi for the time of Goldsby's death. If Pilbeam killed Quintessa, though, then I can't see why Fisher felt the need to blackmail him through Goldsby.'

'Maybe he didn't,' Uckfield replied. 'Fisher could have been approaching Goldsby about something completely different and the boat explosion could have been an accident.'

Horton eyed Uckfield sceptically. The Super returned the gaze defiantly, but Horton knew it was a defensive pose. Uckfield didn't really believe that, he just hoped it because he was jittery about his father-in-law being involved in a cover-up and because he had blabbed about the investigation to

Dyer, who could have told Jarvis. He had no evidence of that and Uckfield hadn't admitted it, but Horton knew him well enough to spot the signs.

Uckfield reached for a glass of water on his desk and removed some tablets from the pocket of his trousers. As he swallowed them Horton assumed they were either painkillers, because of his hangover from another night on the booze, or seasickness pills in anticipation of his rough crossing to dinner on No Man's Fort.

Bliss said, 'Goldsby could have been involved with Pilbeam in Quintessa's murder, which Fisher may have discovered and then used to blackmail them both. Pilbeam killed Goldsby and then killed Fisher and Bray.'

That was a possibility, but if that was the case then why had Adele asked to meet him on the ferry? Maybe she hadn't been pointing him at Jarvis and his guests. Maybe he had got that completely wrong and she had intended meeting him but Pilbeam had prevented her. And, as he had discussed with Cantelli, she could be dead and buried somewhere or her body dumped at sea.

They needed more in order to charge him. He said as much. Uckfield agreed. He consulted his watch. It was just after eight thirty. *Maybe the gourmet dinner doesn't start until nine*, thought Horton.

Uckfield rose and grabbed his jacket from the back of his chair.

Quickly Horton said, 'Has Trueman got anything from the press coverage on Goldsby in April 2005?'

Uckfield snatched another impatient glance at his watch. 'Let's see,' he growled. He strode out, firmly closing his office door behind him, making it plain he didn't intend to linger any longer than necessary.

There was just a core team left in the incident suite for the evening. Walters was sitting alongside Trueman with Cantelli, who had been briefing them on the outcome of their interview with Pilbeam.

Horton asked Walters if he'd got the information of the arresting officers for Fisher and Bray's theft conviction at Hamble Marina in July 2003. He had. It hadn't been Dyer. Horton thought he sensed Uckfield's relief, although his expression gave nothing away.

Walters added, 'Alex Cummings didn't live at the Hamble in 2003. He bought the house he currently owns there in 2012. Back then, he owned a penthouse apartment at Oyster Quays and a house in London, which he still owns, as well as a marina apartment in the South of France.'

'He's doing all right for someone who's got four ex-wives to support,' said Horton, unless they had all remarried. 'Any children?'

'Two from his third wife, aged ten and twelve. We can't find any pictures of him from 1985 but Camper and Nicholsons might have some in their archives from when he did his apprenticeship. We're also checking if he still worked there in 1985.'

Horton addressed Uckfield. 'In 2003 Dudley Goldsby would have been Cummings's Member of Parliament, unless Cummings used the London address as his main residence, but even then, he could have entertained or accommodated Goldsby when he went to the House of Commons. Anything on Jonathan Sloane?' This last he directed at Trueman.

'From his biography on his website and a couple of press interviews, he's aged fifty-eight and single. Originally from Cardiff, he moved to Swindon when his father got a job there in the railway works. He went to a secondary modern school but was clever enough to get a place at Cambridge and gained a first-class honours degree in chemistry, followed by a masters. He founded Grendon Biotechnology in 1986 — one of the first biotechnology companies to commercialize scientific research and one of the early pioneers of genetically modified food. The company is highly successful and Sloane gives talks and seminars around the world. He was and still is a special adviser to the government on agriculture, has a London flat at Chelsea Marina and a large motor yacht.'

Uckfield sniffed. 'Doesn't get us much further.'

Horton disagreed. 'Being a government adviser, Sloane must have known Dudley Goldsby.'

'He's not the only one.' Trueman swivelled his computer screen to face them. 'This is dated the eighth of April 2005.'

Two weeks before Goldsby had died. Horton found himself staring at a double-page local press article with a photograph of a group of men on board a large motorboat in Portsmouth Harbour. In the middle and forefront was Dudley Goldsby. To his left was Peter Jarvis. The short, stout Alex Cummings was next to Jarvis, and next to Cummings were two visiting Japanese businessmen. The photographer had positioned them well to disguise Cummings's lack of height. The man looming above him was Dominic Keats. The others were a mixture of prominent local business owners, senior managers from the industries within the naval base and overseas visitors. There was no sight of Dyer or Sloane. The article was about attracting inward investment and, according to the quotes from Goldsby, demonstrating that the area had a good employment base, excellent infrastructure and transport network. Horton couldn't see the name of the boat or the make. It had probably been hired for the event.

'This could have been what Bray and Fisher saw.' But even as Horton expressed this idea, he knew it wasn't enough. How would they have recognized Quintessa's killer from a press photograph?

Trueman said, 'Aside from this article, Goldsby was photographed at several meetings and with various business people. There are pictures of him at the Camber talking with the fishermen, at the university with students and staff, and with local environmental groups, the harbour conservancy people, at the naval base, the port and at the dockyard.'

Uckfield called it a day. He was clearly anxious to get away. Horton rapidly followed him out and hailed him at the bottom of the stairs.

'You're on No Man's Fort tonight, Steve. See what you can get from Cummings, Jarvis and Keats about that photograph and about Vic Fisher. It could also be worthwhile pumping Cummings's fiancée, Sarah Lemont, for additional information.'

'Anything else you'd like me to do, like search for Lord Lucan?' Uckfield said sarcastically, hurrying towards the station rear entrance.

'I'm quite willing to come with you and assist.'

'I bet you are.'

'Not for the gourmet dinner. I hope they've put up a plate for you.'

Uckfield snorted. 'If I'm lucky, I'll just catch the third course. And I am not going to spend the evening interviewing anyone.'

'We *are* dealing with a killer, and he could be on that fort.'

'He could be in the vicarage.'

That was a possibility. 'If Brandon didn't call his killer after he left here but the killer called him, how did he know Brandon had been released?' Horton recalled Uckfield's hangover on Friday morning at the Spur Redoubt when they'd been at the crime scene. Now was the time to tackle him. 'You were on Jarvis's boat Thursday night for a boozy dinner, weren't you, Steve? Did you tell Dyer? Did you mention Brandon? Did someone slip off that boat that night and meet and kill him?'

'You're saying my father-in-law is a killer! For Christ's sake, get a grip.'

'You talked about Dudley Goldsby's death, though. Dyer probably asked why you'd let an inspector come barging on board to harass Jarvis. I can see that I'm right. Who left that yacht between nine and midnight?'

'No one, and I can damn well swear to that,' Uckfield said stiffly and stormed off.

Maybe he could, but drunk, maybe he wouldn't have noticed anyone leaving.

Horton returned to his office to collect his helmet and leather jacket. As he flicked off the lights he saw Bliss's car sweep out of the car park, followed by Trueman's. Cantelli had offered to take Pilbeam home but he'd refused, saying he'd prefer to walk and get some air.

Horton made for his boat. The rain had stopped. The puddles glistened with the reflection of the street lamps. It had grown colder.

Two police cars swung into the main road with blue lights flashing and sirens blazing. Horton followed them out and headed southwards.

If no one in that picture was involved in Brandon's, Goldsby's and Quintessa's deaths, then, as Uckfield had said, that left the Reverend Simon Pilbeam.

CHAPTER TWENTY-THREE

Sunday

'I've got something on the Dudley Goldsby autopsy that you might find rather interesting,' Gaye announced to Horton the next morning on the telephone. It was just after nine thirty and Horton had returned from his run along a windswept and very cold promenade, where he hadn't been able to resist calling into the mobile incident unit. The officers who had reopened it that morning at seven said there had been no new information before it had closed at 1 a.m.

'I didn't think you'd be working on a Sunday?' Horton said, surprised.

'Why not? Everyone else seems to these days, and we know that corpses don't only come along Monday to Friday. Besides, you said it was urgent. I'm at the mortuary.'

'Be with you in about forty minutes.'

Horton wondered if what Gaye had discovered would be enough to bring Uckfield back from No Man's Fort. He hesitated over calling Cantelli, conscious that it was Sunday and he would want to spend it with his family, but in the end, he rang and said he'd see what Gaye had discovered and call round to update him afterwards.

'Not on your life,' Cantelli replied robustly. 'Remember I was on the original investigation and I want to know what we missed. I'll pick you up at the marina.'

It was just after ten thirty when they were sitting in Gaye's small backroom office.

'The toxicology tests confirm that a high level of cocaine was found in Goldsby's bloodstream,' Gaye announced after the usual exchange of greetings. Horton hadn't doubted that, but he knew she wouldn't have called them here just to tell them what was already in the original autopsy report.

'Taking cocaine by mouth is the least effective method of absorbing the drug,' she continued. 'As you know, it is far more common for someone to absorb it through the mucous membrane, particularly the nose, hence the term "nose candy". It can also be injected. The pathologist who examined the body for an injection mark didn't find one, but that doesn't mean to say it wasn't there. It might have been so tiny that he missed it. If someone injected Goldsby, rather than him injecting himself, he must have been restrained, which he wasn't. There is no evidence of that — but he could have been unconscious.'

Horton sat forward, listening eagerly.

'I've examined the photographs of the body, in particular the areas where an injection could have been administered, but it's difficult to tell from the pictures and it's no good digging him up after all this time, because you still wouldn't be able to find any evidence of an injection. As I told you before, if he had overdosed on cocaine, he would have exhibited signs of hyperactivity and convulsions before falling into a coma and suffering heart failure, which can come on rapidly if given a lethal overdose. If he was injected or given a drink containing the fatal dose, then your killer would have watched him writhing in agony before his death and then, as you said, Andy, he'd have cleaned up the room and laid out the body.'

Horton heard a phone ringing in the distance and the wheeling of a hospital trolley. Voices sounded and faded.

'I've gone over the crime scene photographs. I started with the theory that Goldsby took the cocaine voluntarily, but we run up against several objections to that, one of which you so clearly pointed out. The lie of his body and the room would have shown evidence of his death throes. It didn't. And there are many more peaceful ways to kill yourself. He might have taken an overdose accidentally, being a newcomer to the drug, because there was no evidence that showed him to be a habitual user.'

Cantelli said, 'He was tired and drained so maybe he wanted something to pep himself up.'

'For thirty minutes at the most, if he snorted it, and only five to ten minutes if he smoked or injected it. And he'd have been far more likely to have taken it before the meeting, not after it, unless he needed a boost because he was going to engage in some kind of sexual activity. And there was no evidence of that. We also still run up against the same problem of the room showing no signs of hyperactivity and with him lying quite peacefully and naked on the bed.'

'Go on,' said Horton keenly.

'So, I discounted the suicide and accidental theories and moved on to the idea that someone deliberately injected or gave him a lethal dose of cocaine in a drink in order to kill him. I looked for evidence of why he appeared so peaceful and why he was half-sprawled naked on the bed, aside, that is, from the killer having cleaned the room and placed him there. I checked his medical history. The amount of cocaine found in his system could have brought on a heart attack, which was what the coroner found.'

Horton threw Cantelli a glance. 'But—'

'Patience.' She smiled and sat back with an expression that Horton knew well. She'd uncovered something of significance. His pulse quickened.

'Dudley Goldsby suffered from the skin condition psoriasis, which can flare up under stress, and a forthcoming general election could be considered exceptionally stressful. As a result of which, shortly before his death, he'd been prescribed an anti-inflammatory drug called prednisone, which treats allergic disorders and skin conditions. It's a corticosteroid that prevents the release of substances in the body that cause inflammation. Now, this drug in itself is harmless, but when combined with other drugs, it can cause difficulties. So I looked not only for the cocaine but any other substances in the toxicology tests that might have reacted with prednisone, and I found diazepam.'

Cantelli threw Horton a look. 'Isn't that used for treating alcohol abuse?'

'Alcohol withdrawal symptoms, yes. And I have no note to say that your man was an alcoholic.'

'He wasn't,' Cantelli answered.

'Or that he suffered constant and debilitating seizures, which it is also prescribed for. But the fact that he had been prescribed prednisone recently and that his psoriasis had flared up indicated, as I said, that he was under stress. Oral diazepam can be prescribed short-term for severe anxiety, which affects work performance, sleep patterns and therefore interferes with the quality of life. It's known for its sedative, anxiety-relieving and muscle-relaxing effects. In the case of chronic insomnia, it decreases the time taken to fall asleep as well as increasing the total amount of uninterrupted sleep.'

'Sounds like something I should take,' Horton muttered, thinking of the many troubled nights he'd spent over the last two years, with his suspension from duty, his marital breakup, Catherine's unreasonable behaviour over Emma and the search for the truth behind Jennifer's disappearance.

'I wouldn't recommend it, Andy.' Gaye eyed him with a concerned expression.

'I'll take your advice,' he quickly added with a brief smile.

'Good, because it can become highly addictive.'

Cantelli said, 'So Goldsby was anxious and not sleeping because of the election campaigning.'

'And because of his wife's infidelity,' added Horton. 'He could also have been worried because Vic Fisher, a crook, was blackmailing a friend of his over Quintessa's murder.'

Gaye raised her eyebrows. 'Enough to cause anyone extreme anxiety and sleepless nights, but there are no notes on his medical file to indicate that he *was* prescribed diazepam.' She waited for that to sink in. Horton studied her, mulling this over.

She continued, 'There is the possibility that he was prescribed it privately by a GP friend or hospital medic to get him over the worst of the election campaigning. Maybe he confided in someone that he was fearful his anxiety and lack of sleep was interfering with his electioneering and he couldn't risk that coming out. It could have made him appear weak in the eyes of his constituents and his political masters. And the fact that the diazepam in his bloodstream wasn't raised at the inquest could confirm that.'

Horton said, 'Better to have your Member of Parliament taking an overdose of cocaine accidentally or intentionally than diazepam prescribed by a source that would generate more questions. Cocaine could have come from the street. Diazepam could have been bought over the internet, though.'

Cantelli said, 'Perhaps that was what the investigation ·found when they examined his computer. The higher-ups decided not to rock the boat. The person who prescribed it had to be protected.'

Horton addressed Gaye. 'Or perhaps he was given it by his killer, along with the cocaine.'

She awarded him a beaming smile. 'An overdose of diazepam can be fatal. Overdose symptoms can include extreme drowsiness, loss of balance or coordination, limp or weak muscles, fainting, collapse, and then cardiac failure.'

Triumphantly Cantelli said, 'He overdosed on diazepam, not cocaine.'

'That's my theory, and it *is* only a theory. He could certainly have been given a drink containing a high dosage of diazepam. He felt drowsy, collapsed, and the killer undressed him and laid him out on the bed, *then* injected him with a massive dose of cocaine, so it was the cocaine that everyone focused on. The fact that both prednisone and diazepam were in his system was never raised.'

Horton said, 'Or it was and everyone was ordered to keep it quiet? They were told not to complicate matters.'

Cantelli chewed his gum. 'Maybe the killer had no idea Goldsby was taking diazepam.'

'Oh, he knew all right,' Horton asserted, thinking back to what Uckfield had said the previous day and his own musings overnight on the possibility that the vicar could be the killer. Pilbeam had certainly looked disturbed and drained. Maybe he had realized that his time was running out. But was he really capable of killing Neil Brandon and possibly Adele Goldsby? Horton wasn't sure, but even religious and meek people could be driven to extremes.

He said, 'Half of Pilbeam's parishioners are probably on diazepam. He could have sourced the stuff from one of them. Or perhaps he's been prescribed it himself. Pilbeam had to dispose of Goldsby because Goldsby knew the vicar was involved in Quintessa's death. Vic Fisher had told him.'

'And talking of Quintessa,' Gaye interjected, 'you might want to see the reconstructions that John Lauder and his team have been busy working on. He sent them over to Detective Superintendent Uckfield late last night.'

Uckfield wouldn't have seen them yet, thought Horton, having shot off to his gourmet dinner on the fort.

She called up the file on her laptop, swivelled it round to face them and walked around the desk to stand beside Horton.

He studied the computer images of half a dozen women with differently coloured hair, varying shaped mouths and eyes of diverse colours, but all with the same facial structure: a diamond-shaped face, narrower at the chin, wider across the forehead. It certainly bore no likeness to Jennifer. He hadn't expected it to. Quintessa wasn't his mother.

'Seeing them all together makes it a little confusing,' Gaye said. 'Best to see them one at a time.' She leaned over Horton and pressed some keys. His heart raced at her proximity and he hoped it didn't show.

The first picture of Quintessa came on-screen.

'She's younger than I expected,' Cantelli said.

'That's because you're seeing her without the worry lines, flaws and blemishes. For all we know she could have had moles or birthmarks on her face, a scar even, or bags under her bloodshot eyes.'

Slowly, the pictures changed and the next one emerged. Something struck Horton. 'Keith Harnley told me that when they uncovered the corpse it had blonde curly hair. Call up only the blonde ones.'

Gaye obliged.

'There is something about her,' Horton said, puzzled. 'She looks vaguely familiar.'

'Probably because you've seen something similar to this on social media or a computer game,' Gaye answered. 'That's the problem with this type of reconstruction, as Sergeant Cantelli hinted at. There are no life experiences etched on her. You need to try and imagine her if there had been. The image is, of course, just a starting point. Dr Lauder can come up with many more permutations and is working on them, including adding the worry lines. We could even add spectacles. In fact, here's some images that Dr Lauder did with her wearing glasses. Of course, the shape of the frames can change the way someone looks.'

Again, a sequence of shots slowly unfolded in front of them. Something stirred at the back of Horton's mind. When the pictures came to an end, Gaye made to turn the laptop back round, but Horton put his hand on hers and stilled her.

'Run through them again, more slowly, just the fair-haired ones with glasses.'

She did.

'That one. Stop there.' They were looking at a blonde woman with large square spectacles.

Cantelli said, 'She looks like someone who would be missed and reported missing.'

'Studious, serious, clever, steady,' Gaye furnished. 'A lecturer, teacher, secretary, office worker — put her in a white coat and she'd pass for a pathologist,' she joked.

Horton eyed her so keenly that her fair skin flushed. 'That's it!' he cried.

'She's a missing pathologist?' Gaye cried disbelievingly.

'No, but the last time I saw her she was wearing a white summer dress and spectacles, lighter coloured ones than those, but the same shape. She was younger than Quintessa, about eighteen, maybe twenty, but there's the same shape about the face.' He turned excitedly to Cantelli. 'I think I know who she is. We've seen her before, Barney. In the photograph on the bookshelf in Pilbeam's house.'

'His wife!'

'Yes, and when did he say she had died?'

'Not long before he'd been given the ministry in 1985.'

'And what else do you remember seeing in that picture?'

'Trees and a small boat to their right.'

'And Pilbeam told us his father had a boat. That photograph was taken on Rat Island.'

Cantelli's brow furrowed. 'You think Pilbeam killed his wife?'

'Only one way to find out.' Horton jumped up. 'Thanks, Gaye. I'll buy you a bottle of champagne tonight with dinner.'

'I'll hold you to that,' she called back.

CHAPTER TWENTY-FOUR

There was no sign of Pilbeam in the vicarage or in the church.

'He could be giving a service at another of his parish churches,' Cantelli said as they made for the second of the three churches Pilbeam covered.

The service had been and gone. The church was deserted.

Cantelli drove back to the centre of the city, not far from where Goldsby had lived and to the church where his funeral service had been held. Again, there was no sign of Pilbeam nor of a congregation, but there was a verger who told them, with an anxious frown on his lined round face, that Reverend Pilbeam hadn't shown up to conduct the service and he was getting no answer from his landline or his mobile phone. He gave both numbers to Horton, who tried them as they walked back to the car. He got the same result.

'He must know the net's closing in,' Cantelli said. 'Maybe he's done a runner.'

'Where would he have gone?' But no sooner had Horton voiced the question than he knew the answer.

Cantelli followed his train of thought. 'To the scene of the crime.'

'Yes. Rat Island. The forensic team have finished there. And unless he has a boat, he's driven or taken a taxi.' Horton rapidly recalled the time of the tides. It was now just after one o'clock and high water. If Pilbeam had walked across the spit to Rat Island, he must have done so at low tide, sometime around 6 a.m. 'I'll call Elkins and get him to take me over on the RIB.'

Elkins said he would meet Horton at the port in ten minutes. As Cantelli made for it, Horton called Uckfield and put the conversation on loudspeaker so that Cantelli could hear it. Horton quickly brought the Super up to speed with developments.

'Why would he kill his wife?' asked Uckfield, grumpy at being disturbed. *Probably suffering from another hangover*, thought Horton.

'Perhaps she was having an affair. Pilbeam told us she'd died shortly before he was given the ministry here in 1985. I've asked Trueman to check out the death certificate.' And Horton recalled Cantelli telling him the Christian way of burial, which had been how Quintessa had been found, head to the west, feet to the east.

But there was a flaw in the theory — several in fact, thought Horton, and Uckfield voiced the first of them. 'Why didn't Fisher or Bray recognize Pilbeam before 2005?'

'Neither man went to church, so they didn't see Pilbeam until Fisher saw him talking to Goldsby at a political meeting,' suggested Horton, quickly thinking. 'Or maybe at an earlier constituency meeting.' But that didn't make sense either because Fisher could have approached Pilbeam direct. And, as he'd already expressed, Pilbeam didn't seem a likely blackmail victim. Horton quickly said this as Cantelli turned into the port, adding, 'There is another possibility. Pilbeam discovered through Vic Fisher that Dudley Goldsby had killed Quintessa, because it was Goldsby who Fisher suddenly recognized from the newspaper article. And it was Goldsby who Fisher was blackmailing. Pilbeam overheard the conversation. Instead of being dead, as he told us, maybe his wife had deserted him. He didn't know she was dead or who she had been having an affair with until he overheard that conversation. Pilbeam killed Goldsby out of revenge for his wife's murder. Then he had to kill Fisher and Bray because they knew he'd killed Goldsby. No one would look twice at a vicar on board Bray's fishing boat. If anyone saw him, they'd probably have thought he was blessing it.'

'And the drugs?'

'Pilbeam would have known about Goldsby's psoriasis and the medication he was on, and he could have sourced the diazepam and the cocaine from his parishioners — possibly even from Callum Durrant, whom he knew. And he knows Olewbo. Easy enough for Pilbeam to make the anonymous tip-off to us.'

Horton stared through the rain-spattered windscreen. It was turning to sleet.

'And how did he lure Goldsby to that hotel room?'

Horton had been considering that. 'He called Goldsby giving a false name, saying he knew what Goldsby had done. He threatened that unless he met him, alone, and at a place of his choosing, he'd go to the police.'

'Not sure an astute politician would have fallen for that.'

'Why not? Goldsby was in the middle of a general election campaign. There was a lot at stake. Goldsby thought he could get the better of the man threatening to expose him, which was why he was very careful not to be seen entering the hotel and that room.'

'And the stuff about Adele Goldsby getting you on the ferry with Danby?'

And that was the one thing that had been bugging Horton above everything. His mind had rapidly been working on that and as Cantelli pulled up, Horton said, 'She must have had something to show me that linked Pilbeam to her father's murder. She might not have known her father had killed Quintessa.'

'So you no longer believe Jarvis is involved?' Uckfield sneered.

Horton hesitated. Was that just coincidence? Danby *had* received that hoax call. Had that been made by someone entirely different for a completely unrelated reason? 'We need to find Pilbeam, then we might know the answer to that,' he hedged.

Resigned, Uckfield said, 'Keep me posted.'

Horton rang off without asking Uckfield if he was returning to the station.

The police RIB was waiting for him, and five minutes later, Ripley put it up on the shore of Rat Island. Horton, with Elkins, hurried to Quintessa's grave. There they found the lean, bedraggled vicar staring blankly at the earth.

The sleet was driving hard across the harbour. The wind was cuttingly cold. Pilbeam's shoes and trousers were filthy, which confirmed to Horton that he'd walked the length of the spit to reach here. His thin grey hair was plastered to his head, the rain had soaked through his shabby jacket and his trousers were dark with water. His hands were clasped in front of him at waist height, his head bowed as though in prayer. His thin body was swaying a little. He looked like a man on the verge of collapse.

He turned a harrowed face upon Horton. His eyes were sunk deep in their sockets, his cheeks hollow. It was as though all the blood had drained from him. His skin was as grey as the sea in the harbour.

'This is where she was found,' Pilbeam said so quietly that Horton had to strain to hear him above the wind. 'We used to come here as children on the boat my father kept in the harbour. This is where it ended for her and I did nothing to help her.'

Horton registered the word 'children'. Had Pilbeam and his wife been childhood sweethearts? 'Why don't we discuss this in the dry and warm?'

'No. I have to tell you here.'

'I should caution you.'

'Why?' he asked with a flash of animation. Then he added with a knowing expression, 'You think I killed her. Maybe I did. I'm as much to blame as him.'

Horton eyed him, baffled, and threw Elkins a glance.

'If I had stood by her, this might never have happened. I just abandoned her. Just!' he spat scornfully. 'And I call . . . *called* myself a Christian. She packed a case and left. I shall never forget the pleading in her eyes, the disappointment and sorrow on her face. I should have understood, but I didn't. She accused me of being just like them and I was. All my life I've tried to preach forgiveness and understanding and look at me — what a hypocrite when I couldn't even understand my own sister.' The rain was running off his face. He was shivering violently.

Horton puzzled over this revelation. Had Pilbeam avenged his sister then and not his wife? Gently he said, 'She's not here, Simon. Let's go to the boat.'

Pilbeam looked set to protest, then sighed heavily. 'You're right, Inspector, her bones are in the mortuary, but her spirit is elsewhere. I hope to God that she is at rest.'

He said no more and Horton didn't press him. He'd wait until they were safely in the interview room.

* * *

It was three hours later when Horton rejoined Pilbeam, now dressed in a white disposable suit, sitting forlorn and haggard in the interview room. Uckfield had returned from the fort and had called in Bliss, who was in the station along with Trueman. He had confirmed there was a death certificate for Norma Pilbeam, wife of Simon, who had died of cancer in Ringwood, Hampshire in September 1984. Uckfield had executed a warrant to have the vicarage searched, but Pilbeam had given them consent and Dennings had left to oversee it with Marsden, Somerfield and two uniformed officers.

It was Uckfield who joined Horton in the interview room. The Super had said nothing about his gourmet dinner last night on the fort, which meant he hadn't questioned his host or any of his guests about the deaths of Goldsby and Brandon. Horton hadn't really expected him to. He had briefed Uckfield on what Pilbeam had said. Pilbeam had been cautioned but had barely registered that he was being questioned in connection with the deaths of Neil Brandon and Dudley Goldsby. He'd waived his right to call a solicitor.

Horton began the questioning. 'Tell me about your sister.'

'Claudia was very clever. Much cleverer than me and my parents.'

Horton would always think of her as Quintessa.

'She questioned everything and anything, even the teachings of the Bible, which was sacrilegious as far as my father was concerned. He, like me, was a clergyman. But Claudia had a very analytical mind. She said she couldn't believe in God. She believed in science. She wanted to study it but my father wouldn't hear of it. He didn't even believe that women should go to university. The late sixties were very different from now. I went away to university to study theology. I didn't know that things at home were getting steadily worse. My mother did nothing to intervene. She agreed with my father.

'Frustrated and angry, Claudia went out of her way to do things my father despised. She got a job in a factory, then in a laboratory. Then she took some drugs — nothing hard, some Benzedrine — and my father washed his hands of her. I think she only did that because she was curious to see what it was like. At nineteen, when I was home from university for the holidays, there was a big row and he threw her out.'

'Not a very charitable act for a vicar,' Uckfield sneered.

'No.' Pilbeam looked shameful. 'It wasn't long after that picture was taken — the one I saw you looking at, Inspector Horton, of me with Claudia on Rat Island. I was told never to mention her again. Of course, we prayed for her.'

Uckfield sniffed loudly to show what he thought of that.

'I never heard from her again.'

'Then how do you know she was the woman found buried on Rat Island?' Uckfield barked.

But Pilbeam wasn't ready to answer that question. Horton could see that he had to tell his story in his own way.

'I returned to Portsmouth in January 1985, when I was given a ministry in Somerstown, shortly after my wife, Norma, died. My father had died a year before that, my mother two years earlier. It was a difficult time for me. It was in February 1985 that I saw Claudia, or thought I did, but I told myself I must be mistaken — that it couldn't possibly be her, because Claudia was a drug addict and had descended into a life of sin and debauchery, according to my father. But the Claudia I thought I saw was a successful, accomplished scientist with a master's degree.'

'Is that what she told you before you killed her?' Uckfield asked, his voice gentler now.

'I didn't kill her and I never spoke to her,' Pilbeam said wearily. He stared at his hands resting on the table. His plastic cup of tea stayed untouched. After a moment he continued, his pale, dull eyes searching their faces with sad resignation. 'I was asked by the Archdeacon to attend a conference in the Guildhall on food and the developing world. Famine was and always is a major concern. The Archdeacon felt there might be some new breakthroughs that could help. The late-afternoon speaker was a young scientist called Dr Christina Pickmere, but I knew her as Claudia, my sister. She was a researcher at the Laboratory of the Government Chemist in Gosport. The navy's food laboratories had been centralized at the Royal Clarence Victualling Yard in 1961. They designed, manufactured and tested food. I told myself I was mistaken, that it couldn't possibly be her.'

'Why didn't you speak to her?' asked Horton.

Pilbeam looked even more bereft. 'Because I felt ashamed and I was afraid. I didn't think I could cope with her anger and her hatred. I was feeling low after Norma's death. I didn't want any confrontation. I left the conference hurriedly before she had a chance to see me, and when I was able to think more clearly, I went to look for her.'

'When?' asked Horton.

'Late October.'

'You took your time,' sniped Uckfield.

'I'd like to say that was because of pressure of work, but it wasn't. I was a coward and weak. Yes, I admit that, Superintendent. I finally plucked up the courage to enquire at the food laboratory but was told she had left a couple of weeks earlier to work for a research laboratory in America. They gave me the details. I contacted them but they said she hadn't taken up the position and they hadn't heard from her.'

Uckfield said, 'So you forgot about her.'

'Yes,' Pilbeam said sorrowfully and with shame.

But Uckfield wasn't having it. 'Or maybe you did find her and meet her, you argued, you killed her and then buried her.'

'No.'

Uckfield continued, 'You thought you were in the clear but you were seen — only the two men who saw you didn't recognize you burying the body because you weren't wearing your vicar's clothes and they weren't churchgoers. Besides, they were there illegally, doing a bit of pilfering, and maybe they thought if the killer saw them and recognized them, they'd be next on the list to die. They did nothing, just like you.'

'I never killed her. I couldn't.' Pilbeam eyed them despairingly, his voice weary. 'I pushed thoughts of Claudia aside just as I had always done. I had a new and difficult ministry to attend to. I told myself she wouldn't want to see me anyway. I half-convinced myself that I had been mistaken in thinking it was her. Then in April 2005, I overheard a conversation between Vic Fisher and Dudley.'

'At that public meeting the night Dudley Goldsby died?' asked Horton.

'No. It was a week before. Dudley was at the church hall to hold a small meeting with a number of senior citizens. I was to meet Dudley in the lobby but I popped into the gents' while I was waiting. When I came out, I heard them talking.'

'How did Vic Fisher know Dudley Goldsby would be there?' Horton asked, though he had guessed the answer.

'The meeting was advertised in the local newspaper. I heard Vic Fisher say to Dudley that he'd seen a woman being buried on Rat Island in October 1985 and that he'd keep quiet about it if they could come to some financial arrangement. I didn't hear the rest because they moved out of earshot. I told myself it couldn't possibly be Claudia — why should it be? — but she seemed to have disappeared at that time. And it was a place that she and I used to frequent by boat, even though we were trespassing.'

'Did you tackle Dudley about it? Or Vic Fisher?' asked Horton.

'No, because that would have meant admitting to being an eavesdropper. I could see that Dudley was deeply disturbed by what Fisher had said. I told myself it couldn't possibly be my sister and that Dudley couldn't possibly be a murderer — Vic Fisher was just trying to stir up trouble for him. Then I saw Fisher making a beeline for Dudley the following Friday after the public meeting, as I told you, Inspector, but I couldn't get close enough to hear what they were saying. A parishioner at the back of the hall had summoned me. I could see that Dudley was terribly anxious and Fisher looked cocky.'

'And you didn't think it strange the next morning when you heard Dudley had died, and, two days after, that Vic Fisher and Frank Bray had been killed?' asked Horton.

Pilbeam shifted and averted eye contact. He said nothing.

Horton continued, 'You believed Dudley Goldsby killed Claudia in 1985, and after being blackmailed, decided to end his life.'

'It's what the police said about Dudley's death, and the boat explosion was officially declared to have been an accident. I put it out of my mind — that is, I tried to. It never completely went away, but they were dead. I told myself it would serve no good airing my suspicions.'

Uckfield exhaled loudly to show what he thought about that. He sat back and folded his arms.

Pilbeam continued, 'When those skeletons were found I waited anxiously to see what the police would discover. The news coverage said they were all from the nineteenth century and I began to wonder if, after all these years, what I'd heard in 2005 was wrong. Then you came asking me questions about Dudley and I knew Vic Fisher had told the truth. It had to be Claudia.'

They might never have confirmation it was her, though, Horton thought. There was no nuclear DNA to compare her remains with. Perhaps Lauder would have some luck in extracting mitochondrial DNA. A DNA swab had already been taken from Pilbeam.

Horton said, 'Why did you think Dudley had killed her?'

'I don't know. Perhaps they had an affair and she threatened to tell Prudence and the newspapers. He was standing for parliament in the April 1986 by-election. Maybe he couldn't risk that coming out. And I couldn't say anything in 2005, not after he died.'

'So you just kept quiet,' spat Uckfield. 'Even then you wanted to protect your dead friend instead of getting justice for your sister. And I'll tell you why you said nothing—' Uckfield sprang forward, causing Pilbeam to jolt back — 'because all that about Dudley killing your sister is bullshit. He's dead, so he can't deny or confirm it. *You* killed your sister.'

Pilbeam stared at Uckfield with a pained expression.

'Maybe you didn't mean to,' Uckfield pressed, his voice menacingly low. 'You argued over how your parents had treated her. She was angry with you, scathing towards you for your weakness. You lost your temper and killed her.'

'No. I could never do a thing like that.' His hands were shaking.

'Or perhaps you arranged to meet her,' Uckfield persisted, 'taking a knife with you, intending to kill her, because you didn't want her reappearing in your life. You were insanely jealous of the fact that she was successful — much more successful than you, the blue-eyed boy who had never stood by her. You stabbed her and then took her body to the island. I bet you even said a prayer over her after burying her.'

Pilbeam's grey cheeks paled further. His bony hands tightened. Tears welled in his bloodshot eyes.

Uckfield pressed on. 'You confessed to Dudley Goldsby, who kept it quiet for years, until Fisher said he knew and Goldsby urged you to confess. Only you couldn't. But you asked Goldsby to meet you in private. He agreed one last time. You got the cocaine, and you spiked his drink and watched him die. Maybe you said a prayer over him too. Then you killed Vic Fisher and Frank Bray.'

Pilbeam ran a trembling hand over his face and shook his head.

'You thought you were in the clear until Adele Goldsby called you and said she knew where Claudia was buried. And when Brandon found the skeleton, you called him and pumped him for more information. He quickly worked out you were the killer and he set about blackmailing you, so he too had to die, just as Adele had to.'

Pilbeam dashed a hand across his eyes. His face was a picture of misery and bewilderment. 'I don't understand.' He looked pleadingly at Horton.

'Or maybe,' Uckfield continued, 'Dudley Goldsby over-heard Vic Fisher telling *you* that he'd seen you bury a woman. Goldsby asked you if it was true. You said you needed to explain to him what had happened and asked him to meet you in that hotel bedroom the following Friday. That gave you time to get hold of the cocaine and plan his death. Did you know he suffered from psoriasis?'

'Yes.'

'Did he tell you he was taking diazepam?'

'I—I don't know,' Pilbeam stammered.

'Where did you get the cocaine?' Uckfield barked.

'I didn't. I haven't killed anyone, except Claudia by deserting her.'

'How do we know this conference ever took place? Perhaps Claudia made contact with you and asked you to meet her so that she could show you what she had achieved, and that stuck in your claw.'

'I have the conference programme.'

'Where?'

'In the house, somewhere.'

'If it's there, we'll find it.'

'And the Guildhall must have a record of it.'

'As far back as 1985?' Uckfield scoffed.

'There'll be information on Claudia as Dr Christina Pickmere — you can trace her movements.'

'We will, which is more than you seem to have done.'

Uckfield scraped back his chair and suspended the interview. Outside, with conviction and what Horton thought was relief, Uckfield said, 'He did it. He's our killer. He'll confess and we'll get the evidence to back it up.'

'Why didn't her colleagues report her missing?'

'Maybe Pilbeam told her boss she'd decided to chuck it all in and go and help him with his ministry.'

'Why did Fisher wait for so long to approach Goldsby?' They headed back to the incident suite.

'Or the vicar,' Uckfield said. 'He could have overheard Pilbeam praying.'

'I don't think Fisher would have gone into the church.'

Uckfield shrugged. 'Bray could have done and told his mate.'

They paused at the bottom of the stairs. Horton felt troubled.

'I'll tell Dennings to find that programme, *if* it's there,' Uckfield said. 'Trueman will start digging up whatever he can on Dr Christina Pickmere.'

Horton found Cantelli in CID, where he relayed the interview to him. Cantelli punched the name into a search engine.

'Nothing for Dr Christina Pickmere,' he announced. 'But then, it was over thirty years ago.'

Trueman's team would try to get hold of a list of employees at the long-defunct Laboratory of the Government Chemist, although it was likely to prove difficult. The armed services were exceedingly cagey about who they shared information with, including the police. But Christina Pickmere hadn't been in the navy and she couldn't have been the only civilian employed there. In fact, Horton was certain she wouldn't have been. Something flickered at the back of his mind, but before he could grasp it, Cantelli said, 'Do you believe Pilbeam killed his sister and the others?'

'I'm not sure. If he is innocent and Vic Fisher *did* approach Goldsby, then we're back to asking why he waited until 2005 to do so. And why Goldsby?'

'Because, as we said earlier, he didn't have access to the killer but he knew that Goldsby did.'

'Which discounts the vicar and takes us back to Jarvis, Keats, Sloane and Cummings.' *And possibly Dyer*, thought Horton.

'Not necessarily. It could have been another friend or associate of Goldsby's. It could even have been his GP or the doctor friend who gave him the diazepam.'

Horton groaned at the thought. That meant they'd never get him.

'Maybe Vic Fisher changed his doctor and saw Goldsby coming out of the surgery, where he'd gone to pick up a prescription for his psoriasis.'

'And maybe we're focusing on the wrong thing.' Horton's mind was grappling with several thoughts triggered by Cantelli's words and his interview with Pilbeam. He sat back. 'We now know more about Quintessa, as I shall keep calling her, if those remains are Pilbeam's sister — which we'll assume they are. According to Pilbeam she was determined, analytical, argumentative, inquisitive, rebellious, an atheist and ended up as a talented young scientist. She was going places, working in a government food laboratory. Why would anyone want to kill her, bury her and then cover his tracks so well that no one would report her missing?'

'Well, if you ask me, there are three motives. One, sex. She was having an affair with a married or engaged man and she threatened to tell unless he divorced or broke off his engagement.'

'Which fits with Pilbeam's theory about Dudley Goldsby being the killer.'

'Two, money. She had some stashed away and the killer wanted to get his hands on it. That could be connected with the third motive, drugs. You said Pilbeam claimed Quintessa had taken drugs — perhaps she gave up taking them and began to manufacture them using the laboratory's resources. She asked for a bigger cut from the person she was supplying, otherwise she'd stop working, so she was silenced, or someone thought it was about time they took over from her.'

'And the drug theory fits with what Dr Clayton told us about Goldsby's medication. It was someone who knew not only about Goldsby's skin condition but the effects of diazepam if it was administered with prednisone and before the cocaine,' Horton said eagerly.

'Yes, and if her killer was someone who worked with her at the laboratory, that gives us another motive. Professional jealousy.'

'Pilbeam said she'd just very successfully delivered a paper at that conference in 1985, which the killer might also have attended. Perhaps he was giving a paper, only his bombed. And that really got up his nose.'

'Could have. We all know what a mad lot scientists are.'

Cantelli's words struck a chord with Horton. With rising excitement, he was right back to where he had started — Peter Jarvis and his science degree. But he hadn't worked with Quintessa. Or had he?

'What exactly did that food laboratory do?'

'According to this—' Cantelli pointed at his computer screen, where he had rapidly conducted another internet search — 'they perfected the process of freeze-drying food, including coffee granules into instant coffee and dried fruit and vegetables, such as sun-dried tomatoes. That can't have been all they were working on, though. Scientists are very secretive, especially if they're working for the government or the Ministry of Defence.'

Cantelli's words nudged several more things in place. 'Perhaps Quintessa had discovered something that had huge commercial potential. A year after she was killed, Peter Jarvis started a food processing and packaging company.'

'Coincidence?'

'And before starting his company, he worked for a government research establishment, according to Frieda Chillerton. He could have worked with Quintessa there.'

'Or he could have met her at a conference before the one Pilbeam told us about in the Guildhall.'

Horton's mind swam with thoughts. He felt so close to the truth. 'Let's return to one of your motives, Barney. Sex. Only our man didn't kill Quintessa for sex but used it to get what he wanted. Maybe he worked with her or, as you say, met her at a conference. He struck up a relationship with her in order to steal her work, recognizing she was much cleverer than him. He had an affair with her. He believed that one of her projects, a method of freeze-drying and packaging food, could make him a great deal of money, and he doesn't want to share it with anyone.'

Jarvis was and always had been commercially minded, even now with his venture capital trust, which Catherine had told him about. Horton believed it was for commercial gain and tax considerations rather than charity. He sat forward. 'The killer needed to set the stage for Quintessa to disappear without anyone suspecting. He picked his moment carefully, knowing that she had accepted a job in America. He wanted her research findings. He waited until her last day at work. She'd already given notice at the place she was renting, encouraged by him that they'd live and work together. He met her and killed her. He claimed the research she was working on as his own and eventually became a very wealthy and successful businessman, and one that Fisher and Bray recognized hobnobbing with the local politician Dudley Goldsby on that boat in the Solent before the general election.'

Someone had prevented Adele from meeting him on that ferry. She had even suspected that might happen because she had backed it up by luring Mike Danby on to the same one. By calling Danby first to make sure he was able to go and then calling him, she had made sure that if she couldn't make the rendezvous Danby would tell him he was on his way to see Jarvis. Jarvis, who with his buddies had been on that boat in Oyster Quays and was now on the fort. Jarvis, who had been at that hotel the night Goldsby had been killed and who had been on that boat in the Solent in April 2005. Jarvis, who was a scientist and had made a fortune from food processing.

Horton rose, grabbed his sailing jacket from his office and reached for his mobile phone.

'Where are you going?' Cantelli called after him.

'No Man's Fort. I need to find Adele Goldsby before he kills her.'

But Horton wondered if he was already too late.

CHAPTER TWENTY-FIVE

The icy rain swept off the sea as the police launch bucked and rolled in the swollen waves. Horton had called Elkins on his way to the port and had told him to let the fort manager know they were coming. He didn't know if the manager, Craig, would relay that information to Jarvis, and he didn't much care if he did. There were only two ways off that fort — by boat or by helicopter — and he didn't think the killer would use either. It was far too stormy for a small helicopter to land on the fort's helipad, and the sea crossing, even on the sturdy police launch with experienced sailors like him, Elkins and Ripley, was hazardous.

He should have told Uckfield where he was heading, but he knew the Super would never have sanctioned the visit, not while he thought he had the killer in a cell. And even when Uckfield realized that Pilbeam was not the killer, as he soon would, he would insist on gathering evidence before questioning anyone. By then it would be too late to save Adele. It might already be.

The granite structure of the fort loomed out of the heavy grey sea. Horton's heart pounded as Ripley tried to bring the vessel alongside the landing jetty. In front of them Jarvis's superyacht was bobbing and tossing in the dark swell.

Horton reached out in the stinging, slanting rain to try and secure the craft while Elkins attempted to do the same for'ard, but the wind kept pushing them away. On the fourth attempt, Horton managed it. Craig appeared on the steel stairway clothed in waterproofs and hurried to their assistance as the wind ripped and howled around them.

Eventually the boat was secured, and a few minutes later, they were climbing the steel steps to the entrance and the embarkation hall. Horton gave instructions to Elkins and Ripley to wait for him there and to make sure no one attempted to leave. Craig informed them that all the guests had just assembled for pre-dinner drinks in the mess hall, which was to their left. Horton could hear voices coming from behind the closed doors. But the message that he was on his way had reached the guests — or rather, one in particular — because at the top of the stairs in front of Horton appeared an irate Catherine dressed immaculately in a crimson figure-hugging, very short dress.

'I didn't tell anyone you were coming,' Craig swiftly announced.

That meant Uckfield had discovered where he had gone and had rung Dyer, who had told Jarvis and hence Catherine. Cantelli must have told Uckfield or Bliss where he was heading. Not that he blamed the sergeant for that. Cantelli would have stalled for as long as he could, and Horton knew he would be concerned about him. He'd switched off his mobile phone. Uckfield was more than likely calling Elkins right now, he thought, as he climbed the stairs towards Catherine. Elkins would bear the brunt of Uckfield's wrath and would be ordered to bring him back immediately. He guessed that Catherine had told Jarvis she'd deal with him, assuming his visit to be that of a jealous ex-husband. Maybe Jarvis believed that, maybe not. Horton didn't care.

He met her at the entrance to the atrium. The icy, hard rain was drumming against the glass roof as though someone was hurling rocks at it, making it difficult to hear anyone speaking in a normal conversational tone, but Catherine's fury had taken her pitch way beyond normal. The atrium, with its wicker furniture and glass-topped tables, was deserted.

'You just can't bear the thought of me with another man,' she raged. 'You're intent on destroying every relationship I have. Well, you are not going to come barging in here, embarrassing me or Peter in front of all his guests.'

Horton held her hot, angry eyes, feeling a stab of sorrow that there was never going to be anything but animosity between them and that Catherine would continue to make his life with Emma difficult. He didn't know why she hated him so much. He'd never deceived her or been unfaithful. He didn't think he had hurt or neglected her except for his work, but he knew he had disappointed her and perhaps that was what she couldn't forgive. But then perhaps her anger and her hatred of him was to salve her conscience because it made her feel better about the divorce. After all, wasn't it much more noble to be the wounded party than the one who had wounded?

Rapidly, he considered what she'd said. He hated to admit it but she was right about the barging in bit. He didn't have a warrant and he didn't have enough evidence to charge anyone. And Dyer would stick his fat nose in and it would be Horton who would be escorted away. Profound apologies would have to be made to Jarvis and his guests before he could accomplish what he'd come here for — to find and save Adele, if she was still alive. He needed to flush out the killer, and it suddenly occurred to him that he could use Catherine's appearance to that advantage. She would be bound to relay what he told her.

He spoke evenly, though his pulse was racing. 'Dr Christina Pickmere was a very clever woman, a talented scientist conducting groundbreaking research into food production and processing. Too talented, so she had to die. She was stabbed to death and buried on Burrow Island, or Rat Island, as it is more commonly known. Her death was expertly covered up. No one missed her. No one reported her disappearance. She simply vanished.'

'What has this—'

'Just over two weeks ago, her remains were found along with four others on Rat Island. Four of those remains were from the nineteenth century. Christina's were much more recent — 1985, to be precise. Twenty years later, Dudley Goldsby, the Member of Parliament for Portsmouth South West, suffered a heart attack brought on by an overdose of a drug given to him deliberately. His killer *and* Christina's is on this fort.'

She eyed him incredulously. 'Don't be ridiculous. This is mad. I won't listen to any more of this rubbish.' She started to walk off.

Harshly Horton said, 'I don't care who you sleep with, Catherine, but I will not have my daughter anywhere near a killer.'

She spun back. 'Your daughter!'

The blood froze in his veins. He stared at her. Her skin flushed and hastily she looked away, running a hand through her blonde hair. His stomach churned as a terrifying thought flew through his mind. Roughly he pushed it away, even though it was damn hard, and forced himself to think about the killer. To think about Adele. There were only two women who had been on Jarvis's boat and that she could be — the very thin and anxious blonde, Sarah Lemont, or the auburn-haired chef, Ruby. And he was beginning to see which of them it was. Lemont was Cummings's PA and fiancée. Ruby was Jarvis's cook.

'Was Ruby working on board Jarvis's boat when you and Emma were with him at Christmas?' Horton asked.

'Why should I tell you that? Yes, she was,' she rapidly added, as she caught sight of something in his eyes that made her reconsider. 'What has she got to do with this?'

'Was she engaged by Keats, through the Superyacht Academy?'

'How would I know? Probably.'

'Didn't your boyfriend tell you?'

'No, because Ruby Masters is not employed by Peter.'

That pulled him up sharply. 'But you said she was with you at Christmas.'

'She was, but only when Jonathan dined with us. Ruby is Jonathan's chef, not Peter's, and has been for three years. He has various food allergies. She's a damn good chef and she's not a criminal, so leave—'

'Where is she?' He cut her short, his head spinning. Christ, had he got this all wrong?

'In the kitchen. Where else would she be?'

He picked up a circular-shaped map of the fort lying on one of the wicker tables and rapidly studied it before making off across the atrium.

'Andy, where are you—'

'To look for Ruby. Tell that to your boyfriend.'

He was on the upper level but the yellow stairs would take him down to the lower level and the kitchens. Beneath that was the sea-level bunker. He located the kitchen with ease and found it a hive of activity, but there was no sign of Ruby.

Horton managed to stop one of the chefs and ask him where she was.

'She's gone,' came the short reply.

Horton tensed. Was he too late? 'Have you any idea where she might be?' he asked desperately.

'Try the deck. She likes to go up for some air — she finds it claustrophobic working on the fort.'

'Would she be out there in this weather?'

'No idea.'

Horton swiftly consulted the map and headed back up the yellow stairs to the atrium, which was still deserted. From there he negotiated the twisting stairs to the semi-lit lighthouse, which was also uninhabited. There were seats around the edge and binoculars on the ledge. The 365-degree view gave him a sweeping vision of a swollen black sea, with the occasional pinprick of light from a flashing buoy and a ship moored up off Bembridge. The driving sleet obliterated the Isle of Wight to his right, the shores of Portsmouth behind him and those of Hayling Island ahead and to his left.

He peered out at the deck. It was lit by a series of low-level lights. There was no one there, nor at the hot tub, nor by the hot house. She could be inside the latter but he thought it more likely she'd been disposed of over the side of the fort. Perhaps he was to blame for putting her in danger by showing up on Jarvis's boat. His appearance and questioning had somehow given away her identity. Her death on this fort would be put down to suicide or an accident.

Not if he could help it.

He thrust the map into the pocket of his sailing jacket and made his way down to a door that led out onto the deck. Although he didn't think she was there, he had to check, just in case the killer had bound and gagged her, and was keeping her hidden away already dead or unconscious in the hot house or in a darkened corner, ready to dispose of her body later.

The wind snatched the door from his hand and slammed it shut behind him. He crossed the deck in the driving icy sleet to a walkway that he had seen on the map called Commando's Leap. He was no commando and he didn't intend leaping into the angry sea, but from here he could get a better view of the deck.

A door banged behind him. He spun round, tense and alert.

Catherine had delivered the message. It was sooner than he had anticipated. He'd liked to have found Adele first.

He wanted to believe he would be looking into the face of Peter Jarvis, but he knew that wasn't going to be. His prejudice against Jarvis had distracted and diverted him from focusing on the real killer and on the wrong function at the Solent Waves Hotel. It wasn't Jarvis's dinner party in that hotel in 1985 that had harboured a killer, it was the conference on food and allergens. And one of the guests — possibly even the keynote speaker, given his reputation — was the man walking towards him.

Now he could see how Bray and Fisher had recognized him in 2005. They hadn't been far wrong in the incident suite when they'd talked about the killer having a limp. He had only seen the man seated, but now, as he walked towards him, Horton noted the highly distinctive gait he had of rotating his right leg in an unusual manner. Not only did Jonathan Sloane have so many allergies that he employed his own chef wherever he travelled, but he also had one leg shorter than the other. Whether he had been born that way or it had been the result of an accident, Horton didn't know and didn't care, he only wished that Adele had given him or Danby some hint of it. But even then, Horton might not have witnessed Sloane walking, and even if Adele had told him who her father's killer was, he couldn't have waded in and questioned him.

His heart pounded as he stared at the narrow, pale face. Horton knew that if it came to a fight, he would come out the winner. He was much younger and far fitter. But Sloane's hands were thrust into the pockets of his waterproof jacket, possibly to conceal a weapon.

'What did Christina Pickmere have that was so valuable to you, Sloane?' Horton shouted above the roar of the wind. A squall of stinging sleet seemed to cut into his flesh.

Sloane drew closer. His eyes looked stronger, his face sharper without the spectacles. Horton didn't know whether the glasses were worn to fool people into thinking he was weak when he was really ruthless and calculating or if he'd replaced them with contact lenses for this encounter.

'You know who she was?' Sloane said with surprise.

'Her brother told us.' Horton could see that was a shock. So Pilbeam hadn't told Goldsby about his sister and clearly Christina had never mentioned her brother to Sloane. 'He came across her by accident at a conference at the Guildhall in February 1985, the same conference you were at.'

'She didn't say.'

'No, because she didn't know he was there. Was that the last paper she delivered before you killed and buried her body on Rat Island in the October of that year? How did you cover up her disappearance? No, let me tell you,' Horton continued, stepping a little closer. Sloane didn't move. 'She had another job to go to. Your timing had to be perfect.'

'Catherine didn't tell me how good a police officer you were, or should I say detective, although she did say you were impetuous.'

Horton knew that wasn't the word Catherine had used. It had probably been one far less complimentary. Sloane would have made sure to find out more about him after seeing him the first time when Dominic Keats and Alex Cummings had boarded Jarvis's boat. And after Horton had broken up their lunch on Friday, Sloane would have probed deeper. Then Dyer, thanks to Uckfield, would have relayed Horton's views on Goldsby's death.

When had Sloane realized Ruby, his chef, was actually Adele Goldsby? Maybe he had seen something in Ruby's eyes as she'd watched him leave, or as Jarvis had discussed the purpose of Horton's visit with his guests. He cursed himself silently for being so blind. Jarvis had distracted him and so too had Sarah Lemont's nervousness. From what he remembered of her, and had recently been told of Adele, he had thought she would be anxious, timid and frightened, not competent, assured and confident.

Then last night after that gourmet dinner, Uckfield, drunk, had given that select group more details about the investigation and Sloane would have had confirmation of his suspicions that the woman who had been preparing his meals for the last three years was in fact Adele Goldsby. Perhaps he had witnessed her leaving the boat at the time of the telephone calls to him and Danby, and again on the night Neil Brandon had been killed. It wouldn't have taken much for him to pull it all together.

'Christina was due to take up a research position in America,' Sloane said.

'Instead, you killed her, allowing everyone to believe she'd gone to her new job. What did you tell her new employers?'

'I didn't need to tell them anything. They didn't know about me. They must have assumed she'd changed her mind.'

'What was it she was working on that made you so jealous you had to kill her?'

'It wasn't jealousy, it was lack of commercial foresight on her part,' Sloane said easily as though that was reason enough for murder. The rain was running off his face, as it was Horton's, but Sloane didn't seem to notice. 'We were both scientists working for the Laboratory of the Government Chemist, engaged in researching techniques to extend the shelf life of food products without destroying their chemical structure. We succeeded with several foodstuffs but it was the area of genetically modified crops that really interested me, and—'

'She was far more talented than you,' Horton spat. From the tightening of Sloane's jaw, he'd struck a nerve. There was a flash of anger in the man's eyes. His hands were still pushed into his sailing jacket.

'Is that why you killed her, because she was cleverer than you?' Horton taunted, wanting to goad him into action and steeling himself to meet it. He didn't think Sloane was harbouring a gun. There was no bulge in his waterproof jacket and a firearm would not have been Sloane's natural choice of weapon.

Sloane stepped forward. 'She couldn't see the future for genetically modified food.'

Horton held his ground. The wind howled around them, but the squally sleet had died off a little. Somewhere in the distance he heard a ship's horn, long and low. Was Elkins still in the embarkation hall? Would he come looking for him, if only to warn him of Uckfield's wrath?

'I could see the way it was going in the eighties with the food scares and allergens,' Sloane was saying. 'I knew there were great opportunities in plant agriculture, genetically modifying them to make them resistant to insects, diseases and pests, and to make them tolerate certain herbicides. We worked together on projects. I should have been giving that paper at the Guildhall.'

'But you didn't like the fact that she was conducting her research for the good of mankind, not to exploit for profit.

When you saw she had no intention of profiteering by it, you killed her in order to make sure you could develop it and exploit it through your company to make a fortune.'

'Nothing wrong with that.'

'But there is in murdering for it. You thought you'd got away with killing Christina until 2005, when Vic Fisher saw you on a boat during that visit of overseas delegates, just as Goldsby was doing his PR bit and trying to attract more investment to the area. It was your boat in that press photograph, wasn't it? You were on board it at Oyster Quays.'

By Sloane's flash of irritation, Horton could see that his guess had hit the mark. 'Fisher and Bray happened to be there on Bray's fishing boat. They recognized you from your walk as the man they'd seen on Rat Island burying a body. They didn't know how to get hold of you but they could see that you were pally with Goldsby and the press were all over your little group, so you must have been important. They soon discovered who Goldsby was and where to find him. Fisher threatened Goldsby — he said he would tell the media that Goldsby was associated with a killer unless he gave you a message: pay up, and they'd keep silent. You agreed, using Goldsby as a go-between. Meanwhile, you found out more about Fisher and Bray, discovered where Bray's boat was moored and arranged for it to suffer an explosion. For a clever chemist like you, that would have been simple. How many times did Goldsby pass on the blackmail message to you?'

'Twice.'

'The last was when you killed him.'

'He died of an overdose of cocaine.'

'Which you gave to him at the Solent Waves Hotel, where you were a speaker at a conference on allergens. It was easy enough for you to book a room under an assumed name and ask Dudley Goldsby to meet you in it. You stabbed him with a syringe, just as you intend to do to me. There's one in your pocket, isn't there?'

'Yes.' Sloane withdrew his right hand.

'And you watched your friend die.'

'It was relatively quick and painless,' he said, as if that made a difference.

'Because of the diazepam.'

'Yes. It might not be for you.'

'How did you know where to get the cocaine?'

'It's easy enough when you're a chemist and in the business.'

'And Callum Durrant?'

Sloane gave a sly smile. 'That's simple when you're friendly with a police officer.'

So Dyer was Sloane's contact, not Jarvis's. Dyer had given him the name, no doubt when Sloane had steered the conversation in that direction enquiring curiously about drug addiction and dealers on the patch. Dyer must also have talked to him about the drug squad operation, making it easy for Sloane to give them the tip-off.

'The diazepam and prednisone were enough, but—'

'You thought cocaine would confuse the picture.'

He shrugged.

'Weren't you even the remotest bit concerned how that would look for Goldsby?'

Sloane looked confused by the question. 'Why? He'd be dead.'

'And his family?'

'Prudence was delighted when Dudley died and that little mouse of a daughter got herself a new career instead of being tied to her father's bootlaces.'

'Where is she, Sloane?'

'By now? Probably dead. Just as you will be.'

Sloane dashed forward, but in a quick, fluid movement, Horton lunged to the right as Sloane's hand came up. In a fierce grip, Horton grasped Sloane's wrist and squeezed with all his might.

Sloane cried out and his grip weakened. The syringe fell to the ground. Horton twisted Sloane's arm and pushed it so high up his back that he cried out in pain. Sloane tried to kick the syringe over the edge, but Horton tightened his grip further.

'Walk,' he bellowed in Sloane's ear, and, spinning him round, pushed him towards the lighthouse just as Elkins burst through the door with Ripley behind him. 'Get the syringe and be careful with it,' Horton ordered. Sloane screeched in pain as Horton manhandled him inside the lighthouse. Elkins eyed him, worried.

'Where is she, Sloane? What have you done with Adele?'

'Nothing.'

'Wrong answer.' Horton managed to push Sloane's arm up even higher. He was now bent over double, writhing in agony.

'You won't find her,' he croaked. 'You'll break my arm.'

'Good. Then you won't be able to stab any more syringes containing lethal cocktails into anyone.'

Ripley studied the syringe wide-eyed. He'd put it in an evidence bag.

'I'll ask you one more time, before I break your arm, and then I'll start on the other one.'

Elkins stepped forward, worried, while Ripley looked on alarmed that he might be associated with an officer beating up a suspect.

'You can't.'

'I can and I will, even if it means losing my job. Where is she?' Horton yelled.

'Below.'

'Where?'

'Divers Passage.'

Horton let go and Sloane fell to the ground.

'Cuff him, Dai, and whatever he says, don't let him go. He's under arrest for the murders of Claudia Pilbeam, Dudley Goldsby, Vic Fisher, Frank Bray and Neil Brandon.'

'Brandon?' Sloane looked up, puzzled.

'And possibly Adele Goldsby. Caution him and call for assistance.'

'Already on its way, Andy — that's why I was looking for you. Uckfield's coming with a posse on the Ministry of Defence Police launch.'

Uckfield was coming for him, though, not for Sloane. 'Good, the more the merrier. Tell them to join me at the sea level bunker.'

CHAPTER TWENTY-SIX

Horton raced down the stairs to the dimly lit, suffocating tunnels. He sprinted past the brick arched alcoves containing artefacts and displays from the Second World War feeling as though he'd stepped into a time warp. And time was the critical factor here, he thought, as he halted and hastily consulted his map in search of the Divers Passage.

The smell of the sea, the damp and brick dust clawed at his throat. The oppressiveness of the tunnel made his breath come tight and fast. Where the hell was this passage? Was Adele still alive? Had her body been swept out to sea?

Then he was on it, a very narrow passageway barely wide enough to contain a man, leading out to the sea where divers had once exited during operations.

His heart contracted as he made for the low wall over which divers climbed before dropping into the cold sea at high water. Mercifully it was still low tide, but even so, the sea was slapping and thudding against the brick walls of the fort like heavy gunfire from massive cannons exploding and echoing around the tunnel and chamber.

He reached for his torch and peered down into the black water. He could see nothing and no one. Frantically, he swept his beam left. Again, nothing. Then to the right where there was a ledge. His breath caught in his throat. There lay a woman, gagged and bound.

'Adele, it's OK — help is here. We'll get you out of there. You'll be all right,' he shouted above the monumental crashing of the sea hurling itself against the walls. 'Just hold on a little longer.'

He wasn't sure if she'd heard. It was freezing and she was wet. If she slipped, she would drown — her body would thud against the walls of the fort in the wash and rhythm of the sea.

'I'm going to phone for help, which means I have to leave you for a minute. Just hold on. You'll be free soon.'

He thought he saw her move. But he hoped not. 'Stay perfectly still,' he urged. 'I'll be back in a moment.'

He raced out of the passage hoping to God he could get a signal on his phone, but there was nothing. He cursed vehemently. He'd have to tear back to the embarkation hall or maybe just the next level up where he could summon help.

But then he heard footsteps. 'Down here,' he shouted. 'The Divers Passage.'

And with immense relief he saw Ripley with PCs Seaton and Johnson heading for him. Swiftly he gave instructions for Johnson to call the Coastguard and for Ripley to go into the passage and talk to Adele. 'Doesn't matter if she's uncon-scious — she might still be able to hear you.' Horton knew that hearing was the very last sense to slip away. 'Tell her help is coming and to hold on.'

He didn't stop to ask where Uckfield was. With Seaton following, Horton dived into one of the alcoves he'd passed earlier and there found a stretcher that formed part of a Second World War display. It was perfectly stout. In the next alcove was some rope and a large piece of netting. Returning with the items, he left the stretcher at the entrance, urged Ripley out and went in first with Ripley behind him and then Seaton. Swiftly, he tied the rope around his waist, leaving enough on the end to tie around Adele.

He shouted for Ripley and Seaton to do the same and Seaton to find something stout to secure the end to — robust enough to take one body, maybe two if they slipped into the water. He'd give a tug on it when he reached her, two when he had the rope around her and secured to him. He told Ripley to shine his torch into the hole and for the beam to follow him so that he could at least see his way.

With the netting over his shoulder, he climbed over the low wall and eased his way along the ledge, his back pressing against the slimy wet wall. He hoped he wouldn't need the netting, which he'd have to cast into the sea in the vain hope of being able to scoop up Adele with it if she fell before he could reach her and untie her hands. Sloane must have forced her to walk along the ledge, gagged and with her hands bound, not caring if she slipped. When she didn't, he must have commanded her to lie down. She had, sideways on — there wasn't enough room for her to lie on her back. Then he had climbed over and bound her ankles, leaving her terrified until he could deal with her later. Horton was just mercifully thankful Sloane hadn't simply pushed her into the sea. He had lured her here as soon as he'd heard Dyer say that Horton was on his way. She must have been mad to agree to meet him down here, but perhaps the message that Adele had received had purported to have come from him.

At any moment she could fall, and so could he. The ledge was slippery — he had to take it cautiously — but he was surefooted, having had years of practice on a wet deck on a sailing boat. If he did slip, the rope would prevent him from being lost for ever in the sea. Not for Adele, however, unless he got it fastened to her.

'It's OK, Adele, I'm here,' he said softly. He reached out and removed the gag.

Her eyes flicked open and for one dreadful moment he thought she would panic, thinking he was Sloane, and she'd go over, taking him with her.

'It's Inspector Horton — Andy,' he said gently.

She relaxed. He could feel her shivering under her thin cotton chef's whites, which were smeared with dirt and soaked by the spray.

'I just need to tie this rope around your waist.' Carefully, he took the loose end he'd allowed when tying it around himself, eased it around her and deftly tied a bowline knot. His heart beat rapidly. The pounding, echoing sea was almost deafening him, his claustrophobia making him feel sick. Cold sweat crept on his brow and down his back.

He untied her wrists and ankles. 'Can you stand up?' She'd be cramped from lying on her right side for so long — how long? Twenty minutes? Half an hour? 'Flex your ankles a little.'

She did as she was told, unable to speak.

'It's OK, you won't fall. You're tied to me and I've got two officers in the passage. We're secured tightly. All we need to do is walk slowly along the ledge, keeping our backs to it. Do you think you can do that?'

He was glad that Sloane had kept the syringe of drugs he'd prepared for Adele to use on him instead. Drugged, the operation to rescue Adele would have been far more treacherous and she would probably have been dead by now.

'Take my hand and I'll help you up and keep you steady. Ripley, keep that torch on us,' Horton called out. 'Slowly does it. Good,' he encouraged as she rose hesitantly.

She took a deep breath. 'I'm OK.'

'Right. Now, holding my hand, follow me step by step. Take your time, there's no hurry. The bar will still be open when we get there.'

He was pleased to see a small smile touch her lips.

Inch by inch, they eased their way along the ledge until Horton was back at the low wall and greeted by Ripley's anxious face. Horton could hear voices coming from behind Ripley.

He had to climb over the wall first — they couldn't change places, as the ledge was too narrow for that. 'Stay exactly where you are, Adele. I'm climbing over, then I'll help you over. Just keep hold of me.'

She did, tightly. Within seconds Horton was over the wall. Against the booming roll of the gobbling sea below them, he shouted, 'Right, your turn. Step over. You won't fall. Imagine it's just a low garden.'

With a deep breath she did exactly as he said. Then she was in his arms and he was holding her trembling body tight against him. He nodded at Ripley, who deftly untied the ropes, then with Adele still huddled close, Horton half-carried her out of the passageway.

Only when they were in the circular tunnels did he breathe a silent sigh of relief. Along with Ripley and Seaton were Uckfield and two officers from the Ministry of Defence Police launch, one with a silver thermal blanket which he swiftly wrapped around Adele.

'I don't need the stretcher,' she said valiantly. 'I'm OK.'

'We'll get you to hospital.'

'No.'

'Yes.'

'I have to tell you about Jonathan.'

'Later. Tell me later.'

'Will you come with me?'

Horton looked at Uckfield as he answered, 'Yes.' He again put his arm around her.

Her eyes flicked to Uckfield and then back to Horton. 'Is he dead?'

'No.'

'Did he confess?'

Horton didn't answer. He didn't think Sloane would ever confess.

She frowned. 'He killed my father.'

'I know.' But as Horton dashed a glance at Uckfield before moving off, he could see that Uckfield didn't believe that.

CHAPTER TWENTY-SEVEN

Monday

A tired Cantelli met Horton outside the hospital.

'You didn't have to come. I could have got a patrol car to take me back to the boat,' Horton said, climbing in.

'I thought you might like company.'

'And it was deemed "inappropriate" for me to return to the station with Adele,' Horton said with an edge of bitterness. Uniformed officers had taken her there once the medics had declared her fit half an hour ago.

'How is she?'

'Unharmed but emotionally drained and damaged. And Jonathan Sloane?'

'Keeping mum, awaiting his super-slick London lawyer.'

'I'd have thought he or she would have been here by now.'

'Even money can't get the best out of bed so early on a Monday morning.'

And Sloane would have the best, or rather the most expensive.

Horton's thoughts returned to the events on the fort the previous night. He and Adele had been winched up into the Coastguard helicopter and taken to the hospital. As Horton had watched Adele safely lifted up in to the helicopter, Uckfield had turned to him. 'You've cocked up big time,' he'd snarled. 'You were well out of order.'

'Tell that to my tribunal.' Horton had looked beyond the Super to see Jarvis and his guests watching. His eyes had locked with Catherine's and she'd glanced away. Her words swam into his mind now as they had when she'd uttered them: *Your daughter.*

Cantelli's voice broke through his thoughts. 'Trueman will get confirmation today that Sloane worked at the Laboratory of the Government Chemist at the same time Dr Christina Pickmere was employed there.'

But Horton knew that in itself meant nothing. It was circumstantial, which was what any lawyer, expensive or otherwise, would point out. 'And Keith Harnley?'

'We're still looking for him.' Cantelli yawned. Horton knew Barney wouldn't have got home until the small hours of the morning and then had probably slept little, only to rise at six and report into the station before heading here to pick him up. It was just on 8.15. Horton hadn't slept at all. He'd stayed with Adele even though he didn't need to — a uniformed officer had been posted by Uckfield to sit outside her hospital room. Uckfield had ordered him home, but Horton had refused to go. Adele had slept after talking to him and the doctor had given her a mild sedative. But still Horton had sat and watched, thought and waited. Not all his thoughts had been of Adele but of Jennifer and her fate.

Cantelli indicated right at the traffic lights. 'Uckfield says you're to report to him and Bliss tomorrow morning at eight o'clock sharp.'

'For a roasting and suspension, I expect.'

'I don't see why when you got the killer.'

'Barney, you know that police work isn't done the way I do it. And besides, although we have the killer, I'm not certain we'll be able to convict him. Sloane, through his smart-arsed lawyer, will probably argue that I assaulted him or made him admit to it under duress, not that he actually did admit to killing Goldsby, Fisher, Bray or Brandon, only Pilbeam's sister. But there were no witnesses and he's hardly likely to repeat the confession. And he wasn't under caution. I should have collated the evidence, handed it to Bliss and Uckfield and, when we had enough, brought him in for questioning.'

'And Adele would have been dead by then. Let's hope Sloane can't resist telling us how clever he is.'

But Horton thought Sloane was too cunning and evil for that. There was a glimmer of light, though. 'Perhaps Adele's confession and testimony can help to convict him, and Trueman and the team can get enough evidence to back it up.'

'Confession? Then it's true what Uckfield said this morning, she killed Neil Brandon.' Cantelli flashed him a worried glance.

'Yes.' Horton recalled her steady confession, even though he'd told her to remain silent.

'Don't worry,' she'd said, 'I'll repeat it under caution when they arrest me, unless you'd like to do that now.'

He'd said he'd leave that to Uckfield.

'She told me that Brandon had to be sacrificed in order to get our attention and force us to investigate her father's death. She knew that if she came to us with what she had, we'd dismiss her as a neurotic woman. We might still do that,' he added with bitterness. But she wasn't neurotic. He thought of how he'd seen her through everyone's eyes: Pilbeam's, the nuns, her mother's, Frieda Chillerton's, Mike Danby's, Cantelli's, from his own contact with her in 2005 and from the recent phone call — vulnerable, shy, invisible, obedient, plain, ineffectual, unaccomplished, mousey. But she had been determined and driven because she'd pursued a career with the sole purpose of getting into Sloane's employ to expose him as her father's killer.

Her motivation? Something Pilbeam had said to him explained that. All Adele had wanted from her father was a hint of gratitude, a word, a smile, a loving touch that told her she was doing all right. She'd never got it. Horton felt sick inside for her, and maybe for himself, because he understood so perfectly how that felt. For years he'd obliterated the memories of the love his mother had shown him before she'd disappeared because he'd been told she hadn't loved him enough to stay with him. That had been a lie.

He knew how Adele felt. There was always that empty feeling inside. Adele needed to be able to say to her dead father, 'I did OK, didn't I?' And he was searching for the same. If he could get to the truth, if he could get justice for Jennifer, he too would be able to say, 'I did OK, didn't I?'

And Sloane? Horton's thoughts swung to how he had seen him. He hadn't and that had been his problem. He'd been too focused on Jarvis, seeing what he wanted to see: a man who was devious, ruthless and evil, because that was what he wanted him to be so that he could get Emma away from him. And was he viewing Lord Richard Ames in the same light? He wanted him to be guilty of Jennifer's disappearance and probable death because he needed to blame someone for everything that had happened to him after she had vanished. He wanted revenge for those years of hurt and pain.

He brought his mind back to the incidents of the previous night and continued as Cantelli headed east on the dual carriageway. 'Sloane had looked puzzled when I accused him of killing Brandon. It was then that I wondered whether Adele had killed him. She'd been on Jarvis's boat Thursday night along with Sloane, Cummings, Sarah Lemont, Catherine, Dyer and Uckfield. Uckfield said no one had left the boat, but he wouldn't have thought to include the chef. She wasn't one of the elite, but the hired help. Once dinner had finished and the guests were drinking, Adele slipped off the boat to meet Brandon at the Spur Redoubt, taking one of her chef's knives with her.'

He looked out of the window as they crawled in the rush hour traffic. 'She'd heard Uckfield tell the guests that Brandon was being released. She called Brandon, probably on deck between courses, to arrange the meeting. Brandon might have been in the station at the time of the call, before you and I went back in to re-interview him, or he might have just been released. She said she wanted to talk to him about the skeleton and that she would make it very worth his while, but couldn't meet him until twelve thirty, which was why he spun out the time in the pub and then eating the kebab before catching the bus. At the Spur Redoubt, she stabbed him and pushed him into Long Curtain Moat, hoping to throw the focus on Sloane. Except all I could focus on was Jarvis,' he said with bitterness and sorrow.

Cantelli indicated off the dual carriageway and headed south towards the marina and Horton's boat. 'How did she know Sloane killed Quintessa?'

'At that public meeting she heard Fisher talking to her father. They'd stepped just inside the door leading up to the stage. She heard Fisher say that it wouldn't look very good for a politician to be mixing with a murderer, especially if that man was a very wealthy businessman. Her father said he had a meeting arranged that night with Sloane and would see Fisher the next day. He'd meet him at the usual place. She didn't know where that was, but Fisher said if he didn't show with the money, he'd go straight to the newspapers and show them where the woman was buried on Rat Island. Her father left abruptly without speaking to her.'

Horton recalled her words to him as they had waited in casualty for a doctor. 'She said, "My father often forgot I was there."' In that moment, Horton had seen that all her life she'd strived to be noticed by him.

Cantelli shook his head sadly. 'Makes you wonder why she went to such lengths to get justice for him.'

But Horton understood. Wasn't he doing the same for Jennifer?

He said, 'Fisher and Bray probably intended to black-mail Goldsby once they thought they had them both in their grubby clutches.'

'Why didn't Adele tell us this during the investigation?' Cantelli pulled up at another set of traffic lights.

'I wished to God she'd told me when I broke the news to her, but she thought we'd all call her stupid, tell her she was being hysterical and overreacting. There were no witnesses to that conversation.' Horton's lips tightened as he stared across Langstone Harbour. The storm had abated. There was barely a ripple on the sea. At Easter the small yachts and motor-boats would take up their moorings and the sailing season would begin in earnest. And at Easter, Emma would be with Jarvis on his yacht. He had an appointment with his solicitor this afternoon, which he was determined to keep.

He also thought of the dinner engagement he'd missed last night. Would Gaye forgive him? Would she agree to rear-range it? He had returned her call while Adele had been sleeping in the hospital and had left a message on her voicemail.

The lights changed to green. Cantelli pulled away. Horton resumed. 'Adele knew that the officer in charge of the investigation, Dyer, was friendly with her father. She tried to tell him that she thought her father was being blackmailed and that a man called Sloane was involved, but she could see that she was wasting her breath. She didn't know that Dyer was a close friend of Sloane's. Dyer told her it was the shock of her father's suicide — loved ones often looked for a reason and someone to blame when there wasn't one. It was soon made clear that no one would listen to her and that everyone wanted her father's death forgotten as quickly as possible, including, of course, her mother.'

And Horton wondered how Dyer would feel now. He thought it unlikely he'd experience guilt or remorse. He'd say it went with the job, and sometimes it did, but not this time.

Horton said, 'As she watched Sloane at her father's funeral, she vowed to get to the truth and find evidence to show that he had killed him, because by then she'd also read that Fisher and Bray had died in a boating accident and realized that Sloane must also have killed them. But who would believe her? She left Portsmouth, changed her name, her appearance and got herself a career in the food industry, a subject that she knew was closest to Sloane's heart. She'd dug into his background and discovered his interests, the sea, and his food allergies. She became a qualified chef, and after several jobs, went to work for the Superyacht Academy as a chef on board superyachts. Dominic Keats didn't recognize her. She'd passed the first test. She built an excellent reputation for herself among the luxury yacht owners and charters, knowing that Sloane moved in those circles. She was eventually offered a job with him as his personal chef and he took her everywhere.'

'It's a wonder she didn't poison him.' Cantelli drove slowly through the densely populated streets towards the seafront.

'That would have been too quick and too easy. She wanted him apprehended by the police, charged, tried and convicted for his crime. And she didn't have all the links in the chain — not until she contacted Keith Harnley. She found him from digging in the newspaper archives, where she discovered that Fisher and Bray had been convicted for theft along with Keith Harnley. From Harnley she got more information about Neil Brandon and their jaunts to Rat Island. She tracked down Brandon at the museum at Priddy's Hard and got hold of his mobile number by pretending to be a journalist with an interest in local history. She said she'd been told he was a very reliable and knowledgeable source.'

'Quite an accomplished actress then?'

'No, a very determined woman, driven by the need to be heard.'

'I assume she used a different name when acting as a journalist?'

'Yes.'

'Sophie Kranton?'

Horton nodded. 'When she knew that Sloane had been invited on board Jarvis's boat at Oyster Quays and to the fort for the weekend, it was time to put her plan into action. Ten days before they were due to arrive here, she called Brandon as Adele Goldsby to say she had learned that there was evidence of human remains buried on Rat Island. She'd been told he was something of a local historian and thought he might want to take a look. She couldn't as she was out of the area. There might be publicity as it could be a major find and she didn't want to be involved.'

'And Brandon was only too pleased to put himself in the limelight and take the glory.'

'Yes. She called me after she had arrived at Oyster Quays with Sloane on Jarvis's yacht, because she not only remembered me as the officer who discovered her father's body and who came to break the news to her, but she also knew that Catherine was Jarvis's girlfriend and Jarvis was Sloane's close friend. On the same morning she phoned Danby posing as Sophie Kranton, pretending to be Jarvis's PA to get him on that ferry along with me, taking a chance that we'd bumped into each other. And we did.'

'It must have been a shock when those four other human remains were found.'

'She knew Quintessa was among them and that we would discover her remains were much more recent than the nineteenth century and start to investigate. She didn't know who Quintessa was any more than we did then. Brandon's death put the focus squarely on Quintessa and brought us back to Adele and her father. I told her she'll go to prison. She said, "Before I do, I'll tell the court that Jonathan Sloane killed my father and why, and that will get into the media and on the internet. Someone will come forward who knew Jonathan Sloane from those days, and the police will have more evidence and will be forced to reinvestigate."'

'She's right.' Cantelli pulled into the marina car park. 'Maybe after she's been questioned and made her statement, Uckfield won't tear you off a strip.'

'Oh, he will. But he'll also need to explain why he blabbed about the investigation in the presence of the killer when on board Jarvis's boat. Adele can confirm that, and so can the others when questioned, and I don't think that will do his career much good when I make that known.'

Cantelli grinned. 'Then you won't be suspended.'

'Bliss will be disappointed.' Horton smiled.

He watched Cantelli drive away before heading down to his boat. He thought of Adele and her desperation to find her father's killer and what it had cost her. Was he prepared to pay such a high price? Would he kill to achieve justice for his mother?

He liked to think not, but who really knew what they were capable of until driven and pushed to the limits? And just as Adele had been determined to get to the truth, so too would he. But would he expose it? Only time and what he discovered could answer that.

THE END

Thank you for reading this book.

If you enjoyed it please leave feedback on Amazon or Goodreads, and if there is anything we missed or you have a question about, then please get in touch. We appreciate you choosing our book.

Founded in 2014 in Shoreditch, London, we at Joffe Books pride ourselves on our history of innovative publishing. We were thrilled to be shortlisted for Independent Publisher of the Year at the British Book Awards.

www.joffebooks.com

We're very grateful to eagle-eyed readers who take the time to contact us. Please send any errors you find to corrections@joffebooks.com. We'll get them fixed ASAP.

Made in the USA
Las Vegas, NV
21 October 2022

57839945R00162